PLOTTED AT THE SUGAR MILL MARKETPLACE

Sugar Mill Marketplace Book 2

BECKY CLARK

Foreword

RAT RACE is the prequel novella that bridges Becky Clark's Mystery Writer's mysteries and the Sugar Mill Marketplace mysteries.

Read RAT RACE before you read BOOKED, PLOTTED, and BOUND as it sets the stage for some action that occurs in those early books in the Sugar Mill Marketplace series.

You can buy RAT RACE for 99c or download it for free when you subscribe to Becky Clark's newsletter, *So Seldom It's Shameful News.*

Subscribers also receive FICTION CAN BE MURDER— the first book in the Mystery Writer's series—as well as some related short stories and a Christmas play.

Dena

"FRUIT and white chocolate are their biggest problems?" Dena Russo grumbled to herself as she heard Kober and Hugo lament their trials and tribulations about her bakery and his chocolate shop while they were in the vendor room behind her used bookstore. She heard them even though she was at the front counter in her store with a *real* problem.

Even if Dena had her back door closed, Kober's voice would carry. Kober's voice would carry if Dena was working with a jackhammer instead of an infuriating new inventory tracking program on her infuriating laptop. Hugo was simply trying to keep up.

Dena repeatedly pressed the ENTER key. Nothing happened. "Enter already!"

"What is going on in here?" Hugo stuck his head in Dena's door. "I can hear you yelling over Kober's yelling."

Dena kept jabbing at her keyboard, trying any and all keys. "It's this stupid program. I can't get it to accept any of these numbers. Now I know why the previous owner of this place didn't track his inventory at all."

"Want me to have a look?" Hugo said the right words, but his voice lacked the requisite enthusiasm. He had that conflicted look people get when they feel they should offer help to be polite, but concerned that said politeness will lead to six hours of computer troubleshooting.

"Would you?" Dena stood from her stool and stepped aside. "I promise I won't suck you into my drama."

"Good. I have enough of my own. I can't find strawberries, cherries, or white chocolate." Hugo stepped to Dena's front counter and peered at her computer.

It didn't seem like Hugo's problem was anywhere near the scale of her own, but everyone was fighting their own fight, right?

Dena pointed. "I'm trying to get those numbers into that column."

Hugo tapped the keyboard a few times.

"The manual said—"

"Like that?" Hugo glanced up at her.

She stared dumbly at the screen. "How did you do that? I've been fighting with this thing for an hour."

Hugo pointed. "You need to highlight it then use that arrow."

Dena let loose with an enormous theatrical groan as she gripped the edge of the stool she'd been sitting on. "That's all?" She saw Hugo's eyes widen and realized it must look like she was ready to hurl the stool across the bookstore. She let go and shook out her hands. "Sorry. Thank you. Are you going to be around today in case I have more trouble?"

"Sure," he said, still without enthusiasm. "Unless I can find a supply of fresh strawberries, cherries, or white chocolate within a hundred-mile radius."

"Sounds like Kober is looking for the same stuff. Why don't you guys substitute raisins or something instead? You two are such artistes." Dena smiled sweetly to make sure he didn't think she was mocking him. Hugo made the most divine chocolates and Kober had a huge eclectic menu of decadent bakery treats. But complaining they needed out-of-season fruit—in February in Colorado, no less—seemed like a problem of their own making, easily remedied by a trip to the grocery store. Raisins were in stock year-round everywhere on the planet.

Hugo cocked his head and wrinkled his brow, thinking over what Dena said. He finally shook his head and turned back toward the vendor room, calling, "Hey Kober … Dena said we should use raisins!"

Dena heard them both cackle then Kober said, "Sure, that'll work."

Dena shrugged, not entirely convinced they weren't being sarcastic. But if not, she was glad to help find a solution to their conundrum so easily. Why was it so simple to solve other people's problems and so hard to solve your own?

She went back to her computer program. "But thank goodness other people solved this one," she muttered.

Perhaps she'd be able to cross this one off her lengthy list of Things That Needed To Happen Yesterday.

After their landlord and developer of the Sugar Mill Marketplace, Norbert Wallace, had died, his executor—Wife Number Three—sold the Marketplace jointly to the tenants for a song. Norbert's ex-wife was wealthy, had all the investment property she wanted, but more importantly, knew it would kill Norbert all over again to know how many entrepreneurs, women especially, would be helped by the Sugar Mill Marketplace. Plus, she never again wanted to visit the godforsaken armpit of the country, as she referred to the lovely town of Sugar Springs, Colorado, nestled in the Rockies along the

Arkansas River. She was thrilled to sell off the Marketplace.

Because money was tight for everyone—except Hugo, they'd learned—he had offered anyone who needed it a no-interest loan to cover their share of the buy-in. Dena didn't know for sure if everyone took him up on his generous offer, but the day they signed all the papers, two new haikus had appeared on the white board in the vendor room. She knew she hadn't written either one, so at least two other tenants were grateful.

> Hugo is a … well,
> I won't say "wild card." Perhaps
> Just an enigma.

> Enigma is right.
> But no one can deny that
> He is a true pal.

Dena, Kober, Skyler, Evelyn, Max, and even the typically sad-sack Hugo had rejoiced at the news they'd be the current owners of the Marketplace. They'd already had a joint meeting and decided they'd lease space to any new tenants for a term of two years, then decide whether or not to allow them to buy in. This would help them control and influence the right kind of businesses and owners who'd join them. They'd already been through so much together that adding new personalities to their mix might be troublesome.

As thrilled as she was by their joint ownership, Dena was less enthused that the other tenants had voted her to be the interim Marketplace manager, tasked with finding new tenants to complement the rest of the businesses—her already opened used bookstore, Hugo's chocolate shop, Kober's bakery, Skyler's cheese shop, and Evelyn and Max's photography studio where customers dressed up in period clothing to sit for portraits. They agreed that all their businesses required much more "hands-on" work than Dena's bookstore did, so she should act as manager. Dena's lone hand waving frantically in the air voting against the idea didn't sway any of them. Nor did her pouting, cursing, or begging.

Kober did bring her a plate of fresh cinnamon rolls as a conciliatory gesture, however, although she demanded the plate be returned—washed, preferably—the next day.

Despite what the other tenants believed, even after Dena repeatedly illustrated for them in colorful language, running the bookstore and managing the Marketplace took up more than one hundred percent of her time, especially when she was trying to recreate the entire inventory for Thrice Sold Tales from scratch.

Finding and vetting new tenants was much harder than anyone anticipated, involving research and due diligence into their submitted financials, the history of their business, and even their personal lives. Dena and the others were very wary of the baggage potential tenants brought with them and they've scratched many potentials off their decidedly short list.

Often, after all that, when she did extend an invitation to a promising prospect, they got cold feet or their bank denied their loan and Dena had to begin the process all over again.

After what had happened with the previous management team of the Marketplace, none of them trusted any outsider with this process. Although she complained, Dena actually enjoyed the control over the process of finding new tenants and dealing with the various concerns of the Marketplace. As it became clear that the job of managing the Marketplace was more difficult and time-consuming than any of them truly imagined, though, she knew they'd have to start looking for an office manager—one who would work for the tenants and the Marketplace, rather than their own self-interest.

Despite all the problems they had endured at the Marketplace in the month since their grand opening, business had been good for all of them. The bookstore had a steady stream of customers, today included.

She hoped that the new business she'd officially offered space to last week—an ice cream parlor—wouldn't fall through like the previous five before. Dena was a bit nervous, not completely convinced the guy would be a good fit. The few times she dealt with him he seemed full of hot air. Ironic, for someone who makes and sells ice cream.

At their tenant meeting, Dena and the others had agreed on a five-year plan for the Marketplace. They wanted to lease the remaining three spots on the first floor, and then start leasing the eight spots on the second floor. For now, the public stairs and elevator remained closed off.

Two customers asked Dena about her themed table and she answered with enthusiasm. This was one idea she was proud of. She knew she'd set up tables with normal themes covering holidays, spotlights of classic authors on their birthday, and banned books, of course. But she had also decided to do some funny and perhaps more obscure themes.

She didn't think her current themed table was all that

difficult, though. She'd written "The Green-Eyed Monster" on the small chalkboard on the table.

"These books aren't about envy," the man said, pointing. "I mean, I haven't read them all, but …" He trailed off and Dena saw him raise his eyebrows at the woman next to him.

"I guess that could be misleading," Dena said. "But did you notice that all the covers are green?"

"Yes. But the green-eyed monster is a metaphor or euphemism or whatever for envy," the woman said.

"What should I have written on the sign, then?" Dena asked.

"How 'bout *all these books have green covers*?" the man said.

The woman clucked her tongue at him. "Not very poetic."

They all stared at the sign for a few moments.

"Just leave it like it is, I guess," the man finally said.

Dena handed them both a bookmark with the store information on it. "Think up some good themes and email me. Clearly, I need help." She rang up their purchases.

"That'll be fun," the woman said, grinning at the man. "We can do it on the drive home."

After they left, Dena went back to the data entry, her phone interrupting her just as she gained her rhythm again. When she saw it was her daughter Charlee calling, she smiled, a welcome break.

"Hi, Mom. I just wanted to let you know I'm sending a new shipment of books to you."

"Bummer. I was hoping you'd bring them yourself."

"I can't. I'm swamped. I have a bunch of impossible deadlines. I have two different editors breathing down my neck for two different books. And I'm not even late yet! If they'd quit bothering me, I'd have more time to write."

"I'm guessing what you're telling your editors is fiction too, though."

"Ha. You know me too well. How's everything in Sugar Springs?"

Dena briefly told her the problems she was currently enmeshed in.

"Oh, so that's why you wanted me to come visit … so I could help with your inventory."

"The thought did occur to me." Dena tried to clasp her cellphone between her ear and shoulder so she could continue typing. The phone clattered to the countertop. She put it on speaker. "I'm just so pooped these days. Two full time jobs is, like, one-and-a-half too many."

"It's too bad you have all those pesky customers bugging you all day."

A nearby customer glared at Dena as she scrambled to quiet her daughter and her phone. She held it up to her ear again. "Charlee!" she whispered. "I had it on speaker."

"Mo-om! You're supposed to warn people!"

Dena glanced apologetically at the customers who were in earshot. "Here, have a bookmark. My gift to you. I love my customers." She walked to the very front of the store before coming back to Charlee on the phone. "Crisis averted. Readers do love their bookmarks."

"Why don't you get the other tenants to help with the Marketplace stuff?"

"They want to help, especially since they acknowledge they railroaded me into the job, and they offer, but I just don't know what to ask them to do. Finding these potential tenants is such a big job and it seems like all the pieces are interlocking. Breaking off small bits for everyone is harder than just doing it myself. And I don't mean to complain. Really I don't. I'm getting exactly what I wanted—a busy bookstore and now ownership in the Marketplace. I'd just like to see my bed on a more regular basis. There are times I'm so tired I'd sell this place for a dollar to the first person who walked in and wanted it." Dena meandered through her store, straightening books and displays as she spoke to Charlee, winding up perched on the stool behind the counter again.

A man materialized in front of her.

"Charlee, I've got to go. Talk to you later." She stowed her phone then addressed the man, "Do you have a dollar?"

"What?"

"Never mind. What can I do for you?" Dena stepped out from behind the front counter and saw a beautiful white German shepherd sitting primly by his side.

Dena was momentarily flustered. They hadn't discussed a pet policy for the Marketplace. In the summer there would be a dog-friendly patio area, but in February with a harsh wind blowing across the river, Dena wouldn't send anyone outside. Plus, it would be hard to enforce any rules about pets since Evelyn and Max's charcoal Persian cat, Balaam, spent his days strutting around the Marketplace hissing at everyone he encountered. Unlike this polite and friendly girl, who was so well-behaved.

"And who are you, lovely lady?" Dena let the dog sniff her hand before chuffing her under the chin and rubbing the side of her face.

The man answered for her. "This is Twist. Twisted Sister, technically. Because she's not gonna take it—not treats, not commands, and definitely not your nonsense."

Dena laughed, still petting Twist. When she glanced up and saw the sour look on the man's face, she straightened up. He didn't seem to be joking. "My nonsense?"

"You're trying every which way you know to *defrock* me out of the venture I *cultiformed* out of nothing."

Dena easily had six inches on him. She stared down at him while she tried to decipher what he said. Ah, a word-a-day calendar drop-out, she thought. *You could lead a horse to vocabulary, but you couldn't make him learn.* She didn't want to get all judgmental on him, since it was clear he was trying. *And he's in a bookstore so he's obviously good people.* But she wondered what venture he cultivated out of nothing of which she might have defrauded him.

"Who are you?" she asked.

"Duke Bughata."

The guy she bought the bookstore from. Dena had only talked to him on the phone, but if memory served, he wouldn't let her finish a sentence. "Oh, how nice to finally meet you. Come see what I've done with my—"

"This is my store."

"*Was* your store."

"This is *my* store." Duke raised his voice and several customers looked in the direction of the commotion.

Dena raised her voice in response. "It most certainly is *not* your store."

"You don't know how hard I had to work to get Twice Sold Tales to thrive."

Dena waved her hand at the sign. "I changed the name. It's Thrice Sold Tales."

Duke spoke over her, completely ignoring the fact she even spoke. "I curated an impressive selection of used books. I bought shelves, I even built some. I trained my employees to an implacable degree—"

Dena translated in her head, *impeccable.*

"And now, you just waltz in and try to steal it from me? I think not! Tactiles such as yours might work on other people, but not me, Miz Russo."

Dena wasn't sure what *tactics* he alluded to, unless he meant transferring funds from her bank to his and completing a sales contract with his attorney. You know, like people did when buying a business. She also wasn't sure if this spectacle he was making was funny or frightening.

She glanced around the store and saw almost all the customers were engrossed in this unexpected drama, some outwardly staring and stepping closer, some pretending to read the book they held while secretly spellbound by what was going on ten feet from them. She could only imagine how they would describe their trip to Thrice Sold Tales around the dinner table that night, perhaps talking about it like they would an episode of their favorite dramedy.

It seemed to Dena that Duke Bughata was putting on a performance, as if he'd prepared this scene for his Method Acting class. He did kind of look like he was right out of central casting, maybe as Rocky Balboa's sparring partner. Legs planted, knees bent a bit for optimum balance, ready to take a punch, or perhaps to dispense one. Round balding head plunked atop a thick neck. Beady hooded eyes.

Twist sat between Dena and Duke, looking back and forth at them as if she was watching a ping pong game.

Dena decided she wasn't amused or frightened. She was angry. "What are you talking about? You sold me your business. Now it's mine and I'm running it. I didn't steal anything from you. Remember all that money I gave you? You are absolutely crazy if you think I *defrocked* you. We used Finster—your attorney—for the transaction, for Pete's sake!

By now, all the customers had dropped any pretense of clandestine listening. Everyone stared openly at the two of them. The other tenants had joined them—Evelyn, Kober and Skyler from the front of the store, Max and Hugo from the back.

"I will ruin you! You haven't lived up to the terms of the contract and I want you to hand over the keys to this place *too sweet*." Duke Bughata adopted a low, menacing tone. A sheen of sweat appeared on his head.

He grabbed for the keys sitting on the front counter, but Dena was faster. She batted his arm away and pocketed her keys.

"Assault! You assaulted me! You all saw it." Duke bellowed, glancing around the bookstore looking for confirmation.

"I will do worse—much worse—if you don't get out of here this minute." Dena put a palm on the middle of Duke's back and forcefully guided him out of the bookstore. When they reached the threshold, he stopped short, causing an accidental flourish to her final shove. He stumbled into the Marketplace promenade to the surprised stares of other shoppers who hadn't witnessed the scene inside the store. They *tsked-tsked* and gave her angry looks, shocked at her behavior to a customer.

Duke overreacted to her push, off balance and windmilling his arms, before dramatically falling to the floor with a loud OOF and then a groan. Other shoppers helped him to his feet.

Dena saw phones whipped out of pockets and purses and held to record whatever was going to happen next. She shouldn't have been surprised, but she stared, incredulous, at all the gawkers, ready to post everything they encountered directly to social media. Or perhaps the authorities. She glared—and maybe even bared her teeth —at the videographers closest to her: a twenty-something girl popping gum who kept giggling and clamping a hand over her mouth every few seconds; a kid with a skateboard panning his phone all over the place, seemingly unsure of which action would garner the most attention on his feed;

and a plump woman incongruously dressed up top in a grungy hoodie pulled up over a baseball cap and down below in a pair of elaborately hand-painted knee-high boots with three-inch stiletto heels. Somebody should be shooting video all up in *their* faces, see how they liked it.

When Duke regained his balance, he saw the crowd gathered, cellphones directed his way. He raised one arm directly in front of him and pointed in a semicircle at the shoppers. "You are my witnesses. She assaulted me! You all saw it."

Duke ended the semicircle by pointing his finger at Dena. She glowered as all the phones panned toward her, spasms of irritation flashing across her face.

He repeated, "You all saw," then he fled from the Marketplace.

Everyone watched him leave then began to move about their business again, holstering their phones. As one woman passed Dena, she wagged her finger and said, "That's a shameful way to treat your customers."

"He wasn't my—"

"Shameful," she repeated, more vehemently.

Others hurried past, giving Dena a wide berth, as if they thought she might assault them too. The woman in the boots headed for the outside door, and the twenty-something girl and the boarder boy stood in the middle of the promenade comparing phone screens, probably trying to decide who got the better angle or the most unflattering images of the squabble, and whether any of it was upload-worthy.

Dena returned to the bookstore. She watched as all the customers who had, just ten minutes earlier, been ready to pay for their purchases, instead drop the books they carried like they were coated in three-week-old curdled milk. They scurried from the store.

"What was that all about, dear?" Evelyn pulled a tissue from the sleeve of her mint green cardigan and offered it to Dena.

Dena shook her head, declining the tissue. "I have no idea." She noticed Twist sitting in the exact place they'd left her.

"Is that his dog? If so, he forgot her," Skyler said.

"He doesn't deserve a dog." Dena spat out the words, heart pounding, adrenaline beginning to course through her system.

"You can't keep her," Kober warned. "He's gonna come back and be mad."

Dena turned on her, eyes flashing. "Mad at who? Me? I didn't do anything. And I'm not keeping her … she's just sitting there. Besides, if you forget your dog, you come back immediately. Or you don't forget her in the first place. He doesn't deserve to own a bookstore—especially mine—and he doesn't deserve her!" Dena calmed herself by dropping to one knee and hugging Twist. The dog responded by leaning into Dena's hug.

"Who was that nutjob?" Hugo asked.

"What was all that hoopla about?" Max rasped, hooking his thumbs in his suspenders in the way of eighty-year-old men across the globe.

Dena gave Twist one more face rub before standing up. "Darned if I know. He's the guy I bought the bookstore from. He came in here ranting and raving like a lunatic that I hadn't fulfilled the terms of my contract."

"Which are …?" Kober raised her eyebrows which dislodged the precarious nest of hair on her head. She patted it back into place.

"Which are that I pay him money. Which, for the record, I did."

"There must be something else, dear," Evelyn said softly.

"There's not," Dena snapped. "I'm sorry, Evelyn. I didn't mean to go ballistic on you. I'm trying to wrap my head around what just happened."

"Well, it's over now," Max said. To Evelyn he said, "You have some pirates ready to walk the plank and some cowpokes and saloon girls right after them."

"Oh my! I almost forgot." Evelyn and Max hurried back to their photography studio to attend to their customers.

"Are you okay?" Skyler placed her hand on Dena's shoulder.

"Yes, thanks. Just a bit shook up."

"Let us know if he comes back," Hugo said as he returned to his shop via the back door through the vendor room.

"Better take another look at your contract," Kober said. "And don't keep the dog."

"I'm not—" Dena sighed. "Yes, thank you." She didn't need Kober's advice to reread her contract. She pulled open the two-drawer file cabinet under the front counter and plopped the folder open. Paging through every single piece of paper, she read all the terms of the sale of the bookstore. Not one paragraph or sentence jumped out at her as something surprising, or an item of business she hadn't fulfilled. She closed the folder and refiled it.

When she stood, she glanced around her empty bookstore and prepared some mental sentences—entire paragraphs, actually—to use to reprimand Duke Bughata when he returned for his dog.

Kober

"I CAN'T BELIEVE Dena is going to steal that dog." Kober tut-tutted to herself as she stirred batter for some pecan blondies heading to the oven.

Her disapproval was less about Dena, though, and more about her choice of bakery items. If she had known she wasn't going to be able to find more white chocolate this close to Valentine's Day, she would have made brownies instead of blondies and saved her white chocolate for something more special. It only made her feel the teensiest bit better that Hugo was having trouble with his suppliers as well. If he got his hands on white chocolate, fresh whole strawberries and cherries, and she didn't, she'd … well, she wasn't sure what she'd do. But it would be loud.

She appreciated Hugo's suggestion that if either of them found a supply, they'd double the order and share. She hadn't owned the bakery for very long and was still learning, but fresh, delicious strawberries and cherries in February in Colorado seemed like a tall order.

Hugo wanted to dip his supply of fresh fruit in chocolate. She wanted hers to grace the tops of her beautifully decorated petits fours, each one a bite-sized, five-layered, delicious work of art.

"Oh well," she said to her batter. "At least stealing a dog isn't on my to-do list today."

Kober mulled over the amount of vindictiveness you'd need to steal someone's pet.

She learned something new about the other Marketplace tenants every day it seemed.

For instance, she knew Evelyn had become obsessed with a virtual reality role playing game where she hunted treasure and slayed dragons. And Max liked to sit on the couch and watch her do it all evening.

She also recently learned, when she offered to share her lunch with him, that Hugo didn't like tuna from a can mixed with mayo and pickles like a normal person.

And Skyler could talk for three hours on the phone to her parents at the drop of a hat.

But she never knew Dena could steal a dog. Didn't mean they couldn't be friends, though.

Kober sold a dozen assorted tarts to a customer, then picked up her stainless-steel bowl of batter again. The curve of her ample bosom helped hold it tightly in place as she whisked. She wandered out of the back door of her shop, through the vendor room, and next door through the back door of the bookstore.

"Everything okay in here? Any more assaults going down?" she said too loudly, breathing hard due to the vigorous whisking.

Dena started to shush her then glanced around. There were no customers to be concerned with. "You're such a riot."

"What are you doing?" Kober asked.

"I'm taking advantage of my lack of customers to put a dent in inputting this inventory list."

"Inventory? How industrious." Kober stopped whisking and shook out her hand and arm.

"Are you here to help or just bother me? Or is it wishful thinking to hope you brought me something delicious?"

"Just here to bother you. I can't believe you're stealing this dog." Kober nodded at Twist.

"For the last time, I haven't ever, nor do I plan to, steal anything from Duke Bughata. Not this store, not this dog."

They both stared down at Twist. She stared up at them.

"Did she just wink at me?" Kober asked.

"I wouldn't doubt it. She's kind of amazing."

"I thought you just said you weren't going to steal her."

"I'm not! I simply said she was amazing. That lunatic doesn't deserve her, obviously, but I'm sure he'll be back to get her."

Kober handed Dena the bowl of batter and took a knee next to Twist. She rubbed her velvety ears and kissed her on the snout.

"Oh, I see. You don't want me to steal her so you can." Dena laughed.

"My kids have been on me for ages to get them a dog. I hope your lunatic comes back to get her before school lets out and my kids see her."

Kober's four children hung out at the Marketplace every day after school. The ten-year-old twins *practiced their parkour* which Kober knew was code for hurtling themselves off any surface and giving their mother a heart attack. Fourteen-year-old Wyatt would once again spend his time devising clever excuses for not completing his homework, which would have taken him half the time to complete.

And sixteen-year-old Jain would be here to mother them all, Kober included.

She couldn't wait to see them, but really, truly, absolutely did not want them to see this dog.

"Holler at me when he comes to get the dog." Kober reached for the bowl, but changed her mind, kneeling back down next to Twist for more nuzzling. "I think maybe I'll give him a piece of my mind."

"Stand in line."

Balaam

BALAAM, the smoke-colored Persian cat, screeched to a stop in the Marketplace promenade in front of the bookstore. He stuck his nose in the air. What was that stench?

He investigated further, isolating the odor to inside the bookstore. He hissed at two women walking past, then hugged the wall into the store. He wound his way under tables, stopping occasionally with both his nose and tail in the air.

This was highly unpleasant, he decided. Especially for a store with no food. Now there was absolutely nothing redeeming about this place.

Balaam circled the leg of a table, stopping short at the sight in front of him.

Was that a … a dog?

What in the world would a dog be doing in my Marketplace?

Balaam inched forward, hair puffed so much he looked like a campfire marshmallow.

Unmoving, the interloper stared at him as he crept

closer. Balaam relished a fight and knew with his superior skills, well-timed hisses, and razor-sharp claws he'd be no match for the white blob he saw in front of him.

The white blob raised her head from her paws but didn't stand up.

Balaam hissed.

The white blob blinked.

Balaam hissed again.

The white blob flopped on to her side.

Balaam jumped backward, startled. Was this some kind of trick? Feigning indifference, but coiled, ready to spring at me when I'm not ready? Joke's on you, dog. I'm always ready.

Balaam edged into scratching distance. He prepared to slice the dog's snout, tensing the muscles in one front leg, rearing back with the other, paw ready to slice.

Suddenly, the dog was in Balaam's face. How did it move so fast? Balaam squeezed his eyes tightly, bracing for painful impact even as he scrambled backward.

Balaam ran for the cover of the closest table. What was happening here? He peeked around the leg of the table.

The dog sat back down, watching with ears perked and tail twitching.

Dena tensed, watching them. "Twist, meet Balaam, the world's most evil cat. Balaam, meet Twist. You could learn a thing or two from her."

Dumbfounded, unable to process this information, Balaam remained rooted to the spot under the table, even when Twist padded toward him.

Try it, dog. Just try it. I will succumb to no further tomfoolery from the likes of you.

Twist stopped mere inches from Balaam.

Balaam skittered from the bookstore, scrabbling on the

tile of the promenade, trying to get enough purchase to race into the safety of Evelyn and the photography studio next door.

So help me, there better be kibble and a lap handy.

Hugo

HUGO STARED AT HIS SUPPLIES, trying to determine how he'd be able to salvage Valentine's Day if there were no traditional chocolate-covered strawberries or cherries for his customers.

At least he'd have customers, though. The way those bookstore browsers high-tailed it out of Dena's store after her altercation with that man was immediate. Definitely had an air of finality to it. But that might just be his innate sense of fatalism, which he didn't know he possessed until everyone at the Marketplace pointed it out to him.

Why are you such a gloomy Gus? Evelyn asked on the regular.

You remind me of Eeyore, Skyler had told him at least twice.

Quit being a horse's ass, Max demanded.

Stop it, you'll scare my kids. Kober even jabbed him in the chest that time.

He hadn't even realized. Just the way he was born, he told them. *Well, snap out of it, you're bringing us down*, Dena had scolded.

Snap out of what, he wanted to say. My brain? My entire being?

Dena shouldn't talk anyway. Here she was, again getting into things she shouldn't. Cripes, that woman was a trouble magnet. I'd rather be an Eeyore.

Hugo waited on some customers, selling truffles and some chocolate-covered pretzels adorned with perfectly sprinkled flakes of sea salt.

He watched them leave then waited patiently for the woman peering into the glass case as she tried to decide what she wanted. Used to be, when he was first open, he'd try to steer them toward what he thought they might like, knowing absolutely nothing about them. They never accepted his recommendations, so he stopped making them.

Once word got out that he was actually a nice guy simply because he worked up the courage to ask his father to front the no-interest loans to the other tenants, things changed around the Marketplace. The other tenants felt like they knew him better, although he'd never tell them how hard he had to steel himself to talk to his father. Let them assume whatever they wanted.

Skyler had mentioned to him—nicely, of course, because she was Midwestern nice, even nicer than Coloradoans, if that was possible—that now that he'd shown his marshmallow center, he should try to be nicer to his customers too, that his superior, aloof manner reflected poorly on the entire Marketplace.

Apparently, everyone agreed with her, too.

But now, if anyone mentioned his demeanor again, he could retort—trying not to sound superior and aloof—that at least he had never assaulted a customer.

Not to Skyler, though. He'd never be so crass as to retort anything in her direction. He knew he should cool it with her, put the kibosh on his attentions toward her. He couldn't help himself. He'd had this crush on her longer than anyone knew, certainly longer than he could admit to anyone, but so far it hadn't been reciprocated. He hadn't been completely rebuffed so he still held tight to a tiny shred of hope, which was the amount of dignity he felt he possessed too.

He couldn't help it.

Just the thought of Skyler's smile made it feel like summertime and not February. If he could write poems or songs, he would. And a lot of them. Not to share with anyone, mind you, that would be beyond humiliating.

But he'd love to find something to allow some of this emotion to dissipate into the ether so he wouldn't feel like he would explode like a balloon too full of helium.

Or a fireworks finale.

Or a watermelon dropped from a roof.

Skyler

"THAT POOR WOMAN." Skyler thought about Dena while she put the finishing touches on a cheese tray she was making for the church ladies' Bunko game tonight. She rearranged some wayward almonds, but then the pile of olives looked skimpy so she added another handful. Dena was just minding her own business—literally, Skyler thought, smiling at her little joke. Trouble seemed to seek her out. So much drama just in the short time she'd known her.

It was such a shame, too. It probably made it so difficult to do what needed to be done for the Marketplace.

Skyler wrapped the tray tightly in cellophane so it would survive the trip from the Marketplace to the church basement.

She wondered how she could help Dena with any of her Marketplace manager tasks. But every time Skyler asked, Dena would get bogged down in complicated instructions, finally giving up. "I appreciate your help, Skyler, really I do," Dena had told her, "But I just don't know what would actually help me. It all seems too much to explain."

Skyler nodded, but had passed along to Dena something her mother used to tell her. "In the long run, it's easier to teach a kid to tie his shoes. But short term, it's so much quicker to just tie his shoes for him. It's up to you to decide how long you want to tie the darn things." Skyler had easily heard this adage a million times growing up because on a dairy farm, there was much to teach, and everyone had to do their share. Mom didn't have time to tie anyone's metaphorical shoes.

The fact that Dena didn't even realize she was still tying everyone's shoes didn't mean Skyler would quit asking if she could help. Dena, it seemed, needed all the help she could get.

They all did, if Skyler was being honest. The Marketplace required so much of all of them, and only Max and Evelyn were partners. Everyone else was on their own, unless you counted Kober's kids. They were here after school most days, but the boys rarely helped. Jain seemed useful and interested, but Kober had confided she didn't want the kids to think they were tied to the bakery, like she couldn't run it on her own. Kober especially didn't want her teenage daughter to learn a lesson like that, even inadvertently, so she made it a point to hype Skyler's cheese shop and Dena's bookstore as examples of feminist power whenever possible, and held up Evelyn as both a female and mature role model.

She didn't know about the others, but Skyler felt incredibly uncomfortable when Kober touted her accomplishments. Mainly because Skyler hadn't seen or embraced many of them yet herself.

Sure, she had learned everything she could about cheese before she opened her cheese shop. And, sure, she was making a small profit, but everyone was in this month or so since the grand opening of the Sugar Mill Marketplace. The enthusiasm from the town would wear off soon enough, and then they'd really have to double down and run their businesses like tycoons.

The question was, were any of them up for that?

Skyler couldn't say for certain whether she was or not. And if she wasn't, what would become of her? She'd have to go crawling home to her childhood bedroom on her parents' dairy farm.

She loved those cows, but they could be so judgmental.

Skyler needed a better plan going forward. One that even a cow couldn't find fault with.

Evelyn

WHILE SHE WAITED for Max to find the wayward ping pong ball, Evelyn read the amendments to the haiku anonymously written on the whiteboard in the vendor room.

> In the dark of night
> Or on a bright sunny day
> Sugar Springs ~~provokes~~ ~~delights~~ flusters

She wasn't sure which one she liked best. All were true.

Max located the ball so they commenced playing one of their sedate ping pong games in the vendor room. *Plink. Plonk. Plink. Plonk.* They were too old to play those smashing points like Kober's kids enjoyed. If she and Max hit each other in the face with a ball, it was probably an accident.

Dena sat in one of the folding chairs at a nearby table and watched for a bit.

"Game point, dear," Evelyn said to Max.

When she took the point, he said with a smile, "I just let you win, you old woman."

"Yes, dear. You just keep believing that." Evelyn placed her paddle on the table.

Max held up his paddle and the neon orange ball to Dena. "Care to play the loser?"

"Nah. I'm exhausted just watching you athletes."

Max placed his paddle on the table, trapping the ball under it. "You still thinking about Duke Bughata coming into your store this morning?"

Dena nodded. "Do you guys know him?"

"Not very well." Max sat across from her.

"He only had the bookstore open a couple of years before he shut it down and moved to Colorado Springs," Evelyn said. "As much as I liked having a bookstore in town, to tell you the truth, I wasn't entirely disappointed when he closed it and disappeared."

"How come?" Dena asked.

"I always got a … what do you kids call it? … a vibe about him, I guess. We didn't really know him all that well, though."

"Didn't you go into the store very often?"

"Oh, yes, I did. But he was rarely there. He always had a series of women running it who never stuck around very long." Evelyn looked knowingly at Dena. "Probably because he didn't pay them very well."

Evelyn and Dena held a moment of silence for all the women in the world subject to the pay gap, and all the bosses contributing to it.

"I think Swede's wife used to work there, didn't she?" Max said.

Evelyn nodded. "I think you're right."

"Swede who owns the hardware store?" Dena asked.

"The one and only," Max said. After a pause he added, "I never trusted Duke. Not as far as I could throw him."

"Why not?" Dena asked.

"He always reminded me of that kid on TV, Eddie Haskell. Always said the right words, but it was like the meaning was altogether different."

Dena laughed. "Ain't that the truth. When he was ranting at me, he used the wrong words, like he had a word-a-day calendar, but never actually read it."

"But it was more than that," Evelyn said. "Something down deep."

The three of them pondered that for a moment.

"I hope you're not going to let this bother you, dear," Evelyn said to Dena.

"I wish it didn't, but he said something about the contract I have with him which I can't quite figure out right now."

Evelyn *tsked*. "He's just greedy. Now that you've made a go at the bookstore, he wants it back. Just like after you break up with some guy and his new girlfriend spiffs him up. Happened to me and this old coot—" Evelyn tipped her head toward Max— "after his girlfriend Roberta gave him the 'ol heave-ho. I turned him into the prince you see before you. She did her darnedest to win him back."

Max guffawed. "Remember that time she came over with that cherry pie?"

"And she had nothing on under her coat except her altogether? And you sent her away but kept the pie!" Evelyn laughed so hard she began to cough.

When they both collected themselves, Max said, "Why don't you ever make me a cherry pie?"

"Because I don't have a long enough coat, I guess. Maybe you should give Roberta a call."

DUKE BUGHATA never came back for Twist that day, so Dena took her home for the night. "Surely he'll come for you tomorrow," she murmured as she opened the door for Twist to hop in the backseat of her car.

Dena blasted the heater to warm up the frigid car. She knew there wasn't much for Twist to eat at her house, so Dena stopped at the grocery store. They sat in the parking lot until the car was toasty, then Dena said, "Hang tight. I'm going to find you some dinner."

Twist's ears shot up straight.

Dena was reminded of something she read that said average dogs have a vocabulary akin to a toddler's, with around one-hundred-sixty-five words. "Super dogs" can learn up to two-hundred-fifty. Regardless of where she fell on the scale, *dinner* must have been on Twist's list.

She didn't want to keep Twist in the car too long, for fear it would cool down too much in the freezing February night-time temperature. She penguin-walked through the snowy parking lot, trying not to stumble or slip over any icy ruts. Once inside the store, she hurried for a cart then raced up and down the aisles tossing in a small bag of kibble for Twist as well as some people kibble for her.

When she returned to the car, she was pleased that it still felt warm. Twist craned her neck toward the front seat where Dena had placed the bag of groceries.

Dena drove home. She opened the big garage door using the remote clipped to the sun visor. She pulled into the garage and immediately tapped the remote again, lowering the door behind her. The last thing Dena needed was to open the car door and have Twist run away into a cold, dark February night.

The door from the garage to the back yard was open just a crack. As soon as Dena released Twist from the car, she nudged it wide open with her snout then made a beeline for the yard, immediately relieving herself near the shed.

"Oh, sorry," Dena said, waiting for her to finish. It hadn't occurred to Dena to take Twist outside all day. But in her defense, Twist never asked her to.

In the house, while Twist explored, Dena found two sturdy, non-breakable bowls. She filled one with water which Twist began noisily lapping up.

Dena looked at the mess on her floor then picked up the water bowl, wiped up the spills, then replaced it, but this time smoothed a placemat on the floor first.

She poured kibble into the other bowl and set it down on its own placemat. "Fool me once," she said with a smile, thumping Twist on her side.

Twist investigated the kibble, sniffing every single piece, it seemed to Dena, even using her snout to fling half of it to the floor. But she didn't eat it. She sat nearby, staring up at Dena.

"Eat it. It's food." Dena scooped all the fallen kibble back into the bowl.

Twist simply sat staring up at her, ears on alert.

"No, seriously. It's food, you should eat it."

Dena began to feel self-conscious with Twist boring through her soul like that. "Not hungry? That's okay too. But I am."

She pulled some boxed egg rolls from the freezer and began to heat them in the toaster oven while she chopped some broccoli, onions, and bell pepper for a stir fry. Dena tried not to, but found herself glancing surreptitiously over her shoulder to see if Twist was still sitting and staring at her.

She was.

Dena sat down to eat. "Your food is over there. It's perfectly fine. Go eat it."

Twist didn't budge.

While Dena ate, she began to wonder, is it perfectly fine? How would she know? Didn't dogs have an uncanny sense of smell? Maybe Twist knew something she didn't.

Dena knelt down next to the bowl of food and held a piece of kibble to her nose. She had to admit, it didn't smell delicious. Or even very good.

She stood and sighed, then set her half-finished plate on the counter. "Be right back."

When Dena returned from the grocery store, having penguin-walked through the snowy parking lot once again, she carried a different bag of kibble. She carefully emptied the previously untouched kibble back into the bag, exchanging it for the new brand.

"Try this one. It says vets recommend it three to one." She set it down on the placemat. "Since you probably don't know math, I can tell you that's pretty good."

Dena reheated her leftover dinner in the microwave while Twist investigated the new bowl. But when Dena sat down to eat, Twist was sitting by the table staring up at her again.

"Seriously?" Dena squatted down by the bowl and tried to entice Twist to eat the kibble she held in her hand by making yummy noises and pretending to eat.

Twist finally came over and plucked one small piece from her hand. She rolled it around in her mouth, then daintily dropped it back into Dena's hand.

"Gross." Dena got up to wash her hands, then reheated her dinner again. "Fine. If you're not hungry, you're not hungry." She took a couple of bites, trying to ignore Twist staring at her with those big brown eyes and those expectant ears. "When my kids were little, we'd play Eat It Or Don't. I can teach you the rules. They're pretty easy."

Dena took another bite. "Ohferpetesake."

She shoved her arms in the sleeves of her parka, swirled a scarf around her neck, and pulled on her warmest gloves. She hurried to her car, glad she bundled up. The temperature had dropped considerably each time she'd gone out.

Twist was waiting at the front door when Dena returned with the newest bag of kibble.

Offering the newly-filled bowl under Twist's nose, she said, "This is the last one. It's the most expensive so you may as well choose it. Hope you like salmon."

Twist flicked her tail and went to sniff this latest offering.

Dena held her breath and heated up her own dinner, hopefully for the last time. She tried not to watch while Twist plucked some kibble from the bowl with her delicate front teeth and crunched it. By the time Dena finished her dinner, Twist had almost cleaned her bowl. There was a scattering of kibble left in the bottom, like a tithe.

"You're a very polite girl." Dena thumped Twist on her side. "Picky, it seems, but not greedy."

She tried to decide what to do with the two bags of subpar kibble. Probably donate it to the animal shelter, along with the delicious one, after Duke returned for Twist.

When Dena had finished cleaning the kitchen, she invited Twist to join her on the couch to watch some TV. Twist dozed for a while, then hopped down and wandered the house. Dena took the hint and looked for some blankets to arrange for a makeshift bed.

When Dena finished her show and turned off the TV, she was surprised to see Twist with a sock drooping from both sides of her mouth. Her tail wagged slowly, mischievously.

"Hey, that's not for you."

Twist let Dena get within an inch of grabbing the sock before dancing away with it still clutched in her teeth.

Dena tried two more times before she realized this was a game she could never win. Instead, she ignored Twist while she got into her pajamas. Twist would tire of this game exactly like her children had when they dropped things off the tray of their highchair.

She went to turn out all the lights and make sure the doors were locked. By the time she returned to her bedroom, there was a neat pile of several pairs of socks in the middle of the floor.

"Very funny." Dena scooped them up and plopped them all back into the hamper, this time making sure the lid was closed.

Dena brushed her teeth.

When she circled it to climb in with her book, she kicked over another neat pile of socks. She fake-glared at Twist, and again scooped them into the hamper.

Dena read a couple chapters in her book, then got out

of bed to turn out the light. When she did, she stepped directly into another neat pile of socks.

Twist snored softly on the carpet nearby, but Dena was convinced she saw her open one eye the teensiest bit.

———

In the morning, Dena returned three more piles of socks to her hamper. But at least she didn't need to go out to buy more kibble. Twist happily crunched what she'd been given. Of the expensive kibble, that is.

When she finished, she nudged up to Dena who sat at the kitchen table eating breakfast and drinking coffee.

"You're welcome. I'm glad you enjoyed it." She rubbed Twist's white ruff.

Dena was trying not to fall in love with this German shepherd. She still couldn't believe that Duke would just abandon such a sweet, clever girl. Well, when he came for her today, she would not make it easy on him. He would be forced to listen to her Ted Talk about responsible pet ownership, and then the one regarding false accusations involving sales contracts.

"You're going to stay here today." Dena made sure Twist's water bowl was full, and as an afterthought, went ahead and gave her more kibble, just in case she got peckish before Dena returned.

In the light of day, Dena showed Twist the doggy-door that led to the backyard. When she bought the house several months ago, she hadn't even noticed it. Charlee had pointed it out to her when she, Ozzi, and Lance had helped her move. "I'll just pull out this doohickey here." Dena gave the closing panel, just a solid piece of fiber-board, a tug and leaned it against the kitchen wall. "You just squeeze through there when you need to attend to your business."

Twist looked at the doggy door, then at Dena.

Dena squatted down. She pushed open the heavy rubber flap and pretended she was going to go through. "See? It's easy." She pointed. "You do it."

Twist continued to sit and stare at Dena.

Dena opened the door, then stepped outside on to the small concrete porch with Twist still in the kitchen, then closed the door behind her. She squatted down and called out, "Twist! Come here … time to go potty!"

No Twist.

Dena was freezing to death without her coat, so she came back inside. "It's going to be a long day for you if you can't figure this out."

She stared down at Twist, second-guessing her decision about taking her to the Marketplace, ultimately deciding against it for two reasons. One, she wasn't sure it was good protocol—or even legal—to bring dogs to the Marketplace. And two, she really did not want to make it easy for Duke Bughata to collect her.

She put together something for her lunch, but then decided she better come home to let Twist out at lunchtime. She stowed her Tupperware of salad back in the refrigerator. As she closed the door, she heard a strange noise.

The rubber flap was swaying. Dena stepped to the kitchen door and looked out the window to the back yard.

Twist had figured out the doggy door.

Dena

DENA EXPECTED Duke Bughata to return all that Tuesday. She even enlisted Max to run by her house at lunchtime to make sure Twist was okay and to return with her lunchtime salad. She didn't want to miss Duke when he came by to pick up Twist. She had a lot—a lot—she wanted to say to him.

But Duke never came.

Max had told her that Twist was sitting by the front door when he went over at noon, which pinged Dena's heart a bit.

But when she opened her front door at seven-fifteen that evening and saw Twist sitting exactly as Max described, including the neat pile of socks next to her, Dena's heart broke into several Twist-shaped shards that threatened to cut into her deeply and permanently.

"Well, that does it. Tomorrow you're coming with me."

With a small nod, Twist agreed with her, and trotted off to wait for dinner.

As Dena filled the bowl, she said, "I don't really want

Duke Bughata trooping over here to get you anyway. I'm not sure I want that odious man knowing where I live. Besides, coming to the Marketplace will give you something else to think about than collecting my socks."

Dena frowned. She was positive she'd closed the hamper.

————

On Wednesday morning Dena and Twist raised the security gate in front of the bookstore. It was early, the Marketplace not yet open, but it was Dena's habit to raise it as soon as she got to work. It creeped her out a little bit to work in the store with the gate down. It made her feel like she was in prison.

She tried to get as much work done as possible before the Marketplace opened and customers began coming in. If she didn't raise the gate, invariably she'd get immersed in some project and forget to open the store. It only took that one time when customers began haranguing her from the other side of the gate until she raised it.

And anyway, she'd rather be able to gaze across the bookstore and beyond the promenade where she could see the cobalt Colorado winter sky unobstructed out the huge Marketplace window.

Even when the temperature hovered below freezing, like it had been for more than a week, you'd never know it by looking at the sky. If you didn't know better, you'd think it was July in Sugar Springs instead of February.

Dena didn't think to bring the pile of blankets she'd made for Twist at home, but it didn't seem to matter to Twist. She'd already plopped down in three different spots in the bookstore, immediately falling asleep each time.

Dena had been working, standing at the front counter

poring over the latest responses from businesses expressing interest in leasing space at the Marketplace. She stepped backward to stretch, tripping over Twist who had silently moved directly behind her for a nap. In regaining her balance, Dena kicked the ancient desktop computer she'd stowed under the front counter and felt guilty she hadn't even tried to fire it up. Because of the rush of getting ready for the grand opening in mid-January, Dena simply unboxed the computer which had been in storage with all the books and shelving, forgetting about it until now.

She bent down to adjust the angle and place it less in kicking proximity. It was so ancient that she wasn't even sure it worked. It might even be hand-cranked, she thought with a smile.

Once she determined that her pricing system for the majority of books in her store was the simple calculation of half off the original cover price, she had promptly forgotten about the computer. Her cash register and credit card reader handled all the sales transactions. Charlee's books sold at full cover price, as they were the only new books in the place, on a dedicated table you couldn't miss when you walked in. The rare or first edition Colorado history books she received from Quint O'Dell were all priced by him, using some formula lost on Dena. He made a list, she okayed it and attached it to a clipboard that lived on a shelf under the front counter. They split everything that sold fifty-fifty. Dena's process was as streamlined as she could make it, under the rushed circumstances.

The bookstore also came with a CPA named Ginger. Dena pictured her with flaming red hair, but had yet to meet her since she worked out of an office located in Colorado Springs, about ninety minutes away.

After a brief phone interview soon after she bought the bookstore, Dena decided to keep her on as CPA. Ginger had explained that all the financials Dena needed for the bookstore lived on that antiquated computer. She knew the system and was happy to stay on the job until Dena was up and running, at which point she could guide her in an upgrade. Dena quizzed Ginger about the necessity of using the ancient computer. Thank goodness for Ginger. They negotiated an easy and efficient system without using the ancient computer. Dena emailed her bank deposit receipts and any expenses every couple of days, and Ginger tracked it for her.

They agreed that when things calmed down a bit at the Marketplace and Dena was more comfortable with how she wanted everything to work, she would upgrade to bona fide accounting software to go along with her inventory management program. But that seemed overwhelming right now, especially when her procedures were low-tech and working just fine.

Dena shooed Twist out from behind her and into the middle of the store where she'd be visible and not a tripping hazard.

By moving the computer out of the way, Dena had inadvertently created a monster of the shelves beneath the front counter. She struggled to move everything into better position, now that she understood her needs better. Filled with the entrepreneurial spirit, before she opened the store she had purchased scads of supplies, many of which turned out to be laughably unnecessary. She consoled herself by acknowledging she was surely not the first person who'd been seduced at the office supply store by all manner of colorful, seemingly useful items that actually had no use in the real world. Nor would she be the last.

With a guilty conscience that she'd submitted those receipts to Ginger, she shoved the unopened boxes of colored markers, index cards, and rubber bands to the far corner.

While her head remained buried deep under the front counter, Dena thought she heard someone in the store, even though she was sure she still had plenty of time before opening. She called out, "Just a sec!" but before she could extricate herself, she heard high heels click-clacking out in the promenade.

Twist sat at the threshold staring into the promenade.

Dena walked across the bookstore. She rubbed the side of Twist's head and fake-scolded her. "You should have bit her or something to keep her in here. We need all the customers we can get." As soon as the words left her mouth, however, Dena had a real fear that maybe Twist had scared the woman away. She was walking awfully fast away from the store. Not everyone liked dogs, after all. Even though Twist was white and a bit daintier than some of the enormous black-and-tan German shepherds, Dena acknowledged that she still probably had the ability to intimidate people.

Especially if they wore socks.

Maybe it hadn't been a good idea to bring Twist to the Marketplace after all. It's one thing to have Balaam the cat slinking around on the periphery, but a German shepherd doesn't quite slink. Nor does she stay on the periphery.

It was probably a moot point anyway. Surely Duke Bughata would come for her today.

But by the time Kober's children showed up at the Marketplace after school, Twist was still there. Despite Dena's gentle suggestions from yesterday about getting too attached, the four of them—five, including Twist—were ecstatic. Dena was worried. She didn't have the heart to tell them that all of this was temporary, that Duke would be back for her as soon as the humiliation about his poor behavior ebbed away and he could face Dena (and Twist) again.

Dena made a mental note to mention to Kober that she should start preparing them for Twist's departure.

Dena had her own heart to prepare.

Dena

BUT DUKE DIDN'T SHOW up on Wednesday either.

On Wednesday night, Dena bought Twist a doggy bed to keep at the store so she'd be out of the way and not a tripping hazard.

On Thursday morning, Dena had to cajole Twist into using it. Just like with the doggy door in her kitchen, Dena did everything short of curling up in it so Twist could see how comfortable it was.

Twist sat watching Dena while she explained, pointed, and begged for Twist to just step into it. "You'll see how soft it is. It was the plushest one they had. Look, it's just like a miniature couch."

Finally, Dena laughed and reached a hand under Twist's belly to get her to stand up. "Okay, if this is another game, let's play." Dena straddled Twist and with a slight tug of her collar began walking forward together, as if Dena were riding her. She knew Twist wasn't in any distress because she could feel her tail slapping back and forth against the back of her thighs as they progressed forward.

When they reached the dog bed, Dena said, "I should put a pea underneath, for the princess," and kissed Twist on her hairy noggin. Dena stepped aside and gave Twist a little pat then a push on her hindquarters to get her all the way in.

Twist pawed at it, made three complete orbits, then collapsed in a heap. She rested her chin on the arm of the dog bed and gave a contented sigh.

Dena shot her with a finger gun. "Told you so. Enjoy the lap of luxury."

Wyatt and Jain showed up after school at two-thirty-five on the dot and raced into the bookstore, each carrying one of the gigantic chocolate chip cookies their mother baked. They started cuddling and playing with Twist who acted like she'd never been cuddled or played with before.

Dena's feelings were a bit hurt, but she decided to take the moral high ground. "She sure loves playing with you guys."

"She's the best!" Wyatt held his cookie aloft, where Twist's sniffing nose couldn't quite reach.

"When we moved here, Mom said we could have a dog, but she keeps making excuses, putting it off." Jain's arm was draped around Twist's neck.

Dena had forgotten to remind Kober that she should talk to the kids about Twist just being here temporarily. They'd already grown so accustomed to her, same with the twins. She didn't want to come right out and say it, so she hinted. "The man who owns her will be happy you took such good care of her for him."

Wyatt and Jain gave some noncommittal grunts and Dena realized that their hearts would have been broken if Duke had returned for Twist even just ten minutes after they met her.

Twist was that kind of dog.

Sheriff Keisha Johnson and Deputy Vince Chavez strolled along the promenade, wandering in the bookstore when they saw them there.

The sheriff glanced around. "Quiet in here today."

"Don't remind me," Dena said glumly. She'd been watching all day as shoppers streamed past the bookstore, heading into every store but hers.

"Who might this be?" Sheriff Johnson reached a hand toward Twist to let her sniff before petting her.

Deputy Chavez did the same.

"This little lady is Twist." Dena didn't want to say too much in front of the kids. "She belongs to the man I bought the bookstore from."

The sheriff nodded slightly, in a way that made Dena think she already knew the answer to the question she'd asked.

"My grandparents raised Boston terriers when I was growing up. I loved going over there when a new litter was born," Chavez said.

Everyone stared at Deputy Chavez, trying to figure out what he'd just said. Chavez spoke at triple time. He saw their blank looks and repeated himself, willing his mouth to slow down.

"Ah, Boston terriers," Dena said.

Sheriff Johnson watched as Wyatt and Jain romped with Twist. If Chavez spoke like the hare, Johnson spoke like the tortoise. "I had a dog once. Well, she wasn't actually mine. My roommates at the time trained therapy dogs. One of them washed out, but they loved her so much they couldn't give her up. Instead, they just kept training her."

"Even though she washed out?" Dena asked.

The sheriff laughed. "They trained her to *go next door.*" She used air quotes.

"You trained dogs?" Jain asked.

"Like police dogs?" Wyatt bounced from foot to foot, Twist joining in the dance.

"No, my friends were the dog trainers. This was long before I joined the force. We'd have these late-night games of poker or when we got hungry while watching a movie, all we had to do was stick a ten-dollar bill in her mouth and she'd go next door to the pizza place and they'd bring us over a large pepperoni. We all got a kick out of it."

"That would be awesome!" Wyatt shouted.

"Next door here is a bakery and a cheese shop." Dena turned to Wyatt and Jain. "You guys should teach her that. Way more useful than stealing socks."

Even though Dena was just joking, the kids started working with Twist right that moment, deciding that "next door" would be Kober's bakery because they figured she'd be less annoyed than Skyler would.

After the kids left with Twist, the sheriff came to the point of her visit. "We have something to tell you, Dena."

"That sounds bad."

"It's not good." The sheriff took a deep breath. "Duke Bughata has disappeared. You were the last one to see him after your very loud and public argument on Monday where you assaulted and threatened him."

Dena gasped. "Who told you that?"

"Can't tell you. Anonymous. Sorry."

"For the record, I never threatened him. I was just … trying to figure out what he was saying to me." Dena ran a hand through her shoulder-length hair. "Does it seem weird to you that he hasn't been back to get his dog?"

Sheriff Johnson leveled her gaze at Dena. "Yes, it does."

The look on the sheriff's face was not lost on Dena. This might be serious. Dena thought she'd been on solid ground with the sheriff after she helped her solve Norbert

Wallace's murder. Maybe not friends exactly, but peers, compatriots, on the same side.

"What does this mean? Are you accusing me of something, Keisha?"

Deputy Chavez had the decency to look away, but the sheriff kept her eyes locked on Dena's.

"I'm not accusing you of anything, but I'd like to know everything you can tell me about Duke Bughata."

"I don't know anything about him except his vocabulary stinks and he abandoned his dog here when he started raving like a lunatic that I owed him money or something. Monday was the first day I ever laid eyes on him. I talked to him one other time on the phone. All our dealings went through Finster."

"And the assault?"

"Pure fiction. I put my hand on his back like this—" Dena demonstrated on Chavez. "He was out of control so I steered him out of the store. He tripped and fell down, acting like I'd done it." The sheriff didn't respond so Dena added a clarification, "But I didn't."

Sheriff Johnson nodded at Chavez, then at Dena and they turned to leave the bookstore.

Dena called after them, "I didn't assault anyone and I don't know anything else about Duke Bughata!"

Dena was glad there were no customers in the bookstore as she sat on the stool near the front counter and took deep ragged breaths.

When she had calmed sufficiently and didn't sound like she'd just run a hundred-yard dash carrying a refrigerator, she gathered all the tenants in the vendor room behind all of their shops.

"Son of a funky mushroom."

Normally Dena laughed at Kober's child-friendly cursing, but not this time.

"Make it snappy. I've got a chocolate souffle in the oven." Kober's eyes darted to the back door of her bakery. She held up the timer in her hand and pointed it at Dena. "Two minutes."

"What is it, dear?" Evelyn asked.

"Sheriff Johnson just came by to tell me that Duke Bughata has been reported missing after I *assaulted and threatened him*. Her words."

"Who reported it?" Max asked.

"That's what I want to know." Dena gazed at each of them in turn.

Kober's timer rang loudly, startling everyone. "If you think it was me, you're wrong. Never met the man, don't care about him or his whereabouts." She hurried back to the bakery.

The rest of the tenants stared after her.

"Kober sure tells it like she sees it," Skyler said.

Dena couldn't figure out if she heard admiration in Skyler's voice or if Kober appalled her.

"Kober's right, though," Hugo said. "None of us know him. How would we know if he disappeared?"

"And why would we care?" Skyler added.

Dena glanced at Evelyn and Max. "You guys know him."

"I suppose … I mean, technically," Evelyn said.

"Why would you think one of us reported him missing?" Max rasped. "There were plenty of people in your store and in the promenade out front while the whole debacle was going down."

"Debacle!" Dena wanted to say more but Hugo interrupted her.

"Despite all those people watching, it still doesn't make sense that any of them—or us," he shot Dena a dirty look, "would report his disappearance. His wife or someone would have done that."

Dena mulled over Hugo's words. "I guess you're right. I just …"

"You just jumped to the wrong conclusion … again," Hugo said.

"I know. I'm sorry. It's just that … coming right on the heels of Norbert's murder …"

"We're all a bit unsettled, dear. But don't you worry about Duke Bughata. He'll turn up." Evelyn patted Dena gently on the back as she returned to the photo studio.

"Yeah, he will. Like a bad penny," Max said, following his wife.

Evelyn

AS EVELYN PREPARED for her photography appointment, she worried about Dena, in the middle of something again. How in the world did Dena get herself into these situations?

Evelyn racked her brain trying to think of anything that might help figure out this mystery. She couldn't even remember if Duke Bughata was married. Who did he have who might have reported him missing? And why would it be a secret? Was it anonymous to the sheriff's office, or did the sheriff simply not want them to know who it was?

She could ask Vince later, she supposed.

She'd keep trying to remember anything she could about Duke. Evelyn recognized the information stored in her 'ol brain filing cabinet was all still in there somewhere, but so much hadn't been weeded out for much too long and it was all jam-packed into every little cranny. Why can I remember my phone number from the 1970s, the names of the kids in my third grade class, and exactly how to sew my 4H outfit, should I ever need one again, but ask me what I had for dinner last night, or the name of that author I follow on the FacePlant, or that actor I like … we just saw him the other night in something … what was his name?

"Max?"

"That's my name. Don't wear it out."

"Who is that actor I like in that movie about the thing with all the noise?"

"Daniel Craig."

"Oh, that's right."

"Why?"

"I was just thinking who might know Duke Bughata or where he went."

"You think Daniel Craig knows Duke?"

"No. Never mind." She listened to him chuckle. "And you just hush up."

Evelyn continued to try to access her memory, but still hadn't come up with anything by the time her appointment arrived.

She took one look at the woman herding a man and three pre-teens into the studio and knew she'd have been better off continuing to think about Daniel Craig.

Evelyn tried to remember the name the woman had given when she'd called. She should have checked the appointment calendar before this. It was something cutesy and not at all age-appropriate. Prissy? Boopsy? Mimsy? Evelyn had sensed over the phone the name signaled it would be a difficult shoot.

Whatever her name was, she tapped her foot while she assessed the props Evelyn had pushed into place.

The kids didn't look up from their phones, the man stared off into the distance.

The woman began to wind through the studio, moving the fake hay bales, flipping through the various backdrops hanging. "This won't do at all." She finally noticed Evelyn standing there. "Oh, hello. I'm Bitsy."

Ah, yes, Bitsy.

"You're late." Max growled quietly, so only Evelyn could hear.

Evelyn raised her eyebrows at him, which was short-hand for *pipe down*. But she knew Max's corporate life made him less likely to tolerate people making appointments and not being able to keep them. Many a hopeful employee and salesperson found Max's office door closed with the lights out when they showed up three minutes late.

"I'm all set up for you." Evelyn waved her hand around the space. "The costumes are hanging over there, just take your pick from—"

"We don't want a *cowboy* scene."

The way she said it made it sound like the fake Old West they'd set up in the Marketplace was riddled with real dysentery. Evelyn almost laughed. Instead, she asked, "What scene would you like? I just assumed, since you didn't choose one when you made the appointment, and this is our most requested photo shoot."

The woman marched over to the racks of costumes and began aggressively flipping through them. "Don't you have anything for Valentine's Day?"

Max didn't look up from where he worked at the computer, but said, "Like the Saint Valentine's Day Massacre?"

Evelyn saw the corners of Bitsy's husband's mouth curl upward, as if it was rare that someone spoke to Bitsy that way. She willed herself not to smile along with him. She knew Max was probably grinning wide without even looking at him. She knew if they made eye contact, they'd collapse with a case of the giggles.

"Are you thinking of a specific period of history?"

Evelyn asked Bitsy sweetly. "I can't actually think of one …" She trailed off, pretending she was deep in thought. And she was, but she was thinking about how to get Bitsy out of the studio faster.

One of the preteens, still without looking up from his phone, said, "Let's just play cowboys and get this over with, Mom."

Bitsy tapped her foot more emphatically, then yanked costumes off the racks and tossed them at her family, choosing the sheriff's outfit as her own.

Bitsy kept up a running monologue the entire time they were getting ready. As easily as Evelyn was able to tune her out, she knew Bitsy's family had it down to a science. They may not even hear her voice any longer.

Evelyn didn't dare look at Max because she knew he'd make a face that would force her to laugh out loud. And if she started, she might not be able to stop.

Who *was* this woman? Evelyn felt like she might be in the middle of an SNL skit. She busied herself moving props back and forth, ending with them in the same place they'd begun.

Finally, they were all dressed. Evelyn organized them and their props, but before she had stepped to the camera, Bitsy had already started complaining about the prices and the package deals offered.

"We're going to want *two* eight-by-tens, and *twelve* five-by-sevens."

Evelyn pointed at the package prices listed on a poster hanging on the wall. "None of the packages come with that. I can give you the package with the two eight-by-tens, four five-by-sevens, and eight three-by-fives, but——"

"Fine. But I'll need it at the lower price." Bitsy licked her finger and rubbed something off her son's face. He grimaced and rubbed his cheek.

"The prices are listed next to the package description." Evelyn tried to keep her voice even as she picked up the camera. "Everyone say cheese!" Nobody did, but Evelyn began taking photos anyway.

"But I don't want eight three-by-fives," Bitsy said through a gritted teeth smile.

"No talking!" Evelyn sang out. "You'll ruin the photos."

Evelyn took photos quickly, much faster than she ever had with other customers. The entire time Bitsy haggled, first with her, then with Max when he made the mistake of looking over at her.

When Evelyn had taken plenty of pictures and Bitsy's family had dropped all their costumes in a heap on the hay bale, Max pointed at the package price list.

"So, Package One or Two?" he asked, standing at the cash register.

Bitsy tried and failed to frown at him. Too much Botox, Evelyn thought.

"Haven't you been listening? I *said* I wanted—"

"Package One it is." Max had already rung up their purchase and given the receipt to Bitsy's husband.

Bitsy yanked the receipt from her husband's hand. "No, I wanted Package Two at the Package One price." She waved the receipt at Max who only glared at her, making no move to take it.

"Tell you what…" Evelyn smiled, taking the receipt from Bitsy.

Bitsy relaxed, knowing she'd get her deal.

"We'll give you Package Two … at the Package Two price. Or …" Evelyn paused but didn't break eye contact. "Package One at the Package One price." Evelyn lowered her voice, smile still plastered across her face. "Or nothing."

Bitsy's husband and kids headed for the door without a backward glance.

Bitsy stared at Evelyn. "Package One, then."

"Good choice." Evelyn handed the receipt back to Bitsy who snatched it from her and stalked out of the studio. "Your pictures will be ready in thirty minutes!" Evelyn called after her in a singsong voice.

Evelyn and Max watched until she was gone, then Evelyn turned to Max. "Can you believe the gall of that woman? What a … a … Greedy Gus!"

"Watch your mouth, young lady!" Max's hand fluttered to his face in feigned horror. "Let's make a new package just for Bitsy and her kind. We'll call it The Saint Valentine's Day Massacre."

"I'll run out and buy some Chicago gangster suits and Tommy guns."

While Evelyn processed the photos, she fumed about entitled people who always wanted something for nothing.

Kober

KOBER'S SOUFFLE fell despite her precautions. Now she kneaded what would become a loaf of Italian herb bread. She punched and manipulated it until she'd worked up a sweat thinking about Duke Bughata.

If he hadn't already flown the coop, she'd give him a piece of her mind. He better undisappear himself and get back here to pick up Twist before the kids fall in love with her any more than they already had, she thought with a viciousness that surprised her. She was sure they'd given up on the idea of having a dog of their own and then, like a magician's rabbit from a hat, Twist appeared in their lives.

Every time they clamored all over Twist, Kober was forced to make a new excuse about why they couldn't have a dog. I'm allergic, she'd told them. Your dad is allergic. We can't afford it. I don't have time to take care of a dog; I can barely take care of you hellions. Dog hair! Dog poop! And besides, I never said we'd get a dog.

She knew full well she had promised them a dog after their move to Sugar Springs. But that was back before everything began to fall apart.

The kids were unaware everything was beginning to fall apart, however, or at least she hoped they were. Sometimes they seemed as if they kept the secrets of the Universe and she was the last to know. But a dog. Egad. A dog would create more problems than it solved.

But if Duke didn't come back here and retrieve his dog she'd … she'd …. Kober punched the dough. She didn't know what she'd do. But whatever she came up with, it would make Duke unhappy.

Very unhappy indeed.

Balaam

BALAAM SAT REGALLY, fluffy tail curled around his feet, staring across the room at that creature playing with the noisemakers. What had Dena called it? Oh yes, "Twist," a ridiculous name for a ridiculous creature.

The two youngest noisemakers played tug-of-war, first with the creature, then with each other.

Balaam flattened his ears as they stomped past, ignoring him completely, just as he preferred. He turned and hissed at their backs. Ridiculous, all of them.

He watched as the two bigger noisemakers tried to teach Twist the odd command to "go next door." Balaam sniffed haughtily. He knew exactly how to go next door without any prompting from anyone. He would never demean himself by acting so subservient as to do it on command, however. Clearly, he was more fully evolved, the dominant species.

Balaam's whiskers twitched as a dreadful thought passed through his mind.

If that man didn't come back here to retrieve that ...

thing … would it mean the creature would stay here? Indefinitely? In my Marketplace? With my people?

Balaam hissed in their general vicinity. Perish the thought.

He slunk away, hugging the wall of the promenade, back to the photography studio and Evelyn. She'd know what to do, and even if she didn't, she'd always have a lap.

A woman in high heels marched from the studio, coming perilously close to stepping on his tail. He hissed at her. She hissed back.

Skyler

SKYLER REWRAPPED and priced hunks of cheese, cut from larger hunks, and placed them in her refrigerated display case. She came around the front of the case to wipe away fingerprints marring the view of her beautiful cheeses, a task she diligently performed eight thousand times a day.

She felt guilty that she thought of Dena as she scrubbed away the fingerprints. Surely she hadn't done something ill-advised because she really liked Twist and wanted to keep her? Skyler couldn't imagine what Dena might have done, nor why she would have leaped to such a drastic conclusion.

Skyler refolded her scrubbing cloth. Her mind was on what had happened previously at the Marketplace. She had assumed that one mystery would be their quota at the Marketplace, but now was this another, right on its heels? Would this be the case in perpetuity?

She smiled at her hyperbole. Of course it wouldn't. That sounded more like Saint Mary Mead rather than Sugar Springs. Skyler stopped scrubbing. Saint Mary

Mead? That didn't sound right. Was that where Miss Marple lived and solved crimes?

Skyler dropped her cloth on the counter and picked up her phone for some quick research. But when her phone came to life, she saw the worst thing she could imagine.

Dena

DENA SCRAMBLED into the vendor area when she heard Skyler yelling something incomprehensible.

When they'd all come running, Skyler waved her phone around. "Guys! Hey guys … it's happening again! Listen to this." She began reading. "Former Resident and Business Owner Missing. By Aja Capitano."

Everyone groaned. Aja was a local reporter and a pain in everyone's neck. She and her husband Cap had taken over the *Sugar Springs Courier* from Cap's grandparents. They were young, fresh out of college, and anxious to stir up controversy to focus eyeballs—and dollars—on their newspaper, both online and print editions.

When everyone quieted, Skyler began again and read the entire article.

Former Resident and Business Owner Missing
By Aja Capitano

Unnamed sources at the Sugar Springs Sheriff's Department have confirmed that Duke Bughata, former resident of Sugar Springs, Colorado and owner of the now-defunct "Twice Sold Tales" bookstore has been officially reported as a missing person.

"Twice Sold Tales" was bought last November by Dena Russo and immediately renamed "Thrice Sold Tales," with a single location in the Sugar Mill Marketplace. The January grand opening of the business was marred, as readers of this paper will recall, by the murder of the Marketplace property developer, Norbert Wallace. Wallace's body was discovered by Russo on the second floor of the Marketplace.

A few days before Bughata's disappearance became official, Russo had a loud and public altercation with him. Several witnesses watched this drama unfold as it spilled from "Thrice Sold Tales" into the promenade of the Sugar Mill Marketplace. None of the witnesses wanted to go on record with what they saw, but their statements included phrases such as "shocking to see," "I was afraid for that poor man's life," and "she was out of control," referring, of course, to Dena Russo as she physically threw Bughata to the ground outside her bookstore.

Witnesses inside the bookstore confirm the tumultuous dispute had something to do with money, and perhaps ownership of a white German shepherd, possibly a show dog, who seems to be under the care, custody, and control of Russo.

One witness overheard Russo trumpet with disdain that Bughata, "doesn't deserve a dog."

The SPCA and PETA were asked to comment on the dognapping aspect of this story, but the Sugar Springs Courier hadn't heard from them before deadline.

Our investigation, as well as that of the Sheriff's Department, remains active.

"Today is Thursday." Max hurried into the studio and returned waving the print edition. "Front page here too."

Dena groaned again, this time louder, grabbing the

paper from Max. "Aja is at it again. *Unnamed sources at the Sheriff's Department?* It's only Keisha, Vince, and Gayle over there. *A single location in the Sugar Mill Marketplace?* Like they're dissing me because I haven't franchised yet? I had nothing to do with Norbert's death and they know it. *Physically threw him to the ground?* Absolutely false."

"You did push him," Hugo said glumly.

"I didn't push him, I just guided him out of my store and he tripped over his own stupid feet!"

"You did say he didn't deserve a dog," Evelyn pointed out.

"Twist is a show dog?" Skyler looked at Twist with renewed interest as she sat near Kober's children. "Is that a felony, you think? You know, to kidnap one? Dognap, I mean. If she's so valuable?"

Kober cocked her head at Twist who mimicked her in return.

"I didn't dognap her! He abandoned her here. And if she's a show dog, then double shame on him. Everything in this article is fiction."

"I hate to be the one to say it, but none of that article sounds false, like it's made up, Dena." Max had the good sense to look contrite.

Dena thought back to when Charlee was involved in Peter O'Drool's dognapping and how stressful that was for everyone. To lump her in with a real dognapper truly hurt her feelings, though. She was upset about Duke's disappearance, of course, but he wasn't as likable as Twist. Not even close. It was beginning to get old to be regularly suspected of some ridiculous crime whenever anything went wrong in Sugar Springs. Like she was a continuing character in one of her daughter's books.

"What should I do?" Dena asked helplessly.

"I don't think there's anything you *can* do," Hugo said.

"Except find Duke," Kober said.

Everyone returned to their shops.

Dena helped the lone customer in the bookstore, accepting his money for a copy of *The Truth of it All* by Gwen Florio. How appropriate, Dena thought.

After he'd left, Dena called Sheriff Johnson.

"Keisha, did you see that article in the paper?"

"I did."

"And?"

"And what? Do you want me to tell you it sounds like you stepped in it again? I don't think that's what you want to hear, Dena."

"Definitely not. What can you tell me about Duke's disappearance?"

"Nothing. It's an ongoing investigation."

Dena was quiet for a moment. "Do you think I'm in danger?"

"I think we're all in danger, all the time. Remember, accidents aren't always accidents."

"I was afraid you'd say that." Dena pictured the sheriff shrugging. "I guess I'll be starting my own search for him, then. It's the only way I can clear all this up."

"Be my guest. Just keep me in the loop."

"Does he have a wife or kids?"

Keisha remained silent for a moment before answering. Dena wasn't sure if she was debating what or how much to tell her, or if she simply wanted to make Dena sweat. Regardless, mission accomplished.

Finally, the sheriff said, "You'll probably find out yourself, but no, no spouse or children that we've found."

"Is there anything else you can tell me?" Dena asked.

Again, the sheriff didn't respond right away, but then told her, "I've already checked hospitals, morgues, and jails in the area."

Dena got goosebumps even though she'd begun to sweat.

This morning Dena's life involved dog beds, stolen socks, and books. Now it involved hospitals, morgues, and jails.

Dena

ON FRIDAY MORNING when Dena arrived at the Marketplace, the first thing she noticed when she walked into the vendor area to brew some coffee was the white board. It had a new haiku, written in bright blue marker.

> Could Twist be a real
> Show dog? If so, someone should
> Care for her better.

Again, like all the others, this one was anonymous. Dena had scrawled her share of haikus on the board, so undoubtedly all the other tenants had written their share of them too. Dena had quit trying to figure out the authorship, mostly because it didn't matter, but also because who had the time to solve every little mystery that came one's way?

While Dena waited for the coffee to brew, she gripped a mug in anticipation. It was one of the ugly giveaway mugs that turned out to be the last purchase Norbert Wallace ever made. If he knew that was going to be his lasting legacy at the Marketplace, maybe he would have tried harder. *The Sugar Mill Marketplace … the place you come to market* had to be the worst tagline in the history of taglines. Dena didn't want to think ill of the dead, but sheesh.

Kober came in as Dena poured a cup, so she poured one for her too. Kober, however, wasn't interested in coffee. Instead, she waved her phone around.

"Did you see this?" she bellowed in her normal jackhammer of a voice.

Dena groaned. "Another article?"

"Worse."

Dena grabbed Kober's wrist to steady her hand so she could see what Kober was talking about. She finally took the phone from Kober and saw a video with the clickbait title, "Rando Karen Holds Dog Hostage!" She'd rather poke a sharp stick in her eye, but clicked to play the video anyway.

She watched her own backside straddling Twist and pulling her by her collar through the bookstore yesterday to get her to her new bed. The short video played on a loop over and over, each time with a new outraged comment in all caps with the boldest, blockiest, angriest red font Dena had ever seen. Dena finally stopped the loop when she saw some, then several people, call for a boycott of Thrice Sold Tales.

She knew she shouldn't but began reading the comments.

"They're from all over the world," she said, disheartened. "And so fast."

"Haven't you always wanted to be a viral sensation?" Kober said ruefully.

Dena seethed but continued to scroll through the comments. "Were all these people," she read some of the usernames out loud, "Kennytucky, BarryLovesBaltimore,

PragueBlogger planning on shopping in a used bookstore at the Sugar Mill Marketplace in Sugar Springs, Colorado anytime soon?"

Kober shook her head. "People get worked up over animal abuse."

"Abuse?" Dena squawked, glancing at the screen frozen with her image standing astride Twist. "I wasn't abusing her! I was showing her the new doggy bed I got for her!" Suddenly Dena shivered, staring wide-eyed at Kober. "Do you know what this means?"

"That Twist isn't as smart as everyone thinks if she can't figure out where the only dog bed in the Marketplace is?"

"No! That some creepy stranger was shooting video of me that day!"

Kober's eyes widened to match Dena's. "Or *was* it a stranger?"

Hugo and Skyler walked in while Kober and Dena had horrified eyes locked on each other.

"What's going on?" Skyler clutched Hugo's arm and must have dug in with her fingernails because he flinched.

Kober showed them the video.

"It was only a matter of time," Hugo said.

"Time?" Dena practically shrieked. "It was like eight seconds after Duke disappeared!"

"Somebody knows more than they're letting on," Kober mused.

"Absolutely. But who?" Skyler asked. She released her grip on Hugo's arm and offered him a sheepish apology.

Dena narrowed her eyes and glanced around at her fellow tenants. "Yeah. Who?"

"Oh, stop it," Kober said. "Point your detective nose elsewhere."

Dena sighed. "Maybe you're right. This isn't like Norbert's murder."

"Well …" Skyler shuffled her feet and wouldn't look at Dena.

"What?"

"It's just … well … Sheriff Johnson was asking me questions."

"Like what?" Dena demanded.

"What exactly I heard, a blow-by-blow of the physical altercation you and Duke had—"

"Physical altercation! I wish people would stop saying stuff like that." Dena's chest tightened.

"Deputy Chavez wanted to know if you always wanted a dog," Kober offered.

"What did you tell him?" Dena crossed her arms.

"I told him I've only known you for a hot minute and we've never had a slumber party," Kober snapped. "What do you think I told him?"

Dena calmed a bit. These people were not her enemies. Before she could apologize, though, Hugo began ticking off the things Deputy Chavez had asked him.

"If I'd ever seen you and Duke together before, what kind of relationship did you have with him, what were the terms of you buying the bookstore from him, if you had financial problems … that kind of stuff."

Dena stared at Hugo, then at Kober and Skyler. "Did they ask you those questions too?" When they both nodded Dena threw up her hands in exasperation. "How in the world would any of you know any of those answers? This is ridiculous." Dena set her jaw and inhaled deeply. "This won't stop until I find Duke. If I don't, it'll be bad for my sanity, my bookstore, and maybe even the Marketplace."

Hugo

HUGO STOOD in the middle of Skyler's cheese shop while she talked about her new idea.

"Charcuterie boards are the new thing. People are buying them, so I was thinking maybe I could teach classes about making them. I could charge for the class and include all the supplies, you know, different kinds of cheeses, crackers, olives, nuts. Curly kale and sprigs of parsley and cilantro to make it pretty." She looked expectantly at Hugo, then her face fell. She took a step away from him. "You're right, it's a dumb idea. I'd have to charge so much money—and I forgot they'd need their own board too. Nobody wants to pay that much for cheese and crackers."

Hugo snapped out of it. He was listening to her. Of course he was. He listened intently to everything that came out of Skyler's mouth. But he drifted away for a moment, caught in a memory of her at the FrouFrouFood show. "You're wrong. It's a great idea. You always have great ideas. Remember how worried you were before the grand opening? You second-guessed every one of your decisions, but they all turned out to be perfect." He waved an arm around. "Look at this place … it's gorgeous." Just like you, he thought. He wanted to collect her up in a tender embrace like they do in movies and comfort her, convince her that a charcuterie class would be a smash hit. Exactly what this town needed. Just like deciding to use only locally sourced cheese. Pure genius. Why couldn't she see any of that? "You have to start trusting your own instincts."

"I don't know. Maybe. I guess." Skyler rubbed the curly edge of a leaf of purple kale between her thumb and forefinger.

"Maybe we should plan a trip to the next FrouFrou-Food show," Hugo said.

"The what?"

Hugo frowned. "The FrouFrouFood show? That big convention for trendy food artisans … like you and me?"

Skyler laughed. "We're trendy? You and me?"

"Believe it or not, you and I are the hottest thing to hit Sugar Springs, Colorado in a hundred years."

"That's a pretty low bar." Skyler arranged leaves of kale on a wooden board. "You know, I think I went to that FrouFrou show. A long time ago, before I ever really thought of opening my own store."

Hugo almost reminded her, but instead repeated, "We should go to the next show. I think it's—"

"Oh, hi Jake!"

Hugo had never heard quite that pitch to Skyler's voice before. Certainly not when she greeted him. He turned to see Skyler's cheese supplier, Jake Marchetti, striding in, smiling wide showing a full set of perfect teeth, including that one with the tiniest, most endearing chip in it. Hugo would kill for a chipped tooth like that. Jake carried several boxes. The sleeves of his flannel shirt were rolled up, showing his flexed forearms.

Good grief, he thought, that man is handsome. He's so handsome, in fact, he doesn't even need a coat. His handsome protects him from the elements, probably from everything unpleasant.

Hugo had plenty of self-esteem—or at least pretended he did; fake it til you make it, right?—but knew his female friends were right over all those years when they had commented at one time or another that he was cute, rather than classically handsome. They tried to make him feel better by adding that women were intimidated by men who were too handsome and would always prefer men who were cute, like a gerbil. He didn't point out the obvious: that none of them had a gerbil.

He also noted that Skyler didn't seem the least bit intimidated by Jake.

He straightened his posture but still couldn't reach Jake's height. Hugo felt like he was fourteen years old again. He clasped Jake's offered hand. "How are you, Jake?"

"Still kicking. How's the candy biz?" Jake asked.

Hugo took a beat and refrained from reminding him that his so-called *candy biz* was actually an artisanal chocolate shop specializing in handmade signature truffles, no two of which were ever alike. "The candy biz is fine, Jake. How's the llama juice biz?"

Jake laughed. "Never heard my cheeses described quite like that. But the llamas are fine, as are the alpacas, goats, and sheep."

"What, no yaks?" Hugo asked with a tight smile.

"Funny you should mention that. I'm looking into raising yaks. It's pretty complicated, though."

"How's Penelope?" Skyler asked Jake. "She's my favorite goat. What is she again? A Satan goat?"

Jake laughed. "Close. Saanen." Jake set down the

boxes. "I didn't mean to interrupt you guys. What were you talking about?"

"Skyler was just telling me about her plan to start teaching charcuterie classes—"

"It's probably stupid." Skyler blushed.

"It sounds brilliant," Jake said.

"That's what I was trying—"

"You think so?" Skyler asked Jake.

Hugo sighed. Gosh, it was a good thing Jake came along to tell her the exact same thing I told her. Otherwise, how could she possibly know her cheese board idea was any good?

He listened to Jake and Skyler flirt until he couldn't take it anymore and quit listening. He was torn, though. On the one hand, his ears might start bleeding if he stayed much longer. But on the other hand, he didn't want to cede any potential territory he'd never actually captured to Jake the Interloper.

He excused himself with a sour taste in his mouth. "This has been fun, but the candy biz doesn't run itself, you know."

"So, do you want to?" Jake asked him.

"Want to what?"

"Go skiing. I thought it would be fun, the three of us," Jake said.

"I don't ski anymore." Hugo's voice sounded flat and final.

"Oh." Jake blinked a couple of times and it was clear to Hugo that he wanted to ask follow-up questions. Jake was smart enough to keep the idea in check, however. Instead, he turned to Skyler. "How 'bout you? Wanna go skiing?"

Hugo could tell by the look on her face that she

thought the idea was distasteful as well, and he got a little jolt of smug self-righteousness zipping through his spine.

At least until she said brightly, "I don't really have time to go skiing, what with the hours of the Marketplace, but do you have snowshoes? We could do that just across the river some morning before I have to open the shop."

Jake enthusiastically agreed.

They both turned toward Hugo, but he knew neither of them truly wanted him along as a third wheel on their date. "Nah, you kids go enjoy yourselves." In his attempt at keeping the conversation less awkward, he only ended up sounding like his grandfather.

Jake and Skyler began making plans as he excused himself. Walking back to the chocolate shop he mumbled, "I hope your alpacas organize a coup and run you out of town. Or maybe just stomp the handsome off you."

Skyler

AS SKYLER LISTENED to Hugo talk about going to the FrouFrouFood show, she wished he wouldn't try so hard. She knew he was crushing on her, but she never did anything to lead him on and hoped he'd get over it sooner rather than later.

The last thing she'd do would be to travel to a trade show with him. What kind of mixed message would *that* send?

He'd never even asked her out, though, so maybe she was wrong. How embarrassing to go around believing some guy thinks you're hot but he was just being nice to you because he felt sorry for you. Ugh. But if he did ask her out, Skyler was prepared with her "it's not you, it's me, I think we should just be friends, gosh, we work together and live in the same apartment complex, don't you think that's a bit too much" speech.

She really liked having Hugo as a friend and peer at the Marketplace. All the other tenants were lovely, of course, but Hugo was close to her age and they both had artisanal shops, as Hugo liked to point out. Evelyn and

Max were such dears, but they were fifty years older than she was. Kober had a husband and all those kids to deal with, and Dena was her mother's age with a daughter just about Skyler's age. When she needed motherly or grandmotherly advice, or a perfect brownie, she knew who to turn to.

But Hugo was a great sounding board for her. She tested her ideas on him. When she spoke out loud, explaining to him what was in her head, it helped to solidify her thinking about whatever it was. When the ideas simply spun wildly in her head, she couldn't quite grab hold of them. But when she explained them to Hugo, they began to make sense.

As she told him about her charcuterie board classes, she began to see the entire concept laid out in front of her. She'd hold the classes at seven o'clock, after the Marketplace closed so she could give her students her undivided attention. It would be pricey, but the people this type of event would appeal to presumably had plenty of disposable income. She could order some chi-chi but understated hand-carved, branded cheese boards. Maybe she could even create a package deal in conjunction with the Sugar Springs Bed and Breakfast, enticing people to come for the weekend and take her class.

In her enthusiasm, she became aware she had sidled quite close to Hugo as she spoke. It had been pointed out by the other tenants that she was a "close talker." After they enlightened her about this unconscious—and obviously unwelcome—behavior of hers, she tried really hard to quit doing it. She mostly succeeded, unless she got too excited about something. Then her feet began shuffling as fast as her brain did, and she ended up directly in someone's face. With an apologetic look, she took a giant step backward, putting some distance between her and Hugo.

As Hugo nodded along with her description of the charcuterie classes, Skyler had begun to see the full potential of it all. She knew she had plenty of cheese and design knowledge to pass along to her students. They'd leave with tons of useful information they could deploy for parties of their own, as well as a delicious charcuterie tray, and a custom-made wooden cheese board of their very own they could use over and over again.

But still. What if she built it, and they didn't come?

Thanks to Hugo, she had decided to keep mulling it over, refining and polishing the idea when Jake had dropped in with her cheese order.

She hated how weak her knees got when she interacted with Jake. He was her cheese guy, for heaven's sake, not a Chippendale dancer making a house call. But boy-howdy, that man was almost too much. He made her feel like she was fourteen years old.

She did love talking to him, though. She loved his stories about the exotic animals on his ranch. She had grown up on a dairy farm—hence her love of cheese—so they had that in common. His animals were so superior to dairy cows, however, that it was like the difference between the World Series champions and a tee-ball team.

Jake agreed with Hugo that her charcuterie class was an idea worth exploring further, so that began to make her feel confident, too. Then, when he asked her to go skiing, she had a tiny tingle of hope that maybe he liked her as much as she liked him. The fact Jake had included Hugo in the invitation barely diminished the moment.

As she and Jake spoke, she began to feel greedy. She wanted her shop to be successful and her classes to sell out. Was it too much to want Jake to like her also?

Kober

SON OF A RIPPLED FOREARM, Skyler's cheese guy is here.

Kober was on her way to Dena's bookstore when she glimpsed him in the cheese shop. She reorganized her hair, wiped a hand across her face in case there was any wayward flour, and wondered yet again how she could incorporate some locally-sourced alpaca cheese into her bakery items.

She hurried in through the back door of the bookstore, reminding herself she was a married mother of four and shouldn't be having these kinds of thoughts.

"I'm a married mother of four, I'm a married mother of four, I'm a——" she muttered.

"Ay caramba. Is Jake here?" Dana craned her neck toward the promenade while she straightened her shoulders and fluffed her hair.

"In Skyler's shop."

"Oh." Dena returned to her normal posture. "That man is pretty."

"He's a good reminder that we're not dead." Kober paused. "Hey, listen. I'm sorry if I came off … however I came off earlier."

"Terrible, grouchy, pain in my neck?"

Kober offered Dena a choice between two cake pops she'd been holding behind her back.

Dena chose the red velvet one with cream cheese frosting and chocolate kiss on top. "I get it, though," Dena said. "Another weird problem at the Marketplace when we all have plenty of normal ones. Speaking of problems … now that the bakery has found its groove and you're making money—" Kober quirked her eyebrow causing Dena to ask, "What? You're not making money?" Dena ate her cake pop in one bite.

Kober shrugged. "I'm doing okay, but I just don't think it's going to last."

"You're a worrywart. Of course it's going to last. People love your stuff." Dena waved the empty cake pop stick at her. "You should call these Mary Poppins." At Kober's blank look, Dena explained, "Because they're practically perfect in every way."

Kober grinned. "Practically?"

"Well, since you asked, they're too small and that stick isn't biodegradable."

"It's always something, eh?" Kober licked the chocolate frosting off her chocolate pop.

"But what I was going to ask was, now that you're not so worried about finances, and you've successfully launched the bakery, how are things between you and your husband these days?"

With a noncommittal shrug, Kober offered a noncommittal answer. "Nic is still around. He works a few days a week in Denver, but the rest of the time he's working at home."

Dena thought about Kober confiding in her that Nic was on the brink of leaving her for another woman then asked gently, "Is it possible you projected onto Nic something that's not even happening?"

"I'm not sure anymore what exactly is happening. But I'm trying not to think about it. Let's talk about your problems instead of mine. I need some more fun in my life."

"I'm glad to know I am your entertainment choice du jour," Dena said wryly. "But since you asked, I am worried about the bookstore. This thing with Duke Bughata has blown up in a blink and I don't even understand it. He shows up out of the blue in my store raving that I owe him money or something—which I don't, in case you're wondering. Then I buy *his* dog a dog bed, and now I'm a viral sensation with a boycott called against me. I can't even…" Dena trailed off, shaking her head.

"You said yourself it can't be much of a boycott if none of them were planning on shopping here anyway. On the other hand, some of them are bound to be locals. The internet really excels at showing people stuff it thinks they want to know about. If they read the *Courier* online, that video link will pop up eventually. That's how I found it, anyway."

"Gosh, that makes me feel so much better."

Kober finished nibbling her cake pop just as her ten-year-old twins stampeded into the bookstore.

"Where's Twist?" Leo or Lincoln said.

Dena pointed to the dog bed where Twist was cuddled up, fast asleep. The twins hurried over to start petting her.

"Remember that cat who followed us home that day? Twist is way better." Leo or Lincoln had spoken to his twin, but Kober answered.

"You mean the one you were carrying? That magically appeared in our yard?" She rolled her eyes at Dena.

In unison the boys wiggled their fingers at Kober, pretending to be wizards. "It was magic!" They drew the word out for precisely the same interval and Dena knew this had to be one of their family jokes.

With a laugh Dena said, "I just wish I knew some magic to get people back in here." She wiggled her fingers around the empty bookstore like the twins had.

Leo or Lincoln shouted, "Alakazam!"

The other waved a pretend wand in the air. "Expecto patronum!"

Dena waved a pretend wand too. "Bibbidi bobbidi boo!"

Kober wiggled her fingers and pointed them at the boys. "Presto chango." She looked at her fingers. "Hm. Didn't work." She pointed wiggly fingers at the boys again. "Hocus pocus!" She blew on her fingers. "Third time's a charm."

"Who are you, Bullwinkle?" Dena laughed.

"A la … peanut butter sandwiches!" She ran to the boys and tickled them until they shrieked with laughter.

Twist jumped around them excitedly.

When they caught their breath, Leo or Lincoln asked Dena, "Why do you need magic words?"

"I don't really need magic words," Dena explained. "I need marketing ideas, like for a sale, something fun to get people to come in here and buy books."

The boys thought about that for a minute, then one of them said, "Say you'll shovel their sidewalk if they buy a book."

"Hmm, Leee—" Dena looked to Kober for confirmation. She shook her head. "Leeincoln, that's an excellent suggestion. The only problem with that is the sidewalks are clear right now."

Dena forced herself to remember that Lincoln wore

red today and Leo was in the Broncos jersey. It would certainly help her out if they always wore the same clothes. Or at least had a designated color. Kober could identify them by Lincoln's scar and Leo's mole, but Dena always second-guessed herself. She assumed they'd both rack up exorbitant therapy bills if every time they had any kind of interaction, Dena loomed right up in their faces, searching for scars and moles.

"Make everything one penny and I'll ask my teacher if we can come here on a field trip," Leo said.

"Sell candy instead of dumb old books," Lincoln said.

"Tell everybody you won't sell them books and then they'll want them more. That's how Mom got Wyatt to do dishes one night. Told him he couldn't do them because he wasn't very good at it and Mom wouldn't let him anymore. Wyatt wanted to prove he could do it good and now he does dishes all the time. Mom calls it backwards psychology."

Kober stared at Leo. "Reverse psychology," she said. "Not backwards." She looked with wide eyes at Dena. "I had no idea they were on to me. It's terrifying when your kids get smarter than you."

The twins kept offering sillier and sillier solutions, but then Dena heard something intriguing. "What did you just say?" she asked Lincoln.

"Give people each a bag and whatever they can stuff in the bag costs them a dollar."

Dena bent at the waist and looked him in the eye. "As soon as you figure out how to make a chocolate souffle, you'll officially be smarter than your mother." She gave Lincoln a high five then pretended he broke her wrist with his super strength.

He giggled before running off with his brother to practice parkour. As they ran out of the bookstore, Jain and Wyatt walked in.

As the twins ran past, Lincoln shouted, "I'm smarter than Mom!"

"Get going on that souffle then!" Kober hollered after him. "Where have you guys been?" she asked Jain and Wyatt.

"Robotics club." Wyatt took a knee next to Twist.

Dena shot Kober a melodramatically anxious look. "It's official. You have smart kids. There's no hope for you."

————

Evelyn stood in line at the bakery. When she got to the front, Kober said, "I hope you didn't want a cupcake. I just sold the last one."

"You're going gangbusters here! I'm delighted it's going so well for you, dear." Evelyn bent to stare into the case. "Not delighted I have to make a new choice between so many marvelous treats, though."

While Evelyn assessed her options, Kober asked, "Is this for you or for Max? Because I have it on good authority he's partial to my oatmeal cookies."

"This is for me." Evelyn twisted her face into decision-mode.

"Where is he, anyway? Haven't seen him all day."

"Probably home napping. He's been coming home at odd hours."

"Odd hours?" Kober looked concerned. "At night? At his age?"

Evelyn chortled. "You think he's having an affair? That's hilarious."

"Is it?"

"Oh my, yes." Evelyn pointed into the case. "I'll have a slice of the baklava."

As she readied the treat, Kober couldn't help but wonder if the idea of Max cheating was as ridiculous as Evelyn thought. There was a time she would have said the same thing about Nic.

<h1 style="text-align:center">Dena</h1>

A COUPLE OF HOURS LATER, Wyatt and Jain returned to the bookstore to show Dena how well Twist was learning the "go next door" command. Dena watched and listened, but she was only paying partial attention. After they'd had Twist run through her paces several times, Dena offered kudos for being excellent dog handlers and they romped out of the bookstore again.

Before they'd come in, Dena had been watching that viral video over and over, wondering if it was possible to put a genie like that back in the bottle. She couldn't use magic words, but maybe she could entice people to shop by making them an offer they couldn't refuse.

She hated the idea of giving Cap or Aja Capitano any of her hard-earned money, but she couldn't think of another way to reach potential shoppers. She had to buy an ad in the *Sugar Springs Courier*. She sketched out how she thought her display ad might look.

The newspaper's website was easy enough to navigate, which was handy because Dena was loathe to call them on the phone. She set up an advertiser account, then read through how to set up a display ad. She could send over a print-ready PDF or JPG, or for an extra fee, they'd design her ad. Dena glanced at her sad sketch and decided to pay them to create the ad. For yet another fee, they'd send a proof copy for her approval. She figured they'd do a good enough job whether she saw it ahead of time or not. Besides, she was no designer. She'd save her money and hope for the best.

Time was short. The clock was ticking.

———

Dena began practicing shopping and filling some bags. She'd decided to go ahead with Lincoln's Fill-A-Bag sale idea, but raised his price from one dollar to ten. She filled numerous bags, stuffed as full as she could make them, then tallied up each sale. If she sold each bag for ten bucks, she would have made a small profit on all of her prototype purchases.

But she began to worry. Could a store survive if it only made a small profit? She almost hyperventilated when she remembered the sales numbers that her CPA Ginger told her she'd need to clear every month.

In a panic, she logged on to the *Courier* sales portal to change her ad to read the bags would cost twenty dollars instead of ten. But it was too late, she had missed the deadline.

Other businesses had a loss leader—a really low-priced item to get people into their store where, it was hoped, they'd be enticed to buy more stuff. Fast food places sold ninety-nine cent burgers, then upsold you on fries, a drink, maybe even a milkshake.

Would this be her loss leader? Could it be?

She'd also heard entrepreneurs talk about getting exposure for a business, perhaps in the same way her sale would. But deep down, Dena knew that people died from exposure.

What she really needed was to find Duke Bughata to prove she didn't do anything to him, nor did she steal his dog. Then she could make her own viral video and get customers back in her store buying scads of books.

Dena wondered about Duke. It seemed awfully weird that he just left Twist here. She was a great dog and, try as she might, Dena couldn't come up with one reason why he hadn't been back to get her right away. And now he was officially missing. Had something happened to him before he could get back that day? What did his disappearance even mean? The sheriff said he didn't have a wife or kids, so who had reported him missing anyhow?

Maybe he was so humiliated by his behavior that he was just laying low for a while. Maybe he owed his landlord rent money and took the opportunity to skip town, which would probably be easier without a dog in tow. Maybe he staged the whole thing, knowing that she'd take good care of Twist. She'd had the impression, even as it was happening, that he had rehearsed his entire tirade, perhaps even written a script for himself and memorizing it before he came to the Marketplace that day.

Dena sighed. If there was ever a good time for all this to happen, surely right now was not it. She still had to find new tenants, which was becoming priority number one, especially if her finances were going to take a hit because of that video. She needed new tenants to take on their share of the Marketplace expenses. That would help to remove part of her financial burden. She knew the other tenants would welcome the savings as well.

She was still trying to digitize her inventory which was taking about a thousand times longer than she anticipated.

And she was still trying to keep tabs on her friend Georgia in Santa Fe who finally seemed to be getting back to normal after her hiking accident. It was touch-and-go and worrisome with her broken arm and medically-induced coma. Recovery would be difficult for anyone, but especially hard on a seventy-two-year-old woman. Dena had been trying to catch her to talk, but could only reach her voice mail lately. Not even Georgia's terse text messages came through anymore. Perhaps with her arm healing it was painful to use her phone.

While she was thinking about it—and procrastinating for two more minutes before going back to the inventory software—she dialed Georgia's number. Voice mail. "Hey, Georgia. It's Dena again. Just checking in to see how you're doing. I'd love to hear from you when you get a chance. If it's too hard to hold the phone or something, we can always video chat. Hope to hear from you soon!"

As soon as she put her phone down it rang again. She snatched it up, hoping to see Georgia calling back, but it was an unknown number.

Dena answered anyway.

"Boyd Drummond here."

Dena yanked the phone away from her ear at the loud voice of one of the potential new tenants she'd been vetting.

"Scoops Ice Cream, right?" Dena asked.

"One and the same!" Boyd barked out a laugh and Dena worried about her phone—and possibly her ear— cracking. "I just wanted you to know I emailed you the completed paperwork and dropped my deposit into the Sugar Mill Marketplace bank. They said they'll hold it in escrow until you give them the word our deal is final. I'll be there next Friday and I'll open the next day, if that's okay with you."

Dena thought about how long it took her to get organized enough to open the bookstore. "You want to open next week? The day after you get here?"

"If it's okay with you."

Dena's palms suddenly began sweating. She did not think this guy would be right for the Marketplace, but couldn't articulate why. Maybe it was simply nerves, since everyone else she'd vetted had fallen through and he would be the first tenant she accepted into their fold. It was all happening too fast. Plus, he was as loud as Kober. Could the Marketplace handle that?

"There's no rush, you know. We're not in any kind of hurry."

Boyd responded with another loud laugh.

"You really think you can get to Sugar Springs on Friday and open for business on Saturday?" Dena asked.

"I know I can," Boyd boomed. "I'm bringing my ice cream freezer cabinet with me. I have all my recipes, and my compressor can make two-and-a-half quarts of ice cream in thirty minutes. I have a business license, an EIN, and I expect I'll have my sales tax permit and health department paperwork by the time I get to Sugar Springs."

"And when will that be?"

"I told you … next Friday!"

Dena had been hoping she'd misheard him originally. She truly doubted everything he expected was going to happen, but oh well. The Marketplace needed another tenant and here was one with money, or so he said. She pulled up the contract on her computer and began going over it with him, but he interrupted her.

"Told you, already emailed it to you. Signed, sealed, and delivered. It all seemed copacetic to me."

Dena checked her email. There it was, attached to a

message, just like he said. "Did you have an attorney look it over?"

"No need. I'm sure it's all in order. I trust you."

"You really should have an attorney go over everything with you."

"No need!"

Dena took a deep breath and in what she hoped was a firm voice insisted he write down Finster's information to contact him. "He's the attorney we use for all the Marketplace business. He's very familiar with our contract and everything you'll need to launch your business."

"I told you, there's no need for all that formality."

"Mr Drummond—"

"Boyd."

"Boyd," Dena began again. "Please call Finster. He can make sure you have everything in order before you get here. Your timing is awfully tight. You don't want anything to go wrong and delay the opening of your ice cream shop."

"Fine. I'll call. But there's no need. Everything always works out for the BoydMan!"

They hung up after Dena made him recite back Finster's information, so she knew he actually wrote it down. She regretted ever answering Boyd Drummond's query about leasing the space, no matter how much she liked ice cream.

Why can't the emails you don't want just disappear into your spam folder? Then you'd never have to make hard decisions about them.

She called Finster's office but got his voice mail. "I just wanted to let you know that a man by the name of Boyd Drummond will be calling you. He wants to lease space for an ice cream store at the Marketplace and I need you to go over the contract with him to make sure he knows what he's getting into. And if he doesn't call you, please call him no later than Monday." Dena gave him Boyd's contact information then added, "Also, unrelated, I need to talk to you about Duke Bughata, since you were the attorney we used when I bought the bookstore. I need to find Duke. Please call me back as soon as you can. Thanks."

Dena

DENA LEANED against the entryway to her bookstore looking out into the crowded promenade filled with Saturday shoppers. People were streaming into the bakery and cheese shop and waiting in line at the photo studio.

Risking stepping out of the store and missing any potential customers—fat chance of that—she hurried around the corner to see a long line at Hugo's chocolate shop spilling out into the promenade on the other side of the Marketplace.

Dena walked dejectedly back to the bookstore. It was that article and the stupid video. She returned to the entryway and leaned in the same place again. Locals wouldn't meet her eye, simply scurried past, even the ones who had rejoiced at the grand opening and bought armfuls of books from her. She was positive it wasn't her imagination.

Everyone in the Marketplace seemed suspicious of her and acted as if setting foot into her store would cause them immediate and permanent damage. Like trooping over a lava flow. Or wading into a pool of piranhas. Or sitting at an elementary school lunch table.

Dena knew if a resident of Sugar Springs hadn't been an eyewitness to the altercation between her and Duke, they immediately heard about it from a friend or neighbor.

There was a time Dena relished moving to a small town. The pace was slower. Neighbors were neighborly. No traffic. But lately the bloom had slid off that rose. Was this the way it would be in Sugar Springs going forward? People who didn't know anything about what really happened, but automatically making her out to be a pariah anyway? Why wouldn't they give her the benefit of the doubt? These were her customers and neighbors, people who should know her by now. Granted, it had only been a couple of months, but she didn't get the impression Duke Bughata was a beloved resident or business owner of Sugar Springs.

The residents of small towns also knew everyone's business. Gossip was often a full-contact sport.

Dena's hand fluttered to her mouth. "I'm being cancelled," she murmured with dread.

Terror about her finances made her stomach roll. She was suddenly beyond grateful for Boyd Drummond and the money he'd deposited in the Marketplace bank account. Dena had confirmed full receipt.

She stepped away from the entryway to the bookstore and gave up staring at the shoppers not entering her shop. She picked up her phone from the front counter and dialed Finster's office, hoping he might be working on a Saturday. She knew his wife had recently retired and tried to get him out of the house as often as possible. Maybe today was one of those days he was getting on her nerves.

The phone immediately rolled over to voice mail, making Dena think that signified he was in his office talking on the phone. Maybe to Boyd Drummond, if she could be so lucky.

Dena hurried through the back door to the bakery, waving at the kids playing with Twist in the vendor room.

Kober moved like a well-rehearsed Rockette while she handled customers and pulled bakery items from the oven. She acknowledged Dena with a nod, but no high kicks.

Dena sidled next to her while she rang up a customer and whispered, "Would it be okay if I asked Jain to watch the bookstore for me for a little bit? I'll pay her and it should be pretty easy since I don't have any customers anyway."

"Sure, she'd like that." Kober handed a woman some change. "I'll be here if she needs me."

"Seems like you have your hands full."

"Yeah, it's been crazy. But I'm sure she can manage to sell books for you. She knows how to run the register and she has lots of opinions about books. She'll be fine."

"I'm sure she will, assuming anyone comes in." Dena moved a bit closer, confiding, "I'm not exaggerating. Literally ... zero customers."

"A temporary glitch." Kober turned her attention to a man who called out, "Are those cookies fresh?" to which Kober had to reply, loudly, "Son of a chocolate chip! Of course they're fresh! What kind of a joint you think I run here?"

Dena returned to the vendor area and beckoned to Jain. "Your mom said it would be okay, but I wanted to ask, do you want to be in charge of the bookstore for a bit while I run an errand?"

Jain's eyes widened. "Seriously? You'd trust me to do that?"

"Of course I would!" Dena didn't have the heart to tell her there'd be nothing for her to do except stand there and wait until she got back. "And if it's not, um, busy, feel free to grab a book and read for a while. My treat."

"Awesome!"

"Oh, but I'm going to pay you too," Dena quickly added.

"Seriously?" Jain's grin split her face. "This'll be my first real job!"

Dena laughed. "You work in the bakery."

"Totally different. You're not my mom."

———

Dena hurried over to Finster's office, hoping his wife shooed him out of the house and he'd be sitting at his desk. When she opened the door and saw him wearing his uniform of sedate suit-and-tie at his messy desk, she wanted to high-five someone, maybe do a jig. Instead, she waited patiently, catching her breath while he finished a phone call.

He turned to face her and she was momentarily astonished once again at just how large his ears were. His hearing must be magnificent. "I've been expecting you. I got a call from—"

At the same time Dena said, "Boyd Drummond," Finster said, "Duke Bughata."

"What? Duke Bughata called you? Where is he?"

"At home, I suspect." Finster shoved a pile of papers out of his way and began searching his desk for something.

"When did he call?" Dena became excited.

"Last week."

"Oh."

Finster continued searching his desk and spoke without looking at her. "Duke told me you were having second thoughts and might come over here to talk to me about voiding your contract with him." Finster finally looked up at her, over the rim of his glasses. "You can't do that, by the way."

Dena let out a weird noise that embarrassed her. But only a little. "I don't want to void any contract. Duke Bughata is nuts!"

Finster chuckled.

"Duke came into my —emphasis on *my*— bookstore and ranted about that contract and how I still owe him money. I have no idea what he was talking about. My contract with him is airtight … like you promised when I signed it?"

Finster nodded, still pawing through the piles of papers on his desk. "Ah, here it is." He waved a packet of papers at her. "Your contract."

He began flipping through the pages, but Dena watched as his placid smile vanished, replaced by a nervous frown.

"What?" Dena asked, alarmed.

"Maybe Duke was talking about this?" Finster pointed at a clause.

Dena grabbed the papers from Finster's hand and looked closer at the provision in question. It stated Dena was to pay Duke five hundred dollars every month. She read it four times before saying, "I would never have signed something like that after giving him all that money up front. That lump sum I paid was to own the store free and clear."

Finster adjusted his glasses and reread the clause too. "Are these your initials?"

Dena snatched the papers back. "They look like my initials, but why are they in blue there, but everything else is signed in black?"

Finster shrugged, holding out his hand for the contract. "You must have signed it on a different day."

Dena dropped her voice. "I signed everything at the same time."

"There was a lot to sign. Maybe you dropped your pen or it ran out of ink and you used one of mine."

Dena was suddenly so discombobulated. She racked her brain, staring at the cup of pens on Finster's desk, trying to remember everything that happened that day. People constantly scolded her for being rash, making decisions without thinking them all the way through. Was this one of them? That day with Charlee in Sugar Springs, with so much going on all at once. Is that really what happened? Had she signed this contract without understanding all the bits and pieces? Hadn't Charlee read over the contract too, or was that a fuzzy memory?

"Maybe," she said with a slight shake of her head. "But I want you to find Duke and talk to him about this. I can't have one of your clients coming to my place of business, yelling at me, and then disappearing."

Finster shrugged. "If he yelled at you in public, he was probably right to get out of there."

"No. Disappearing like missing persons disappearing."

"What? Says who?"

"Sheriff Johnson." Dena took a pen from the cup on Finster's desk and wrote her number on the back of one of his business cards in the holder next to it. "This is my cell. You get a hold of Duke, find out where he is, then you call Sheriff Johnson and tell her. Then you immediately call me with the same information."

The nervous look had disappeared from Finster's face. "That's privileged information," was all he said, even after Dena began arguing with him. She almost grabbed

Finster's Rolodex because she knew he had Duke's contact information in that ancient thing.

Dena glanced down at the business card still in her hand that Finster hadn't taken from her. Her stomach roiled. She took a few more pens from the cup, used each to make a scribble. She looked across the desk at him. "All these pens are black. Even if I would have used one of your pens, my initials wouldn't be in blue ink."

She stared at Finster who stared back at her for a moment, but then began shuffling papers on his desk again.

Dena knew without a doubt that not only had she never seen that clause of the contract, she hadn't used a blue pen to sign anything.

What in the world was going on between Finster and Duke Bughata?

Skyler

SKYLER AND JAKE met early Saturday morning for their outdoor recreation date. They had agreed that Jake would bring coffee, and Skyler would bring some of Kober's cinnamon rolls. They sat on the tailgate of Jake's pickup while they had their picnic and watched the sun rise. Skyler was careful to only sip a little of her coffee because she knew there were no facilities where they were headed. She didn't want to make *that* kind of impression on their first date.

She did consume one of the huge rolls and licked her fingers with gusto when she finished.

After Jake finished his coffee, they stashed their trash in the cab of the pickup and strapped on their snowshoes. Between the two of them, they had their Ten Essentials. They knew that even though they only planned to be out for a couple of hours, the Colorado mountains often had other plans for ill-prepared adventurers. In her backpack, Skyler carried a personal locator beacon, a compass and first aid kit. Jake carried a knife, waterproof matches, and a small tent. They both wore sunglasses, and stowed water, granola bars, headlamps and extra clothes in their daypacks.

They made sure their boots were tightly tied before stepping into the bindings of their snowshoes.

"Ready?" Jake handed Skyler her poles.

"I'll race you."

"Then I'm just going to wait in the car," he said with a laugh. "I haven't done this in ages."

"To tell you the truth, I haven't either." Skyler started off. "We're going to be sore tomorrow!" she called behind her.

"I'm already sore!" Jake called.

They walked for a long time in sparkling powdery snow. The only sounds were the whoosh of their steps over the snow, the crunch of their poles into the snow, and, almost immediately when they began, their heavy breathing because of the whooshing and the crunching.

Coming to an area where they could choose to remain on flat terrain, or begin to ascend into the trees, Skyler stopped. "Which way?"

Jake leaned on his poles to catch his breath. "You're barely breathing! I feel like I've run three marathons in a row!"

Skyler laughed, choosing not to tell him how her hips, groin, and arms began aching after their first hundred yards or so. "Shall we rest a bit?" Skyler pointed at a fallen log nearby.

They settled on the log. Skyler handed Jake a bottle of water and a granola bar then opened one for herself.

Jake's eyes rolled to the back of his head. "Oh my word, this is the best meal I've ever tasted!"

"I'd forgotten how much work it is to snowshoe," Skyler said. "We've probably burned seven million calories."

"Ha. We probably haven't even burned off those cinnamon rolls. That woman sure knows how to bake."

"She does indeed."

"So how do you like owning a business in the Sugar Mill Marketplace?" Jake asked. "I watched them refurbishing that place and couldn't believe how beautiful it turned out."

"It's fantastic. I dithered and dithered about whether or not to take the plunge here. I mean, I've never owned a business before and this was a brand-new place in a brand-new town. Well, for me, anyway. I came out to look at it with my dad."

"And he told you it was a good idea?"

Skyler laughed. "Absolutely not. But he kept asking questions until I felt like I landed on the right answer."

"Sounds like a wise man."

"I guess, but he and my mom run a dairy farm, not a store. I mean, they sell stuff, but it's not the same. Despite their confidence in me, I can't help but think they're misplacing their trust. I'm constantly second-guessing myself."

"I get that. Every time I think I've got a handle on everything, my brother says something to totally undermine my confidence. I haven't figured out if he's doing it accidentally, or if he's just a jerk." Jake held out his hand for Skyler's granola wrapper then shoved both his and hers deep in his coat pocket. "My folks liked the idea I was going to be a rancher, but when I told them what kind of animals I was going to raise, they really didn't know what to say. To their credit, they loaned me money anyway."

"My parents loaned me money too, but I still had to take out a bank loan. It's very stressful." Skyler wrinkled her nose.

"Every time I come into the Marketplace, you have a

ton of customers in your shop. And now, with your idea of running those classes, I don't think you have anything to worry about."

Skyler tried to cross her fingers on both hands, but her gloves wouldn't allow it.

"I envy you having Hugo and everyone there. It must be great being able to rely on everyone and not just yourself all the time. You must help each other out all the time."

Skyler shrugged. "I'm not great at asking for help. Growing up, I had to be pretty self-reliant. That's not an easy habit to break. And I'm not sure I really want to. I like learning how to do things for myself. I think the videos on CrowdCube are made solely for me. I mean, I learn everything there—tap dance, knit, how to cut hair." At Jake's surprised look, she reconsidered. "Okay, that one didn't go too well. But you know what I mean."

Jake took a deep breath. "If only there was a Crowd-Cube video to get us back to the truck."

Skyler looked around, alarmed. "We're not lost. Didn't we come from there?" She pointed at their tracks.

"I guess I don't need CrowdCube as much as I need a teleportation device. I'm beat. This was way harder than I thought it would be."

Skyler poked him in the belly of his thick parka. "That just means we have to do it more often."

"Okay, but only if I survive." He stood and pulled Skyler to her feet.

She braced herself for a passionate kiss, and leaned slightly toward him. She completely misjudged the situation and blushed furiously as he reached for his poles instead.

"Okay, let's head back." She took off back down the single file track they'd already made in the powder.

"Hey, wait up!"

She slowed down only when she had convinced herself he completely missed her faux pas. Her furious blushing could be explained as exertion.

It would be terrible to have to close her cheese shop due to a terminal case of utter humiliation, the likes of which corporate America could only imagine. She'd end up living in a back ally in Paraguay or Patagonia or Pittsburgh under an assumed name where nobody could find her. She'd dye her blonde hair jet black and grow out her bangs. Her only friend would be a nonjudgmental ring-tailed lemur who would never ask her about that fateful day when she thought Jake was going in for their first kiss but he only had snowshoeing on his mind.

How would she explain that to her creditors?

Dena

AFTER FORCING Finster to take her cell number from the shaky hand she thrust across his desk, Dena walked out of the attorney's office.

She started to return to the Marketplace, but then had a change of heart. Instead, she called Jain who told her all was well, that there had been no customers. Dena wanted to explain that was the opposite of "all was well" but decided a lecture in economics could wait. "I won't be much longer."

"Don't worry about me. I'm reading *The Westing Game.*"

"Ellen Raskin. Excellent choice. That was always one of my daughter's favorites. It might be why she started writing mysteries."

Dena walked over to the hardware store to talk to Swede's wife, Uta.

Swede offered her a cup of coffee to warm her up. Dena remembered how it dissolved her tastebuds exactly like turpentine dissolved paint. "Not today. I need my tongue intact." She turned toward Uta. "I understand you used to work for Duke Bughata at his bookstore back in the day."

Uta made a noise of disgust. "I did. Worst ten years of my life."

Swede laughed. "You were only there for four months."

"Seemed like ten years. Why do you want to know?" Uta blushed. "Oh. Right."

Dena sighed. "I didn't do anything to that man. And despite what the internet might have told you, I didn't steal his dog either. I'm trying to find him to clear all this up. There's been some weird misunderstanding that's blowing up my life right now."

"Sounds like Duke." Uta shrugged. "I don't really know what I can tell you. He only came in every so often to clear out the register and drop off my measly paycheck."

"You don't know how to contact him?"

Uta shook her head, then stopped. "Oh, wait. Maybe I still have his number in my phone." She scrolled, then smiled and held it out to Dena. His number was labeled Jerk Boss.

Dena entered the number into her own contacts then dialed. "Ugh. Disconnected."

"Sorry."

"Thanks for trying," Dena said.

———

Back at the bookstore Dena held out a twenty-dollar bill to Jain.

"I can't take that." Jain waved her hands at Dena. "All I did was read and play with Twist." Jain closed up the book and moved to replace it on the shelf.

Dena intercepted it. "At least keep the book. And if

you want to discuss it with Charlee afterward, she'd be thrilled." Dena opened the book and slipped the money inside before handing it back to Jain.

"Thanks!"

After Jain left with Twist, Dena pulled out her contract with Duke Bughata again. Just as she thought. She hadn't missed anything. No clause, no initials, no blue ink.

Assuming Finster and Duke were in cahoots somehow, Dena didn't expect a call from Finster with Duke's whereabouts. She began an online search of Duke Bughata's name and was surprised at the remarkable number of Bughatas she found.

She began contacting them one by one. After the fifth Bughata who claimed not to know anyone by the name of Duke, Dena realized it had to be a nickname, perhaps one he only used in Sugar Springs.

Dena called Swede and Uta and asked if they knew of any other name Duke might go by. Neither did, but Uta said she'd been thinking about it ever since Dena had stopped in earlier and remembered the names of two gals she worked with at the bookstore on occasion.

Dena called them both, but they didn't have any information either. One accused Dena of ramping up her PTSD by asking her about Duke.

"Duke Bughata gave you PTSD?"

"Not officially. But probably only because I quit before I got my first paycheck."

"Yikes. He was that bad?"

"No. He was worse."

Dena couldn't decide if the woman was particularly melodramatic, but realized it didn't matter. She still didn't know Duke's whereabouts or any other name he might have used.

Dena went next door to the "Step Into History" studio

and waited until Evelyn and Max had thanked a family and handed them a packet of photos.

"Do either of you know if Duke Bughata was his real name?"

"You mean like an alias?" Evelyn's eyes sparkled.

"No, more like a nickname."

"Oh. Boring."

Evelyn and Max thought about it for a moment then both shook their heads.

"Do you remember anyone besides Uta who worked for him?" Dena asked.

Evelyn gave her the name of one of the women she'd already talked to, the one without PTSD.

Dena returned to the bookstore and called Ginger, her CPA. While she waited for her to pick up, Dena wondered if she really was a redhead. Maybe she was blond. Or completely gray. But when she answered, Dena asked a more important question. "Do you know what Duke Bughata's given name might be?"

"Hm. I only ever called him Duke. Never heard anyone call him anything else." Ginger laughed. "I guess that's not technically true. I've heard Duke called a lot of names. A lot. But none of them very nice."

"Not even on his tax returns?"

"Nope. As far I know, his given name is Duke. Why? What's going on?"

Dena explained.

"I can try to find his old employees," she offered. "I probably still have their W-4 forms they filled out when they were hired."

Dena perked up. "Would they be on my ancient computer?"

"No. I did all the payroll here."

"Bummer. But I'd appreciate it if you could look for

me. Anyone who worked for him or anything with a name different than Duke."

"I'll let you know if I find anything."

Dena turned back to her internet search. No marriage license. No professional licenses. No criminal history. At least not in his nickname.

An alarming number of pop-up ads interrupted her search, advising she could pay for a detailed background search on any name. Dena was tempted, but she was more worried that she'd end up in some sketchy website, maybe that Dark Web Charlee and Lance talked about all the time. As a writer, Charlee was intrigued by what went on there. As a cop, Lance was always trying to shut something down.

Thinking about Lance triggered a new thought. She should ask Sheriff Johnson to do it. The police had access to all kinds of official databases. Dena's measly free internet resources wouldn't turn up anything important, or maybe not even anything very accurate.

Dena called Sheriff Johnson. "Hey Keisha, could you check Duke Bughata's name in your big-deal databases? I'm trying to figure out what his real name is." The sheriff didn't respond. "If you're too busy, I can come over and do it myself."

"No way. Are you nuts? I'll say this again, Dena, to make sure you understand. We're not working together on anything. You're not on my staff, remember? Plus—"

"Yeah, yeah, yeah," Dena said glumly. "I'm under investigation too. I just thought—"

"What? That just because of what happened with Norbert Wallace that you're some kind of quasi-professional sleuth attached to the Sugar Springs Sheriff's Department?"

"No, but ..."

"But what?"

"But I thought we were … getting to be … going to be … friends."

The sheriff was quiet for a moment. "Dena, we are friends. When the weather is nicer you can come over for a barbecue in my back yard. But right now, I have a job to do. Like I told you before, if you want to play Nancy Drew, I can't stop you. But you and I have very different roles in this. It's my job to investigate Duke's disappearance. Your job is to run a bookstore."

"But that's just the problem. If one of us doesn't find Duke, I may not have a bookstore much longer."

"Then let's both get back to our jobs, okay?" Sheriff Johnson disconnected.

Dena glanced around her empty bookstore. With renewed enthusiasm worthy of both Nancy Drew and her perky sidekick Bess, she tried an online search of the bookstore. She began with Twice Sold Tales, since that's what it was called when Duke owned it. Unfortunately, that was a very common name for a used bookstore, which is why Dena had changed it. Despite its popularity, there were no hits for a bookstore with that name in Colorado.

She typed in Thrice Sold Tales, thinking maybe any old mentions of Duke's store might have transferred over to hers. Dena was dismayed to see that the video of her "dognapping" Twist popped up immediately and began playing at full volume. Even though she was alone, Dena hastened to silence it. She was even more dismayed to see additional cellphone video of her argument with Duke, along with more calls to boycott her store.

She considered changing the name of her store to shield it and the Marketplace from all this hoopla, but the cost, she knew, would be prohibitive, especially given the fact she had no income. Protecting every penny might be her new vocation.

Dena deleted her internet search, knowing full well that nothing ever went away on the internet.

Her phone rang loudly, startling her. She saw Ginger's number and kicked herself for turning up the ringer so she wouldn't miss her call. Like that would happen.

"Hey, Ginger, did you find something?"

"Sorry. I didn't see any other name for Duke."

"What about any of his employees?" Dena asked.

"Again, sorry. I must have purged my files when he sold the store. I can keep looking if you want …" Ginger's voice trailed off and Dena knew it was a dead end.

"No, that's okay. I guess I'm grasping at straws. Thanks anyway."

Dena drummed her fingers on the front counter, watching shoppers continue to stream past her store. She needed to figure out more creative tactics. She straightened up. She could try a social media search—FacePlant and Chirpy—of "Twice Sold Tales Colorado." Perhaps an ex-employee of Duke's had posted something about working for him in their biographies on the platforms.

Dena groaned when she saw the message pop up on the FacePlant site, "Did you mean Thrice Sold Tales Colorado?" It helpfully showed the business page for her bookstore. While she was there, Dena decided to scroll.

She should have known better.

She saw some posts Charlee had made on her behalf, but the trolls were there too, with links to Aja's article and the videos. An icy chill ran through her. There might be more terrible comments about Thrice Sold Tales on other platforms where she didn't even have an official presence!

She scrambled to type in the names of all the likely social media candidates.

InstaFab and PostAPic both had the same screenshot from the dognapping video. SplishSplash had many versions of the actual video, some enhanced by angry red scribbles and devil horns. ReadR, because it was an online community of book people, was trending with a horrifyingly large number of links calling for a boycott, with the caption DO YOU SHOP HERE?

Even though she was trembling, Dena gently placed her phone face down and glanced around. Nope. Nobody shopped here.

Hugo

HUGO WAS busy making chocolate truffles and other confections all day, but that didn't keep him from wondering how Skyler's outdoor adventure with Jake went.

She had come into the Marketplace looking rosy-cheeked and brimming over with good health. He hoped it was simply the result of snowshoeing and nothing else. But then he kicked himself.

"She can do anything she wants with anyone she likes," he muttered to the milk chocolate drizzle he whisked. Then he kicked himself again for not joining them. He'd been invited, after all. It probably wasn't a full-throated, enthusiastic invitation, but it was offered in good faith and he'd have been well within the rights of a polite and well-mannered gentleman to accept.

He was only fooling himself, he knew.

Skyler and Jake wanted to be alone. He knew that. Didn't mean he wished it was different, though.

As Hugo artistically drizzled melted chocolate over a tray of heart-shaped chocolate truffles, he remembered the story Dena had told them about going speed-dating when she still lived in Santa Fe. By the time he finished making a tray of peppermint chocolate bark and a batch of pecan fudge, he'd decided he'd do something like that too.

Not something ridiculous like speed-dating, of course, but maybe he'd find a club in Colorado Springs with some live music he liked. If he didn't meet anyone, at least he'd hear some good music on a Saturday night. Hugo felt downright jaunty as he cleaned up the shop and waited on some last-minute customers.

Dena

STILL UNNERVED BY everyone calling for a boycott on her bookstore, Dena slammed shut the lid of her laptop. She kept making mistakes with the inventory program, too unfocused and furious to remember where she was or what she was doing.

She stood to get a cup of coffee, which was the first excuse she could think of to distract herself, and saw Twist fast asleep in her doggy bed. She envied how peaceful she looked, cozy and cuddly with all four feet tucked up under her chest.

In the vendor area she poured herself some coffee and took it out to the comfy armchair across the promenade from her store. She sat sipping, trying—and failing—to clear her mind of the online mess she seemed to be mired in.

She caught sight of Balaam strutting around the Marketplace, sneering and hissing at everyone like he was a Russian oligarch. She watched as Balaam strutted into the bookstore.

Suddenly Dena jumped up, sloshing coffee from her cup. Twist!

Balaam seemed to have taken an intense dislike of Twist when they met the other day. Dena hurried in to try to stop any carnage before it began.

Twist was already on her feet in the center of the bookstore. Her ears were perky. She stared intently at the cat.

Balaam's hair had floofed, making him twice his normal size. He made concentric circles around Twist, hissing louder with each step.

Twist didn't move, simply followed Balaam with her eyes.

"Hey, hey, hey, you two. Let's be friends, shall we?" Dena didn't want to get in the middle of anything, unsure of what she could do if they went all homicidal on each other.

The animals completely ignored her. There were no customers in her store. Kober's children had thankfully disappeared as well. Innocent bystanders getting mauled by animals who probably shouldn't even be in here in the first place would surely cause her liability insurance rates to skyrocket.

Before Dena had a plan, Balaam had diminished the space between him and Twist to almost nothing. They stood a foot apart, Balaam hissing, Twist absolutely still.

Suddenly Twist advanced on Balaam, closing the gap between them in the blink of an eye.

And booped him on the nose.

Balaam leapt eighteen inches in the air, then scrambled away to hide in the stacks.

Twist pursued, slowly stalking, stealthily peering around the corner of the shelves.

Balaam streaked out the opposite direction and, still hissing defiantly, hid behind Dena.

Dena stepped away, immediate crisis averted. "I'm not getting in the middle of this. You started it," she said to Balaam. "If you weren't always so cranky, maybe this kind of stuff wouldn't happen to you."

Balaam looked up at her and narrowed his eyes.

Twist padded forward toward him again.

Balaam fluffed himself again, his copper-colored eyes wide with anger or fear, Dena couldn't tell.

"Twist," Dena said. "Be nice to him. He's just—"

Before Dena could finish her sentence, Twist had booped Balaam on the nose again. Twist stared at the cat for a moment, then padded back to her dog bed. She circled the bed three times before plopping down and closing her eyes.

Dena looked down at Balaam. He looked up at her with utter bafflement on his face. Dena shrugged at him. "Seems not everyone is intimidated by you, my feline friend."

With a haughty swish of his tail, Balaam left the bookstore.

Dena squatted down next to Twist. "Brave girl," she said, cuffing Twist's velvety ear and gently pulling it through her hand.

Watching Twist and Balaam interact made Dena start thinking about where Duke got Twist. Dena knew that Evelyn and Max chose Balaam from a litter of kittens at the animal shelter. Before they could adopt him, he was required to be microchipped. Perhaps Twist was chipped too. She wore a collar but didn't have any tags hanging on it.

Dena called the Sugar Springs vet clinic.

"Bet's Pets, this is Elizabeth."

"How would I go about determining if a dog is microchipped?"

"They often have a tag on their collar."

"She has a collar, but no tags."

"You can try to feel for one."

"Really?"

"Yes. It's about the size of a grain of rice. If she has one, it would be on her neck or upper back between the shoulder blades, just under the skin. If you can't feel it, though, it doesn't mean she doesn't have one. If you want, you can bring her in and I can scan her."

"Okay, I'll give it a try. If I decide to come in, do I need an appointment?"

"Nah. It's not busy today and it just takes a couple of minutes. We're open until eight tonight."

Dena walked over to Twist's bed.

She blinked sleepily at Dena.

Dena put her left hand on Twist's side and with her right hand, began gently prodding and rolling the skin on her lower neck and upper back. She manipulated and palpated her for so long that Twist sighed and fell back to sleep. Twist probably hadn't expected an afternoon massage, but she seemed to enjoy it.

Dena felt nothing under Twist's skin, though.

After she closed up the bookstore for the night, she headed for the animal clinic with Twist.

A woman wearing scrubs with cartoon cats and dogs sat behind the reception desk reading a fat paperback by Libby Klein. She closed it and looked up as they walked in.

"I'm Dena Russo. I called earlier about checking for a microchip?"

"Ah, yes." She came out from behind the desk and knelt next to Twist. "I'm Elizabeth. Is this the stray you found?" She greeted Twist who responded by licking her cheek. "Ooh, kisses. Thank you."

"She's not really a stray. She was left in my care ...

accidentally, I think. But it's been longer than seems reasonable, so I thought I'd try to contact her owner."

The woman stood. "Are you a dogsitter?"

"Nope. I own the bookstore over at the Marketplace." At her confused look, Dena began to explain further, but the woman's confusion morphed into recognition.

"You're the one from that video."

Dena sighed. "I am."

The woman stared at her for a beat, then said, "Well, let's see what we can find out. Bring her back here and I'll grab my scanner."

Dena and Twist followed her into an examination room. While Elizabeth dug around in a deep drawer, Dena glanced at the framed diplomas hanging on the wall. They all bore the name Elizabeth Doolittle.

Dena chuckled. "How fitting that you're a veterinarian."

"My destiny, I guess." She smiled and pushed some buttons on what looked like a computer mouse. "But I thought Bet's Pets sounded better than Dr Doolittle's Animal Clinic." The scanner beeped and Dena saw something flash across the screen. "My husband didn't like either name. He wanted me to call this place The Hairy Godmother." She turned to Dena with mock horror on her face. "Can you imagine?"

The doctor again knelt next to Twist and ran the scanner about an inch above Twist's skin. She slowly moved it up and down, side to side in a wide pattern all across her neck and shoulders. There were no more beeps or flashes. She tried in other places on Twist's body. "Sometimes these chips can migrate over time. But that doesn't seem likely, since this beautiful girl doesn't look too old."

She finally stood. "Let me just make sure ..." She

passed the scanner over the test chip again, causing it to beep. Numbers crawled across the screen. "My scanner is working, so I think I can say with confidence she is not chipped."

"Darn it."

Dena and Twist followed the doctor back out to the lobby.

"Can you check to see if you have any records on her?" Dena asked. "Her name is Twist, and her owner is Duke Bughata."

She typed in the information, then shook her head. "No record of Duke Bughata or Twist ever having been seen there. I'd definitely remember having a white German shepherd as a patient."

"Who breeds white ones?" Dena asked.

"Nobody. It's simply a recessive gene. It shows up every once in a while in a litter of black-and-tans."

"You can't breed them?"

"I suppose you can, if you got two white ones, but it would be hard because you don't know what color or pattern a white German shepherd is masking. Who knows what percentage of the puppies would even turn out white? The ACK won't let you show them, they still think they're less desirable. They used to think they were albino or unhealthy in some way, but at least they've progressed from there." The doctor paused. "I can give you a list of the reputable German shepherd breeders in the area."

"What about the disreputable ones?"

"You're on your own there."

When Dena got home, she decided it was still early enough to contact the names of local breeders she'd been given. She dialed every number, but couldn't find one reputable breeder who placed a white German shepherd in the last couple of years. Just like the vet, none of them would give her a list of any disreputable breeders in the area even though she assured them she wasn't after a puppy, just Duke Bughata.

Hugo

HUGO GOT to the club in Colorado Springs just as the jazz trio finished their set and announced they'd be back after their twenty-minute break. Hugo ordered a gin-and-tonic at the bar and took it to a table facing the stage. The fact that he got a good table so easily on a Saturday night did not bode well for meeting anyone tonight. He tried to check out the other patrons without seeming to. He needn't have worried about glancing around the room. Nobody even noticed him.

Hugo sighed and pulled out his phone to look up more of the reviews of the band. He'd only given a cursory glance when he looked for a club to go to tonight. They seemed okay.

As he scrolled through his social media, biding his time until the band returned, Hugo began to feel self-conscious. The volume in the room had risen with voices laughing and talking. And here he sat alone, checking in at the club on FacePlant. He saw several people he knew online. "Anyone looking for something to do in Colorado Springs?" he typed. "Come join me. First drink's on me!"

Hugo felt a presence over his shoulder and looked up into the face of a young woman wearing a low-cut sweater smiling down at him. "I'm looking for something to do," she said, tucking a brunette curl behind her ear.

Hugo shut down his phone and turned it face down on the table before waving toward the empty seat at his table. "Please, sit down." When she did, he held out his hand. "Hugo Dekker."

"Hi. I'm Stephany. With a Y." They shook hands.

Hugo caught the bartender's eye and asked her, "Can I buy you a drink?"

"Sure. Whatever you're having."

"Gin and tonic." He raised his glass and the bartender nodded.

"So, Hugo Dekker, what do you do?" She pushed up the sleeves of her sweater at the same time she shimmied her cleavage at him.

"I own a chocolate shop in Sugar Springs."

"Get out!" Stephany with a Y put both hands on her waist and stared at him with wide eyes. "How do you stay so skinny around all that heavenly chocolate all day?"

It took all of Hugo's willpower not to show how irritating that question sounded to him. If he was a fat guy who owned a gym, would she say, "How do you stay so fat around all that gym equipment?" Doubt it. And Hugo expected more from women, but now that he thought about it, the majority of people who mentioned this were women. Why did people feel the need to comment on his appearance anyway, especially women? Weren't they in the middle of a movement where they tried to get people— particularly men—to see beyond how they looked?

He must have controlled his expression because she continued, "I *wish* I could stuff my face with chocolate all day and still look good."

The bartender brought over the drink. It seemed to Hugo that he was trying not to laugh as he set it down in front of Stephany.

Hugo tried to change the subject to the club and then the band, but Stephany didn't want to talk about the band or what kind of music she liked and kept steering the conversation back to the chocolate shop and the Marketplace. He wanted to turn his phone over to check the time, but he refrained. Shouldn't the band be back by now?

They both had finished their drinks and Stephany kept hinting at getting another. Finally, she said, "Shall we get another round?"

Hugo did not want to have another drink with this odious woman and said, "Actually, I'm going to step out and make a call. It seems my date must have gotten lost. It was nice to meet you." He picked up his phone and his coat and went out the front door to make his pretend call.

"Hey, buddy. Forget something?" The bartender stood in the doorway scowling at him.

"Oh, I'm not leaving. I just needed … some air."

The bartender guffawed. "Stephany has that effect on people," he said, closing the door.

Hugo stood outside in the cold air, hoping that Stephany had turned her attention to someone else. He heard the music start up again and peeked into the venue. An older couple was sitting at the table he'd vacated, and he didn't see Stephany lurking nearby, waiting to hear more about his deeply captivating life as a chocolatier and small businessman.

He made his way through the room and found a stool at the end of the bar where he could see the stage. Blessedly, there was no empty seat for Stephany. So much for going out to meet someone tonight.

"Another?" the bartender asked.

Hugo nodded.

When the bartender brought his drink he said, "I should have warned you." He tipped his head across the room where Stephany sat with another man.

"I wouldn't have believed you." Hugo sipped his drink. "What's her deal, anyway?"

The bartender shrugged. "She's harmless ... I think. And you're totally her type."

"What type is that?"

"Pumping blood above your shoulders. Male. Willing to buy her a drink. And, let me guess ... you own your own business." He ticked them off using his fingers.

"How'd you know that?" Hugo asked, surprised.

"Stephany, it seems, is looking for a sugar daddy."

Hugo laughed.

"What's so funny about that?"

"I own a chocolate shop."

"Earlier she was hitting on Gunther." The bartender pointed at the man sitting next to Hugo.

When he heard his name, Gunther looked away from the band. "Yeah?"

"I was just telling this guy about Stephany—"

"With a Y," Hugo and Gunther said in unison, and laughed.

"She almost got her hooks in ..." The bartender paused, not knowing Hugo's name.

"Hugo." He shook hands with Gunther.

"What's your business?" Gunther asked.

"I own a chocolate shop. You?"

"I'm a shoe designer."

"Really? I didn't even know that was a thing. I mean, I'm not a complete idiot. I knew that someone had to design shoes. I've just never met one."

Hugo and Gunther spent a pleasant evening listening

to some jazz and chatting. At the end of the evening, they exchanged business cards.

"If you ever think about opening a brick-and-mortar store for your shoes, give me a call," Hugo said. "We'll be looking for tenants at the Marketplace for the foreseeable future, I suspect."

Dena

THE MARKETPLACE OPENED late on Sunday, giving Dena a chance to relax before having to go in. *Relax* was the wrong word, however, because Twist had not lost one iota of interest in her sock game.

Every time Dena turned around since the day Twist came to live with her, she'd find a neat pile of her socks with Twist sitting nearby. Sometimes Dena thought Twist had a look of pride on her face, as if she'd done Dena a favor by herding all the socks to the corral for her. Other times Dena could have sworn she'd seen Twist looking at her with a *isn't this a fun game* grin on her face, with a touch of *what are you gonna do about it?*

But this morning Dena had a brainstorm and before she even showered, ran out to buy Twist her own socks— red ones with pictures of cartoon bones on them. Twist was overjoyed with her gift, immediately scooping them into their own tidy pile, and sitting proudly next to them.

Dena breathed a sigh of relief and collected her own socks before heading to the shower.

She came out to the living room, ready to have a

leisurely breakfast while reading a copy of the Sunday *New York Times* which she picked up along with Twist's socks.

Dena kicked over a new pile of her socks.

"What's all this?" she asked Twist.

Twist sat up on the couch where she'd been asleep.

Dena pointed. "How did you get these?"

Twist hopped down from the couch and, using her nose, rearranged the socks into a neat pile again.

Dena was baffled. She could not figure out how Twist continued to get her socks. She never left them laying around anymore, not since she realized how very much Twist liked the sock game. She even thought to place three heavy books on the lid of her dirty clothes hamper. Somehow Twist still got in without knocking down the books. Dena narrowed her eyes at Twist. Unless she removed then replaced the books on top.

She laughed, feeling a bit paranoid. Ridiculous. This was a creature without thumbs.

Dena scooped up her pile of socks to drop them back in the hamper. She studied them closer. These weren't socks she'd worn recently.

She glanced again at Twist who wore a look of complete inscrutability.

"Good grief. If you've learned to open drawers, I'm so screwed." Dena returned her socks to the drawer and again introduced Twist to her very own red socks with bones embroidered on them.

She poured kibble, thinking breakfast would distract Twist from the game.

Dena ate her own breakfast and read the paper, only mildly surprised to find a neat pile of her socks next to a neat pile of Twist's new socks in the hallway.

Dena

A pair of socks can
Become a true way of life
If you just let it.

ON MONDAY, in the vendor room before the Marketplace opened, Dena replaced the cap on the dry erase marker and wondered how and where Twist learned the sock game. Did someone train her to herd socks? Had she come from a house full of toddlers whose parents needed help collecting them? Did Duke train her to pick up socks? Did she just enjoy it?

Are dogs like Twist born or are they molded? Nature or nurture? Where would one find a quirky, intelligent dog like Twist?

Dena remembered about StevesList, that unwieldy, unregulated no-man's-land of buyers and sellers. She opened her laptop and tried to keep her eyes to barely-opened slits to mitigate the chances she'd see something that might scorch her eyeballs before she found the Colorado dog pages.

Of course, if Duke didn't get Twist in Colorado, there may be no possible way to track down the breeder, shelter, or seller. Or, by extension, Duke himself. Dena tried not to think about that.

While she waited for StevesList to load, she noticed Hugo leaning against the wall near the coffeepot staring across the room into Skyler's cheese shop. She felt her pulse race. She thought that was all over and done with. Skyler had told Dena that she wasn't interested in Hugo romantically, but it wasn't clear that Hugo had received the message. As temporary Marketplace manager—and mother—she needed to make sure nothing weird was going on.

"What are you doing, Hugo?" Dena said sharply.

He jumped a bit and quickly sipped from his mug. "Just getting my morning jolt."

"Of what?" Dena gestured with her head toward the cheese shop.

"Coffee. Just coffee."

"You're sure." Dena didn't ask it like a question.

"Don't worry." Hugo refilled his coffee and walked over to where Dena sat. "Nothing's going on. I get it."

"Are you sure? Because it looks to me like you're all moony for someone who already told you she just wants to be friends."

"I'm not all moony. Just not awake yet."

Dena stared into Hugo's eyes to ascertain how much truth he was telling, a skill she hadn't used much since her children were young. She assessed Hugo's truth meter at above sixty percent, but less than one hundred percent.

He leaned over Dena's shoulder. "Looking to buy another dog?"

"No. I'm trying to figure out where Duke might have got Twist. It could help me find an address or something for him." Dena scrolled the pages and squinted. "This says the listings never get deleted, but I can't figure out how to see the old ones. If he bought her off StevesList it would have been a year or two ago. I don't really know how old Twist is, but I don't think she's more than two. Not quite a puppy anymore, but not quite a mature dog."

Hugo set down his mug and pulled Dena's laptop closer to him, peering at the screen. He clicked a few times and accessed the archived notices. With Dena pointing and Hugo scrolling and clicking, they found someone in Colorado Springs selling a white German shepherd puppy within the correct time frame.

Dena's pulse raced. She picked up her phone to call the number listed.

"Time for me to get to work, I guess." Hugo collected his coffee mug.

"Thanks for your help." As he walked away, she added, "Hugo? Seriously. Quit with the puppy eyes around Skyler. It freaks me out. And it might freak her out too."

Hugo nodded and stepped into his chocolate shop, making a point of closing the door behind him.

Dena called the number. "Hello, I'm looking for the person who breeds German shepherds and had a white one listed for sale on StevesList a couple of years ago."

"That would be me, but I'm not a breeder. Just someone who doesn't get her dogs spayed in a timely manner."

Dena tried to temper her enthusiasm, but she suddenly felt fidgety. "You remember having one?"

"Very clearly. I'd never seen a white one before. I asked the vet if something was wrong with her. I remember that puppy, though. She was so smart I almost kept her, but I already had too many dogs running around here. Luckily, I have a few acres they can roam." Concerned, she added, "Why? Is something wrong with her?"

"No, nothing like that. I have her, but I can't find her owner. I was hoping you'd have some information about the transaction."

"Maybe I do, give me a sec." She came back on the line. "I give my dogs away rather than selling them, but I take photos of each adoption. I don't have any names or addresses or anything, but I found the photo. I'll text it to you."

Dena thanked her and when the text came through, she saw a photo of a woman standing close to Duke who was holding puppy Twist. They were all smiling.

She showed the photo to Evelyn and Max. Neither had seen the woman before.

Dena texted the photo to Uta and Ginger. Neither recognized her.

She texted the photo to Sheriff Johnson with the message, "This is Duke and some woman with Twist as a puppy. FYI. Maybe the woman knows something." She didn't expect a response from the sheriff, but she had told Dena to keep her in the loop. Whatever that meant.

Dena checked the time and saw she had half an hour before the Marketplace opened. There was time to run over to Finster's office and ask if he recognized the woman in the photo.

When she showed him the picture, she studied his reaction to see if he was acting. She didn't think he was, but she'd been wrong about people before. She had no choice but to take him at his word that he'd never seen her before.

On a whim she stopped into Corky's sandwich shop. Anyone who spent any time at all in Sugar Springs ended up at least once at Corky's. The door was unlocked, but he was prepping in the back. Dena was always glad to see food service workers wearing hair nets, but she'd learned to overlook the fact that Corky could use some hair sleeves while he worked.

"Hey, have you ever seen this woman?" Dena enlarged the photo and held out her phone to Corky.

"Yeah, she's been in here." Corky went back to chopping onions.

Dena felt her eyes begin to water. "Seriously? How long ago?"

Corky shrugged. "Six months maybe? She had a conniption when she found out I didn't have a liquor license."

"Who is she?"

"No idea."

Another dead end.

She thanked Corky and hurried back to the Marketplace, hoping the ad she placed in the *Courier* wouldn't be a dead end too. She'd seen the online version of her ad late last night. It looked nice. Not snazzy or anything particularly fancy, but clean, easy-to-read, and hopefully effective. It had a bold black frame with the copy she'd uploaded with the details of the sale: "Monday only! Buy a bag for $10 and take home however many books fit inside!"

What's not to love about a sale like that? Dena thought on her way to open the bookstore. She was sure this would be the jolt her business needed right now to make people forget about the online trolls spewing their nonsense.

While she waited for the crush of customers jamming Thrice Sold Tales to fill their bags, Dena stood at the front counter with her laptop open. She made a quick profile page in FacePlant she titled, "Where is Duke Bughata?" She added a photo of his face, cropping out Twist and the woman next to him. Using the same photo, she put a free ad in StevesList with the same question and a direct link to the FacePlant page.

She figured one of two things would happen. She'd get comments from people who recognized Duke, or Duke would see it, get mad, and then contact her. It was a long-shot either way, but at least she felt like she was doing something. She stared at her screen, wondering how long it would take to get traction with the FacePlant algorithms, but almost immediately received an email from FacePlant advising her that her page goes against community standards and they shut it down. They also blocked her from the site for thirty days.

"I'm in FacePlant jail," she murmured. "I didn't even think that was a real thing."

She edited the StevesList ad to delete the link to the FacePlant page. After several minutes of hand-wringing and debate with herself, she included the URL for the contact page for the Sugar Springs Sheriff's Department instead.

As she was considering whether it would be better to get forgiveness or permission from Sheriff Johnson, a voice asked, "Are you open?"

"I am!" Dena said much too enthusiastically.

The woman took a step backward as Dena rushed around the counter waving a bag in the woman's face.

"You saw the ad? Here's your bag. Only ten dollars. Stuff it as full as you can!" Dena was practically giddy with relief.

"That sounds like a great promotion, but that's not why I'm here."

"Oh." Dena twisted the polyethylene bag in her hands, looking hopefully into the promenade for her anticipated crush of customers. "What can I do for you?"

"I'm Joanne Dunning." At Dena's blank look she added, "Your book buyer?"

"I have a book buyer?"

Joanne Dunning gestured around the store. "How do you think you got all these?"

"From a storage unit when I bought the store."

"So .... Duke didn't explain his ... process?"

"Nope. Just gave me the code—and the final bill—to the storage unit. What *process* are you talking about?" Dena looked at her suspiciously.

She didn't fit the stereotype of what Dena pictured in a book buyer. Her only experience with a book buyer, of course, was Quint O'Dell, that rumpled elderly man who had a penchant for first editions and rare copies of books about Colorado history. This woman in expensive high heels and a tailored suit didn't quite fit in.

Joanne cleared her throat. "Let me start over. I'm one of Duke's regular suppliers, well, I was until he closed his store. I just assumed he'd pass along my information and I'd do business with the new owner. That's you, right?"

Dena nodded. It occurred to her that she'd been so focused on digitizing her inventory, that she hadn't thought about where she'd get more inventory. "Explain to me how you did business with Duke."

Joanne Dunning described how she went to estate sales and bought entire libraries of books all at once. Then she'd search through for anything valuable, which she would then sell directly to collectors. The rest she'd sell to Dena, the price dependent upon the size of the haul and the overall quality.

Joanne stepped toward the table of Colorado histories Dena consigned from Quint O'Dell. She inspected several of the items. "These are good. Where'd you get them?"

"I have a guy."

Joanne laughed. "No need to be so cryptic, I'm not going to steal him from you. But now that I know you have a dedicated space for local history, I can keep my eye out for more." She stared at Dena. "I get it. This is a dog-eat-dog business. If you want to keep your sources to yourself, that's fine. If I see something I think you'll like, I'll bring it in."

"I'm not trying to be cryptic. It's just that I really don't know anything about rare books. I trust my guy to value books properly and then we split the profit. If you bring anything in here, I'll just hand it over to him to work his magic."

"Fair enough." She cocked her head at Dena. "Do you think we can do business?"

"Sure. Let's try it and see how it goes. I'm probably not going to buy some rich guy's entire library for a while, though. I'm trying to digitize and organize my inventory and sales practices first."

"Yikes. That sounds like a big job." She grinned and leaned toward Dena conspiratorially. "If you do that, though, people will want you to be accurate all the time. Lotsa pressure, there. Might be easier to keep it like Duke had it. If some books accidentally fall off a truck, well, then so be it."

Dena leaned away from her. "Are you saying Duke stole books?"

"Not at all. But he never asked where I got mine."

Dena's eyes widened. "You're saying *you* steal books?"

"No! I'm a legitimate book buyer. It's just as I told you, I buy mostly from estate sales. In fact, if you want to go with me, I'm going to an auction this afternoon. That's why I'm dressed like this." She gestured at her suit and high heels. "I'm normally in jeans and sneakers, but I like to make an impression on people, make them think their books are going to good homes."

"Their books *are* going to good homes," Dena said with a huff.

"I'm not coming off so good right now, am I?" Joanne chuckled. "I was just joking about Duke. I thought you knew him."

"Not at all. In fact, do you have his contact information? I've been looking for him."

"Sure." Joanne scrolled on her phone then held it out to Dena.

Dena began to put it in her contacts, until she saw it was the same disconnected number that Uta had already given her. She sighed.

"You don't seem convinced that—"

"No, it's just that's the same number I already had for Duke. Disconnected." Dena stared at this woman, all dressed up to go buy some rich guy's library full of leather-bound, gold-edged books. She didn't entirely trust her, but she would need someone to supply more books to her at some point. The grand opening and last few weeks had depleted her supply, but until business picked up, she certainly had plenty of books on the shelves. "I don't really need a bunch of fancy books."

Joanne laughed. "Oh, they're not fancy. Think garage sale, but not out on the lawn. Estate sales can be fancy, yes, but most are just regular people's houses that are getting packed up when someone dies or has to downsize. They hire an auctioneer or professional estate sales agent to organize everything and do all the work. Like I said, though, I'll keep anything valuable myself to sell to rare book dealers. The rest of the lot goes to you."

"I'll tell you what. Leave me your card. I'll either need

more books in a month or two, or I'll be out of business." Dena paused. "I've had some … um … setbacks."

"I'm sure it's just temporary." Joanne Dunning pulled out a business card and handed it to Dena. As she closed up her handbag, she gestured at Twist sitting nearby watching them. "That's a beautiful dog."

Dena frowned slightly. Shouldn't this woman have met Twist before? Then she remembered that Duke never ran the bookstore when he owned it. Plus, he'd been out of business for a while. Perhaps he hadn't bought books from Joanne Dunning since he'd acquired Twist. Probably not, in fact, if she only had that old phone number for him.

Joanne looked at Dena with a peculiar look on her face that Dena couldn't quite name. "Well, I'll get out of your hair now. I hope we can do business soon."

They shook hands and Dena listened to her high heels clacking along the tile floor of the promenade.

She felt a tad ashamed that she mistrusted Joanne Dunning so much. She hadn't even acknowledged her compliment about Twist. The woman was simply trying to make a living, same as Dena was. The taint of her dealing with Duke had hung over their conversation, coloring Dena's perception of her.

And Dena was no closer to finding him.

She should ask Sheriff Johnson again about doing a database search. But could she ask for a favor like that while keeping the secret of adding the sheriff's office URL to the StevesList ad? She reluctantly called the sheriff. At least she couldn't accuse Dena of not keeping her in the loop.

"I wanted to tell you something about Duke Bughata," Dena began. "I'm still having trouble finding him and I wanted to—"

"We're not looking for him anymore."

The sheriff spoke in her slow manner, which somehow seemed even slower to Dena as she tried to process the meaning of her words. Dena didn't know whether to be relieved or annoyed. Or both. Rennoyed. "I don't mean to be snippy, but you didn't think to tell me?"

"Again, you don't work for me. Plus, I was pretty sure you weren't involved in his disappearance." She paused. "Were you involved in his disappearance?"

"No."

"I thought you'd be happy."

"I'd have been happy if you would have thought to tell me sooner."

Sheriff Johnson sighed. "Why? What's your problem?"

"My problem? Try problems, plural." Dena didn't know where to start. "For starters there was that article in the *Courier*, the viral video, internet trolls, trending lies and innuendos, and a complete lack of customers."

"I'm sorry you had to deal with all that, but it's not illegal for someone to go off the grid. When he resurfaces you can take it up with him directly."

"Wait. You didn't find him?"

"No."

"Then why were you investigating in the first place?"

"I told you. We got an anonymous report that seemed to warrant investigation. We looked into it and found nothing suspicious."

"Nothing suspicious? Not even abandoning his dog?"

"Also not illegal. I'd say it was an atrocious act, for sure, but Twist landed with you. I can think of worse things."

After they hung up Dena deleted the StevesList ad which asked, "Where's Duke Bughata?"

Seemed to be a rhetorical question at this point.

In her mind, Dena began to list all the reasons someone might want to go off the grid. Hiding from someone. Hiding from something. Sick of people. Annoyed by society in general. Distrustful of the government. Scared. In trouble. On the lam after a crime spree.

She came to the same conclusion about all of them—something fishy was going on. And the stink was wafting over her bookstore. But, she reasoned, if Duke had gone off the grid, he probably didn't want to steal her store anymore, and maybe she could concentrate on her business instead of searching for him.

She'd start by clearing up that contract language with Finster.

But how?

Evelyn

A COUPLE with two small children walked into Step Into History just as Evelyn was wondering if she should start worrying about the lack of appointments on their schedule.

"Welcome. Do you have an appointment?" Evelyn hoped they were walk-ins and that she or Max hadn't screwed up the calendar somehow.

"We don't," the woman said in a worried tone. "Is that okay?"

Evelyn made a pretense of checking the appointment book even though walk-ins were perfectly fine. Plenty of people got their photos taken impulsively as they roamed around the Marketplace and stumbled on the studio. But she'd asked about an appointment and now felt like she needed to carry the charade to the logical conclusion. "Let me just …. You're in luck! We have an open spot. What can I do for you?"

The man said, "We're here for a week of skiing in Aspen while the kids stayed on their grandparents' ranch. We heard about this place so we thought a fun photo would be a nice surprise for them to say thank you for babysitting."

"I'm sure they'd love it," Evelyn said. "Did you have a theme in mind already?"

They shook their heads.

"No worries." Evelyn waved them toward the racks of costumes. "Run some of those up your flagpole and see what sticks."

She watched them narrow down their choices, then let them discuss the pros and cons between their final decision, pirates or cowboys.

After protracted negotiations, settling on pirates, Evelyn sorted through the backdrops. She pulled down the seascape with rough waves and ships in the distance before she and Max pushed the props into place—treasure chest with gold coins and jewels spilling out, prow of a ship, helm wheel, plank to walk, lots of thickly coiled ropes.

After some discussion, they decided nobody wanted to walk the plank, so the man pushed it off to the side.

"Shiver me timbers," he said. "None of us want to visit Davey Jones' locker!"

"Aye, matey." The woman picked up a rubber cutlass and after slicing it through the air, tossed it to her daughter who caught it and brandished it, to the cheers of all of them.

It was a fun photo shoot and Evelyn was sure she got some splendid pictures of this charming family.

They removed their costumes and while the adults decided on which package was best, the kids continued to sword fight.

"Have you decided on a package?" Evelyn asked.

The man huffed a few times without saying anything while he glanced furtively at his wife who began twisting her wedding ring on her finger.

Evelyn recognized this as nervousness, but was unsure as to the cause. She cut her eyes at Max who gave her a confident wink.

The package prices were clearly mounted on large posters on the wall where they couldn't be missed. Plus, this couple did not look as if they needed to worry about money. One look at the rock on that woman's finger told Evelyn as much. And didn't they say they were here for a ski trip to Aspen? That wasn't cheap.

She kept her mouth closed and hoped Max would too while they waited for them to speak. Maybe money wasn't the issue at all.

Finally the man said, with more than a little irritation, "What kind of deal can you make on Package B?"

Max took a half-step toward him, but Evelyn pointed a finger at him behind her back and he stopped.

"Package B is an excellent choice. It's our most popular. But if you're looking to spend less money, Package D might be the better choice." Evelyn pointed to the pricing poster on the wall. Maybe they blew their fortune in Aspen. Stranger things had happened.

"It's not the money. I have the money," the man said gruffly. "I just know that small businessmen, er, people, can offer deals and discounts whenever they want to whoever they want."

"Interesting." Evelyn spoke evenly, staring at him with a placid expression. "I hadn't heard that." She wanted to make them walk the plank, but tried not to show it.

After some quiet murmurs, the couple decided on the package they wanted. Max made sure to run their credit card first, giving Evelyn a tiny nod when it went through.

Evelyn offered them one of the coupon pages Skyler had created. She toyed with the idea of withholding it from them as punishment for their greedy behavior, but knew it was less a gift for her customers, and more a marketing piece for the other tenants. Step Into History customers were kind of captive in the Marketplace while they waited for their photos. Evelyn had written the date and TODAY ONLY in oversized letters, circling it all three or four times before telling the couple, "Here's something the other tenants put together for our customers. Every store in the Marketplace has a special deal, just for you because you got your photos taken today."

Kober offered buy-one-get-one cookies. Hugo gave a small box of toffees with the purchase of a large box. Skyler offered a free box of gourmet crackers with the purchase of one of her wedges of cheese. And Dena offered a buy-two-get-one free deal until she could think of something more interesting for the bookstore.

Evelyn pointed out the perks the other tenants offered. "I'll be no more than an hour," Evelyn said. What she didn't say was that, so far, it had never taken her more than about half that time to get a package together. She padded the time in case she had other customers interrupting her process. She was tempted to tell this greedy couple it would take her two hours, but she was not raised to be petty and spiteful. Even when she really, really wanted to be.

Before she got busy on their photographic prints, Evelyn stared at the pricing poster and mused to Max. "Am I the greedy one, or are they? I mean, are our prices actually reflective of—"

Max cut her off. "They're the greedy ones. Greed has become a full-contact sport here in America."

Evelyn had a disturbing flashback to their son. "Greed isn't a new phenomenon, Max."

"I know, Ev. I know."

She heard the thickness in Max's voice and wished she'd kept quiet.

Dena

DENA PLOPPED herself in front of Finster's desk and stared at him, dead in the eye. It was high noon and she was the gunslinger in the white hat.

She had asked him about the doctored contract between her and Duke and vowed not to speak until he did.

It was taking quite a long time, though, and she felt her palms begin to dampen. She was convinced this would work. She knew that contract had been fiddled with, perhaps by Finster himself. If so, his attorney's license might be at stake.

"Is Duke Bughata really worth losing your license over?" So much for vowing not to speak first.

Finster squirmed in his seat which Dena took to be an excellent sign.

"Listen, Dena, I honestly don't know what happened. I was as surprised as you were to see those changes on Duke's copy the other day. But I've been thinking about it nonstop ever since."

"And?"

"And I think Duke pulled a fast one on me. I told you I had to step out and take a call."

Dena nodded.

"I think he set me up, told them to call me right then to give him enough time to make that change about you having to pay him every month. I feel so stupid."

Finster looked like he was about to cry. Dena couldn't help but feel sorry for him. He seemed so sincere, but …

"Who called you?"

Finster's lips disappeared. "Can't tell you that. Attorney-client privilege."

Dena stared at him some more. "Will you enforce this bogus contract? Do I have to pay anyone every month?"

Finster shook his head. "As far as I'm concerned, the contract you have in your possession is the enforceable contract. In fact, give it to me and I'll make a copy for my file where I'll include a note."

Dena looked at his outstretched hand. "Where's the copier? I'd rather do it myself."

"Fair enough." Finster pointed her to the copier in the other room and waited while she made the copies.

Dena brought along a red pen in the hopes this would happen. Nobody just happens to have a red pen with them. It should alleviate any more shenanigans. She signed the new copy with red ink and added a red ink signature to her original. She handed Finster the red pen.

"Highly unorthodox," he said.

"But legal?"

Finster nodded. "You can use any color to sign documents, but black and blue photocopy the best."

"But red makes it obvious when someone messes with a contract."

Dena

THE NEXT DAY Dena stood in the vendor room fluttering one of her bags at the other tenants. "I couldn't even get anyone in for my *fill a bag for ten bucks* event," she lamented.

Hugo glanced down at Twist sitting at her side. "Probably afraid of your stolen dog."

"Nobody even saw your ad," Skyler said. "It came out online on Sunday and the sale was only for yesterday? You should have made it for the entire week." She must have seen Dena's face tighten. "I mean, probably. Maybe. Oh, goodness. I don't know." Skyler walked over to the coffeepot across the room and stood facing it without pouring any coffee.

"Now, dear," Evelyn said soothingly to Dena, "It's February. And a Monday. Nobody wanted to leave their toasty house."

Dena shook her head. "The Marketplace was packed yesterday. Kober even sold out of bakery items."

Kober glanced up from her phone long enough to say, "That's because I only had enough supplies to make half of what I normally make."

"Does anyone actually work here?" a voice bellowed from the cheese shop.

"Coming!" Skyler hurried through her door.

Dena reached down to pet Twist. She'd found having a dog to be quite comforting, more than she would ever have imagined. Even if Twist wasn't technically hers. Or was she? Was this a case of Finders Keepers? Possession being nine-tenths of the law?

Dena had been convinced that her dearth of customers was solely a result of all the bad press swirling around her and the bookstore. Perhaps Hugo was right, though. "Maybe customers *are* afraid of Twist."

Everyone looked at Twist sitting there. She cast her eyes demurely away from their gaze.

"Maybe I should just lock up all my socks and leave Twist at home instead of bringing her here every day."

Kober snapped her head from her screen. "Don't you dare! My kids will be devastated. They race here after school to play with her."

"I thought you were worried that your kids would fall in love with her, and now you're worried if she's not here every day?" Dena said.

Kober shrugged. "Motherhood. What're you gonna do?"

They commiserated for a moment. Kids couldn't possibly know everything you did for them. How much you worried. The things you never said.

Dena gave Twist a head rub and Twist gazed up at her with adoration. She knew Kober was right about the kids, but more importantly, Twist would be devastated. She'd already made herself at home at the Marketplace. "Look at that face! Who could be afraid of that?"

"Maybe you're the one scaring away customers," Hugo

said. "I've seen your face and heard you when you're working on your computer."

"Very funny."

"I wasn't joking."

"Great. Very motivating. But I'll take the high road and play the Glad Game. At least with no customers in the store it will be easier to get my inventory set up." Dena saw Hugo open his mouth. "Don't say it. I heard the irony as the words left my mouth. I do understand that without customers I don't actually need to worry about my inventory."

"Why aren't you just migrating everything to your laptop?" Skyler asked. "At least then you might not scare any customers."

Dena sighed deeply, something she'd done way too much lately. "My CPA pointed out she'd already set up an inventory program on that ancient computer that came with the store, but it's so old, it won't upgrade any further and a bunch of these books are already listed in there. I'm trying to figure out how—or if—I can export the info from the old computer into the new program on my laptop. Of course, even if I figure it out, it probably won't match what's actually on my shelves. She thinks I should just input any new inventory I get and forget about what's on that old computer, but it just kills me not to know what I have here. Without a computerized system, if someone comes in asking for something, I won't have any idea whether I have it or not. It would be no better than me standing next to them and reading titles on the shelves." Dena tried not to, but sighed again. "The alternative is to memorize everything in the store."

"Oh, my. That sounds dreadful, dear," Evelyn said.

"It is. How do you think I found out that Kober ran

out of everything yesterday? I needed to talk to a brownie about it and there were none." Dena used a sinister tone on the last few words while she cut her eyes at Kober.

"Geez, I'm sorry." Kober went back to jabbing at her phone, muttering loudly, "The whole world needs brownies these days. You're not some kind of special snowflake."

———

Since she had fired up the ancient computer, Dena took the quiet time to go over all her accounts, trying to find where—or if—she could save money. Inventory could wait.

She munched from the plate of brownies Kober had brought her. They were invaluable in keeping her face and voice calm, in case any customers came around. She smiled when she'd seen Kober come in the bookstore carrying the small plate, trying to look gruff but failing. She and Kober had a rocky start, but it seemed they might be friends after all.

Same with all the Marketplace tenants. They were beginning to gel as friends and peers—even sadsack Hugo. Dena again felt that knot in the pit of her stomach when she thought about the potential new tenant, Boyd Drummond. Would he fit in or would he drive a wedge through their fragile coalition?

Dena sighed … yes, again … and polished off the last brownie before turning her attention back to the ancient computer.

Just as her eyes began to cross, she saw something that caught her attention. An automatic monthly withdrawal for the local gas company. She cocked her head, trying to think of any natural gas usage at the Marketplace. As far as she could tell, everything there was electric.

She made her way to the other shops to ask everyone. Nobody else paid a natural gas bill, so Dena gleefully made her way back to the bookstore. It wasn't a huge monthly bill, but every little bit helped, right?

Dena looked up the number for the gas company that serviced the Sugar Springs area. After listening to several minutes of hold music and being assured repeatedly that her phone call was important—duh, does anyone call with an unimportant problem?—someone finally answered.

"I bought a business recently and have an automatic monthly withdraw that your company is taking, but I think it must be for his old location, not where I moved my store."

"What is your account number?"

"Um … hang on a sec." Dena searched the screen, but saw nothing that looked like an account number. "I can't find it."

"Let's try the service address."

"Like I said, I don't have any gas service here."

The customer service representative took a beat. "Then you shouldn't be getting a bill."

"Exactly."

"So what's the service address?"

Instead of saying what she wanted to say, Dena told him the address of the Marketplace. "But you won't—"

"I don't see any service at that address."

"That's what I'm trying to tell you. Try the name of the old business, Twice Sold Tales."

"That business name doesn't come up."

"How about Thrice Sold Tales?"

"Nothing."

"Can you look up the account by my name instead? Try Dena Russo."

"I don't see any service under that name."

"And yet you're taking my money every month."

"Ma'am, I'm not taking anything from you except this phone call."

Why was it that so many customer service representatives seemed to think they were the ones with the problems instead of the person they were supposed to be trying to help?

Dena chose her words and her tone of voice carefully. "I guess I'll look for my account number and call you back."

"You do that." The man changed his tone of voice to one much more accommodating and caring. "And on behalf of our company, I'd like to thank you for your business." He must be required to say that at the end of every call.

Dena thought about calling her bank to cancel the charge, but then worried she did have gas service somewhere and called her CPA instead.

"Hey, Ginger. I was going over some of my account stuff, and it looks like I'm being charged every month by the gas company. But they can't find any record of it."

"The store pays for gas usage at your house. That's how I set it up for Duke too."

"Oh!" Dena paused, thinking. "But I have an electric stove."

"Hang on. Let me see if I can figure out what's going on." When she came back on the line a couple minutes later, she said, "You have a gas clothes dryer. You never noticed?"

Dena laughed. "Never even thought about it. It was there when I moved in. Wait. Is that legal to have the bookstore pay for something personal?"

"Yep. One of the perks of owning a business. It's called

an owner's withdrawal. Perfectly legit." Ginger paused. "Uh oh. You didn't demand they turn off your gas, did you?"

"I don't think so, but who knows? It was like I was speaking ancient Aramaic. Or maybe they were."

Ginger laughed. "No worries, I'll get it straightened out. That's my job. You go sell some books."

Dena didn't have the heart to tell her that didn't seem to be on the agenda at the moment.

Ginger called back about fifteen minutes later. "All good. The problem was just a typo in your name. Mea culpa. Anything else I can help you with?"

"Nope. I try to only have one problem per day."

"How's that working out for you?"

"Not that great, actually."

"Bummer. I was hoping maybe you'd share your secret."

"The minute I figure out how to bottle it, we'll go into business together." Dena paused. "But don't hold your breath."

Short of finding the magic elixir, Dena decided she'd simply try to pay better attention to her online statements.

Dena kicked herself for not asking Ginger about her hair color. It wasn't the most important thing in the world, but it was beginning to feel rude not to know. On the other hand, Ginger hadn't asked Dena what she looked like either. Maybe Ginger was picturing her with peroxide-blond dreadlocks. And maybe that was okay.

She heard the clickety-click of high heels in the promenade. She glanced up, expecting to see Joanne Dunning, the book supplier from yesterday. Instead, three women—two wearing heels—veered into the bookstore. She gaped at them and then realized she must look like an idiot. After all, people were supposed to come into her store. That was the whole point of having it.

She stepped out from behind the counter to greet them. "Wow. Love your shoes." She pointed at two of the womens' feet. One wore a pair of highly polished red and black Oxford pumps, and the other, a pair of cobalt blue Victorian-style boots with buttons, buckles, and zippers but knee-high and sharp-heeled. Probably not within the imagination of any Victorian woman.

"Thanks," they said automatically in unison. They must get the same compliment regularly.

"What can I help you find?" Dena asked.

The third woman, the one wearing sneakers, said, "We saw the ad about the ten-dollar bags."

Before thinking about what she was saying, Dena told them the sale was only for yesterday. The women turned to go.

"Wait," Dena said. She ducked behind the counter and pulled out three bags and handed them to the women. "Don't tell." They absolutely looked like women who would tell so Dena thought a bit of *backward psychology* might work on them. "Ten dollars for anything you can stuff in here without tearing the bag. Price goes up to fifteen bucks if the bag tears!" Dena was joking but thought that might be a little bit of genius she'd add to the promotion if her business didn't fail before the next issue of the *Courier* was published and she got the chance to run the ad again.

Dena pointed out the various sections of the bookstore and the women began laughing and fluttering around the store. She pretended to work, but she was secretly listening to them as they shopped. They were a fun group, obviously old friends who enjoyed each other's company. Dena could totally picture them having all sorts of shenanigans together.

The Oxford pumps woman kept talking to Twist while she browsed, asking the dog for advice about authors and titles. Twist followed her around the store, but never responded, as far as Dena could tell, which did not deter the woman in the least.

The women finally plunked their bags on the front counter, happily paying the extra cost for ripping the plastic on their bags due to their overzealous shopping.

The woman in the sneakers said, "I wasn't really in the market for used books, but when I saw the ad, it seemed like something fun the gals and I would like."

Oxford Pumps said, "If I'd have known this adorable creature was here, I would have come much sooner."

Although Dena had a healthy ego, she assumed the woman was talking about Twist and not her. She almost mentioned her theory that customers might be afraid of Twist, but she decided not to interrupt them while they talked about how much they loved Twist. Every girl needed to feel special, after all. Even canine ones.

"She's so polite," the woman in the sneakers said.

"She'd look fantastic in my living room," Oxford Pumps said.

"My grandkids really want a dog. One like this would be perfect," Blue Boots said.

"Wait. I didn't see this." The woman in the sneakers walked over to the display of Charlee's books. The other women followed her.

"Those are the only new books in the store. My daughter writes those." Dena couldn't keep the pride from her voice.

The women began picking up the books and reading the back cover copy out loud to one another.

The woman in sneakers actually squealed. "This one's signed!"

Oxford Pumps opened another front cover. "So's this one!" She began collecting one copy of each title, verifying each had Charlee's signature.

"Don't be so greedy!" Blue Boots laughed.

"We almost know a celebrity!"

"They're all signed," Dena said.

All three women collected an armful of each title and plopped them on the counter on top of their bags of books.

Dena jotted down everything each woman bought as she rung it up. She wanted to know which titles they bought, not only to do some math, but also to start paying attention to any sales trends. It would be good to know, even anecdotally, which genres sold the best for her. It might be the closest thing to having a computerized inventory she could muster for the foreseeable future.

After the women thanked her and said long goodbyes to Twist, Dena calculated she'd made a respectable profit on each of their fifteen-dollar bags. Adding in Charlee's books, it was a lucrative forty-five minutes, even considering the cost of the ad. "Maybe things are looking up," she said to Twist. "At least until Duke gets wind of this," she added ruefully. "He'll probably get back on the grid simply to hurry in here to yell at me some more about wanting his bookstore back."

It reminded Dena of that old joke—want to have a million-dollar business? Start with two million!

After politely escorting the women out of the Marketplace, Twist wandered back to curl up in her bed.

Dena returned to the perusal of her online financials. After scrolling for several minutes and finding no other opportunities to cut expenses, Dena saw the names Beau

Gudthak and Ahab Duktgue. "Those can't be real," she muttered. She stared at them, knowing something was off about the names.

After a bit, she gasped, grabbing for a pen and piece of paper to confirm her theory.

Both names were anagrams of Duke Bughata.

Dena

DENA PICKED up the phone and dialed her CPA. "Ginger! Duke is stealing from me!"

"What? No way!"

"Way! I was going over those old accounts and found more automatic withdrawals like to the gas company. They're different though. Instead of being the same amount on the fifteenth of every month, these are all random. But get this … between the two of them they add up to five hundred dollars in both December and January! That's the amount Duke told me I owed him!"

"You owed him? What are you talking about?"

Dena explained how Duke had come in there yelling at her that day.

"What are you saying, Dena?"

Dena lowered her voice. "I think Duke has been embezzling from the store all along."

She heard Ginger's intake of breath and then a quiet expletive. "Are you sure?"

"Well, I didn't see him do it, if that's what you mean, but yes, this seems pretty solid. Don't you think?"

"I don't know! This is just crazy. Hang on a minute, let me check my records and see if anything jumps out at me."

Dena practically thrummed out of her skin, waiting for her to come back on the phone. When she did, all Ginger said was the same expletive she uttered earlier. Then, "I think you're right."

"Did I already ask if you had Duke's address or phone?"

"I only mailed stuff to the bookstore address, but here's the last phone number I have for him." Ginger rattled off a number that Dena jotted down. "He's not my client anymore, Dena, but let me look into it further. I feel responsible. I should have caught this. This is terrible. Absolutely terrible."

Dena heard the dread and anxiety in Ginger's voice. It broke her heart. Dena realized this could ruin Ginger's business. Something like this couldn't be good for an accountant's reputation.

Dena realized Ginger had been talking to her. She didn't know what she'd been saying, but interrupted her anyway. "No, Ginger. This is my problem. Let me handle it. I'll let you know if I need anything, but I don't want any of this to splash back on you."

"Dena, I can't ask you to do that."

"You're not asking. I'm telling. I'm going to handle it. I'll figure it out without getting you involved."

"Dena—"

"It'll be fine. There's plenty of evidence against him."

"Have you gone to the police yet?"

"Not yet."

"After what you told me, he sounds a little unhinged. Don't do anything half-baked, Dena."

"Oh, I'll be fully baked, don't you worry! Wait. That

didn't come out right. Seriously, though. Don't worry. Duke Bughata will get what's coming to him!"

Dena's queasy stomach roiled. As she put her phone down, she noticed Jain and Wyatt standing there, gawking at her. She realized she might have sounded a bit like Kober just then, too loud and too hyperbolic, but those kids should be used to it by now.

The kids scurried off. Twist chased after them.

Dena dialed the number for Duke that Ginger had given her. It was disconnected too.

She had a brainstorm. After some checking on her phone, Dena picked up the empty brownie plate and went to see Kober in the bakery.

Handing her the plate she said, "Can Jain babysit the store for me again?"

"Sure. She went on and on about it the other day. Couldn't believe you paid her and gave her a book for doing nothing."

"That's the kind of stellar businesswoman I've become."

Kober snorted. "If you're not back by closing I'll lock up for you."

Dena gave her the code to her security gate and ran to find Jain.

If she hurried, she could get there before they closed. Plenty of time to get this all cleaned up.

Dena

DENA GOT to the IRS branch office in Colorado Springs with forty-five minutes to spare. She was anxious to report this—whatever *this* was—thinking it would be as big a deal for them as it was for her. The full force of the Internal Revenue Service would descend like a swarm of angry bees flashing tiny badges. They would find and arrest Duke Bughata. Dena pictured a very public perp walk, vindicating her and erasing her online mess.

She tried to temper her expectations, remembering Charlee's online mess, and how it was still a thing. Not a big thing, but a thing nonetheless.

Dena waited impatiently in line behind a couple. When it was finally her turn, she rushed the counter as if she were trying to get tickets to a Taylor Swift concert.

"I think a man has been skimming from my company," she said breathlessly to the bored bespectacled employee. She knew his day just got exponentially more interesting. He'd have something exciting to talk about to his wife and kids at dinner tonight. It would break their interminable streak of boring conversations about his job.

He blinked twice at her. "Fill out form 3949-A."

Dena blinked back at him, waiting for him to hand her the form and point her to the Agent in Charge, the person she'd ceremoniously hand it off to once she'd competed it.

"Online," he said, still looking bored.

"Wait," she said. "Let me get this straight. I'm here to tell you about criminal internal revenue-y behavior." Dena waved vaguely at the IRS emblem painted on the wall behind him. "Verifiable information about a notorious tax cheat and all you want me to do is fill out some rinkydink online form?" Dena breathed heavily.

He continued to stare at her, his expression never wavering. Finally, he said, "Ma'am, who is your appointment with?"

"Don't you think I would have asked for the person I had the appointment with if I had a—" Dena realized he was fully aware she didn't have an appointment because she saw a slight shift in his expression. It was less bored, and definitely more smug. But his eyes never left her face.

"Online. Form 3949-A. Really easy."

Dena glanced around the lobby, searching for someone in line behind her who might sympathize with the treatment she was receiving. Nobody in line but her. But Dena did see another employee standing near the wall watching her, trying to suppress a laugh. The woman wore the uniform of beleaguered civil servants everywhere—light blue long-sleeved button-down shirt, khaki slacks, and sensible shoes.

Dena marched over to her, hoping she was the Agent in Charge. Maybe she'd get recognition from her industry in catching a criminal for them.

"I didn't make an appointment because this is kind of an emergency. Someone should know about this and take my statement."

"Your statement?"

"Or whatever happens here."

The IRS employee uncrossed her arms while assessing Dena for longer than felt comfortable. She checked her watch. "It's your lucky day. My appointment didn't show up." She beckoned Dena to her cubicle, gesturing for her to sit, then taking the chair behind the desk.

Dena saw her desk nameplate read "Krystal Ball." Before she knew what had happened, Dena said, "So, you knew I was coming. That's why you were waiting out there?"

The look on Krystal's face told Dena she'd heard every single joke about her name. Krystal must have had a real Dad Joke kind of dad when she was born. Someone who always said *must be free* to a cashier having trouble with their scanner. Or *looks like we'll have to amputate* when she got an owie. Or *no, your other right* when she mistook left for right.

Dena was glad Krystal hadn't acknowledged the comment and truly wished she could unsay it. Unfortunately, that wasn't how language worked.

Instead, Krystal said, "You really do only need to fill out Form 3949-A, but I can walk you through it."

"Listen, Agent … Officer …"

"Mrs."

"Oh, wow. Did you marry into that name?" Dena apparently had no control over her mouth at the moment.

Krystal sighed.

"Mrs Ball … Krystal … there's been some kind of misunderstanding. I'm happy to fill out a form, but this is much bigger than that."

She folded her hands on the desk in front of her and stared at Dena. "How so?"

"There's a guy—"

"Isn't there always."

"Yes … ha ha … but yes. There's a guy who has been skimming from his business which means he probably never paid taxes on that amount." Dena wanted to make sure to get Krystal's full attention so added, "And if I know him, he probably hasn't paid his taxes at all. Like, ever." Dena knew this was most likely a blatant lie, since Duke employed an accountant, but she was trying to drive home a point. The IRS could ascertain how much truthiness it held. Besides, she felt like she owed Krystal something.

"And you know this how?"

Dena wrinkled her nose. "I don't know it for a *fact* fact, but I'm pretty sure." Clearly, by the look on Krystal's face, the IRS was only interested in fact facts. "Okay. Let me start at the beginning. I bought a used bookstore from a guy named Duke Bughata and he came in ranting and raving and—well, that's not important. But I've subsequently realized that he's been … well, I don't know exactly, but writing checks to himself, taking automatic deposits from my account."

"That's sounds like a theft case. Not a tax case."

"But he's probably been doing it long before I bought the business from him. I just need the IRS to go find him and get him to … I don't know, stop whatever he's doing."

Krystal swiveled her chair to face her computer monitor. "What's the name of the bookstore?"

"When he owned it, it was called Twice Sold Tales."

"And now?"

"I changed it to Thrice Sold Tales."

She squinted at Dena. "Who sells a book three times?"

"I don't know." Dena gave an exasperated sigh. "But is that important right now?"

By way of answering, Krystal began typing. As she did so, her face became more serious. She asked for the correct spelling of Duke's name as well as Dena's name, the address of the store, her social security number, her Employer Identification Number, and other information Dena didn't know off the top of her head.

Finally, she stopped typing and stared across the desk at Dena for long enough that Dena blurted out, "I pay my taxes!"

"But Twice Sold Tales didn't."

Relieved, Dena said, "I told you."

Krystal Ball furrowed her brow. "Maybe you didn't hear me. Twice Sold Tales didn't pay their taxes."

"Yes. That's exactly what I came to let you know."

"And you own Twice Sold Tales now."

"No, I don't. I own *Thrice* Sold Tales. Three times, remember?"

Krystal stared at Dena, waiting patiently for Dena to understand something she was not grasping at the moment.

But the only thing Dena had figured out was that this IRS agent staring at her seemed to think she was the one who hadn't paid taxes, instead of Duke Bughata. "You didn't even know about Twice Sold Tales until I just now told you." Dena's voice was thin and reedy.

"Yes, I want to thank you for that. But now we need our money. We're greedy little buggers."

"But Duke Bughata owes it, not me. I own a completely different bookstore!"

"That depends on how your contract was written and how the businesses and liabilities were structured. You should probably check you contract and have a conversation with Mr Bughata. But right now, it sure looks like you owe the United States government some money." She glanced at her monitor again. "And quite a bit, too, it seems."

"But I don't have it and I can't find him! I wanted *you*

to find him. That's why I came here." Dena tried to keep from whining, but all of this felt as unfair as the bullies on the playground hogging the swings. Maybe even as unfair as Krystal Ball's name. Dena took a deep breath to calm herself and to think. "Can you give me the contact information you have for Duke Bughata?" She waved toward the computer.

Krystal laughed, then stopped abruptly. "Wait. You're serious?"

"I guess not." Dena thought some more. "Will you give me a chance to find him? Seems he's disappeared. Gone off the grid."

"Sure, take all the time you need."

Dena perked up. "Really?"

"No. But we're the government. Wheels turn slow here." Krystal perked up too. "Better get a move on!"

She sounded so chipper Dena realized she had just dropped Krystal a big, fat gift—maybe a promotion—right in her lap.

And Dena either had to come up with a big, fat check, or produce Duke Bughata.

Dena

AT FOUR IN the morning Dena heard a thump. She felt like she'd barely fallen asleep, as she tossed and turned, worrying about what to do about Duke and the IRS problem. She roused herself from her toasty warm bed, thinking maybe she'd left the panel in the doggy door and Twist needed to go outside. Cleaning up an accident wouldn't make her life any easier right now.

The panel was not in the doggy door but a quick glance out the window of the kitchen door didn't show Twist in the yard. The porchlight was out, however, so the yard was barely illuminated by a half-concealed moon in a cloudy sky.

She checked around the house, but Twist wasn't in any of her sleeping spots. Dena grabbed the flashlight from the counter she'd been using until she got around to replacing the porchlight bulb. So far it hadn't served as much of a reminder.

It had stopped snowing, but the temperature was supposed to have dipped well below zero overnight, so Dena kept the door closed and shined the light out the window. It was a strong beam but flashing it around the yard didn't show Twist. Dena sighed and opened the door, bracing for an Arctic blast.

As she opened the door, calling softly to Twist so she wouldn't wake the neighbors, Dena saw partially covered pawprints from last night when she had let Twist out before bed. She was alarmed to see a fresh set of tracks as well.

Next to Twist's pawprints, Dena saw a set of footprints. With heightened foreboding, she called again more anxiously to Twist, continuing to shine the flashlight beam around the yard.

Dena squatted and aimed the flashlight directly at the set of footprints. It made no sense, but she was sure they were made by a pair of pointy-toed high heels. There were two sets of footprints, one leading up to the doggy door, and one leading away.

More alarming, though, was that there was only one set of Twist's pawprints.

Wearing only her slippers, Dena leaped over the footprints, then rushed into the yard, stopping where she could see the entire area, enclosed by a chain link fence. A dark lump covered the middle of the sidewalk.

The gate hung open.

The flashlight beam bounced as Dena ran to the open gate. She jogged in a wide berth, making sure to only step in untrammeled snow. She knew enough not to ruin any potential footprint evidence. She shined the light directly on the lump. Only a broken pine branch. Dena stood near the fence, scanning up and down the street.

No Twist.

She shined the light at her feet to make sure she wasn't stepping on any other prints and made her way slowly toward the open gate. But when she was a few feet away, Dena's heart clutched. Twist's pawprints and the high heeled footprints led directly out the gate. Dena had shoveled her sidewalk after the last storm, so the prints ended at the gate, but she could envision what had happened.

Some woman in high heels had snatched Twist! The dognapper had parked her car at the curb, led Twist through the yard, opened the door then drove off with her.

But that was crazy.

Dena used the flashlight beam to follow the footprints to the kitchen door. It wasn't her imagination.

She called Twist's name, knowing it was fruitless. But it was the only thing she could do.

Dena

IT SEEMED LIKE A YEAR, but when Dena was finally able to reach Sheriff Johnson, the sun had barely begun peeking over the horizon.

"Keisha, somebody stole Twist last night. There are footprints all over my backyard and it's a woman!"

"Dena, I can't understand you. Slow down."

Dena took a breath and exhaled slowly. She felt her chest loosen. "I heard a noise around four this morning and went to check on Twist. She was gone, but there were footprints from high heels in my backyard."

"High heels?"

"Yes. Definitely."

"You're sure it's not bunny or squirrel tracks? Maybe a raccoon or a bird?"

"No. Absolutely not. Those tracks were from women's shoes." As the rising sun began to spill across the kitchen table and fill the room where Dena sat, her confidence began to ebb.

"Was your gate open?"

Dena nodded, then said yes when she remembered she was on the phone.

"Dena, I'm sorry about Twist, and we'll keep an eye out, but there's not much we can do. Dogs run away all the time."

"It's not like her. Twist didn't run away."

The sheriff spoke quietly. "You've only had her for a hot minute. You have no idea what she's like. She probably got up to pee, there was some unusual critter on the back porch, and she chased after it. You're probably lucky whatever it was didn't make its way inside through the dog door. But if it'll make you feel better, I'll send Vince out to drive around and look for her."

"Thanks. I'll do the same, now that it's light."

Dena didn't know why she said that. She knew Twist didn't open that gate chasing a raccoon. She sipped her coffee and nibbled a piece of toast thinking about those piles of socks Twist made. Dena still hadn't figured out how Twist was able to get into drawers and hampers she was sure she'd closed tight.

Had Twist figured out how to open the latch on the gate? It was very simple. Just raise up the U-shaped hook and give it a nudge. Voila ... gate was opened.

Dena opened the back door and squatted down near the prints. She'd been so sure they were made by high heels, but now, after hearing Keisha talk about the wildlife roaming around Sugar Springs, maybe it was an animal print.

She grabbed her camera and snapped some photos for reference, and so she'd still have them when the snow melted.

She sat back down and searched "raccoon tracks" online. No way. They looked like little handprints with long tapered fingers. Nothing like what was in her back yard.

"Let's try squirrel." Nope. As she scrolled, the image of a large poster with silhouettes of a variety of animal prints popped up. Dena zoomed in. The only one that came close was a springbok, but she was fairly certain they didn't have those in Colorado.

She squinted at the image of a moose print. Maybe, but only half of it. She doubted that some bowlegged moose made its way across Dena's yard and up to the back door.

Dena searched for actual images of snow tracks of every animal she could think of. None matched what she saw.

It was definitely a high heel print.

She considered driving around calling and searching for Twist, but deep down she knew some woman lured her out the back door and drove her away in a car. Twist loved a car ride, after all. As soon as a door was opened, Twist was sitting in the seat. In fact, Dena had to make sure to open the back door for Twist before she opened the passenger door to put her purse or a package down. Otherwise that purse or package rode on the back seat. Twist was not to be dislodged until she arrived at her destination.

Dena's eyes began to swim. "Where are you?" she whispered.

Kober

SCHOOL DAYS SHOULDN'T BE this hectic, Kober thought.

She knew if she was more organized herself, probably the boys would be too. Maybe they could all learn a thing or two from Jain who always seemed to have plenty of time to get ready, eat breakfast, and read whatever novel she had her nose in these days.

Kober envied her daughter. She couldn't remember the last time she curled up with a cup of tea and a good book. Maybe college? Certainly not since the twins were born. And while there were lots of quality children's picture books, she didn't count those.

She wanted to spend some time with a sweaty romance, maybe historical with lots of *miladys* and *thees* and *thous*, or at least a juicy murder she could try to solve. Until she opened the bakery, she was a bit concerned her brain would soon turn into oatmeal.

Organizing the store and creating and refining recipes gave her the mental workout she felt she needed. Some days, however, it seemed to be too much of a mental workout, and she lamented her fitness at anything that required deliberation or logic. Luckily those times were few and far between, even more so as the grand opening of the Sugar Springs Bakery faded into the background.

These days Nic and the kids hardly ever needed to make her a comforting bowl of tomato soup or drape a cool cloth across her brow.

She smiled at the image. She could star in her own romance novel. At least as far as wilting down to a velvet-covered divan to control a case of the vapors.

Kober found herself short of the romance part of the romance novel these days. Nic continued to work long hours, mostly at home, but some back in Denver. Those were the hours she wondered about.

She felt almost certain he was having an affair, but when she spoke her fears out loud to Dena recently, every-thing sounded so preposterous. As she heard herself answering Dena's questions—*no, no proof ... I don't know why I think that ... our relationship is good, actually*—she felt ridiculous.

Kober couldn't put her finger on why she had the suspicion constantly nagging like a broken record in the back of her mind. When Nic was in Sugar Springs he was supportive of the bakery, even though he purposely stayed out of her business, reminding her it was *her* business, not his. He was a kind and attentive father and partner. He wasn't always sneaking off to make furtive phone calls in the middle of the night or anything. When he was at home, he was fully at home.

The snooze alarm rang—again—and Kober smacked it.

But when Nic was in Sugar Springs working remotely, she was at the bakery all day. Maybe that's when he made his furtive phone calls to some paramour.

"Son of a snowplow." Kober placed a hand on Nic's empty side of the bed. He was in Denver yesterday and today.

She felt ridiculous all over again.

She shoved her feet in slippers and zipped a hoodie over her pajamas. The kids were making their typical morning noises around the house. Kober smelled burnt toast.

"Good morning, monsters," she said to Leo and Lincoln, kissing the tops of their ten-year-old heads. "Good grief. When was the last time you washed your hair? You smell like cattle. Your mother should be hauled before the authorities."

"Our mother actually makes us live in the barn. We have no access to soap," Lincoln said, spreading a thick layer of peanut butter across his toast.

"And she won't even fill the horse trough with water." Leo gave a melodramatic pout.

"But she does fill the pantry with peanut butter," Kober said. "I think that makes her Mother of the Year." She pulled a carton of eggs from the refrigerator. "You guys want me to scramble you some eggs?" Without waiting for an answer, she bellowed up the stairs, "Wyatt? Jain? I'm making eggs … you want any?"

"I already ate," Jain called from the living room.

Wyatt thumped down the stairs. "Three, please. But can you make them French toast instead?"

"She won't even fill the horse trough and you think she's making French toast?" Leo said, dancing away as Kober snapped a towel in his direction.

The twins ran off, doing whatever twins do this early in the morning. Jain remained curled up in the corner of the couch with her book. Wyatt popped some frozen waffles in the toaster. And Kober scrambled a bunch of eggs which she and the boys greedily gobbled down while talking about the twins' current events homework.

Everyone cleared their own dishes and she put the skillet in the sink to soak before she went off to take a shower.

While she lathered, rinsed, and repeated, she thanked God for her marvelous children. She was so relieved that she wasn't the only one who appreciated them. None of the tenants at the Marketplace seemed to be bothered by their constant presence, although Hugo tried to pretend he didn't like them one bit. She knew, though, that he made special truffles for them, designed with their initials on top in some kind of magic chocolatey swirl.

Max and Evelyn were like grandparents to them, Skyler like a cool aunt, and Dena treated them like adults, which she knew the kids loved. In fact, Jain couldn't get over the fact that Dena put her in charge of the bookstore when she had to step out lately. Kober had seen her pull out that twenty that Dena had paid her and just stare at it with that goofy teenage grin of hers. Kober was so proud when Jain told her that she tried to refuse the money but Dena insisted she take it. What kid does that?

Of course, Kober knew Dena never would have considered putting Jain in charge for two minutes if she had any kind of regular traffic in the bookstore. She wondered if Dena's mess with Duke Bughata would be cleared up before she went bankrupt. Kober lathered her hair and wondered what other business might take the space next to her if Dena had to bail. Maybe a hip boutique. Tattoo parlor? Oooh, maybe a falafel place. There was not a decent falafel to be found in Sugar Springs. Kober caught a glimpse of her figure in the shower door. "Okay, maybe not a falafel place."

If Dena went out of business the kids would sure miss

Twist. So would Kober. Twist was the reason Wyatt was actually getting his homework done for a change.

Wyatt was a bit infuriating these days because Kober was pretty sure he was a genius, but he had no use for homework so his grades were in the toilet. When he had a mind to, of course, he was able to get it done before he even left school for the day. That was as rare as a white peacock, unfortunately.

Typically, Wyatt's modus operandi was to ignore any and all homework he was assigned. But once when Kober had hollered at him in frustration, "No playing with the dog until your homework is done!" it had lit a fire under him and he immediately completed his work. She had told him similar things in the past, telling him no TV, no snacks, no playing outside, no video games, no going anywhere with his friends … none of it made any difference. His homework remained undone. But with Twist and that nonsense "training" he and Jain were attempting? That did the trick.

Kober also appreciated Twist's influence over Jain. She became more of a kid around Twist rather than the tiny adult she had suddenly turned into over the last few months. Kober knew that was almost completely her fault —since Kober needed an adult in her life—and Jain had recognized that. Kober loved watching her play with Twist, but tried not to let her notice. Every time Jain saw Kober looking at her, she'd ask her mother, "Do you need me to do something?" The difference between working for Kober and working for Dena was that Jain got paid and didn't have to mother her own mother.

Twist was good for the twins too, because she forced them to settle down. One afternoon she went to check on them and found all three of them on the floor of the bookstore. Dena had held her finger to her lips and pointed at them. They rested their heads on either side of Twist—who was sound asleep—and the boys were each engrossed in a Fleur Bradley mystery that Dena gifted them when they left.

God bless Twist. What would they do without her?

Dena

DENA POURED MORE coffee and plated one of the enormous cream cheese and guava empanadas she'd bought from Kober yesterday. She needed fuel while she began brainstorming a list of all the suspicious women she had encountered recently. The more she thought about those footprints, the more she was sure someone had targeted her and Twist specifically.

While it was possible Twist had figured out how to open the gate, she decidedly did not wear high heels.

The first people on the list were those two women in the store yesterday, Oxford Pumps and Blue Boots. She could still hear their stilettos click-clacking along the promenade as they came and went. They'd made such a fuss over Twist. And didn't one say that Twist would look good in her living room? Like she was a statue or piece of furniture or something? That was exactly the kind of person who would steal a dog. Some numbskull who wanted a trophy to show off.

Dena thought back to the conversation. The other woman said her grandkids would love a dog like Twist.

Well, duh, Dena remembered thinking. Who *wouldn't* want a dog like Twist?

They'd all paid cash for their purchases, though, so Dena stuck a pin in them until she could figure out how to track them down.

What about all those people who called for a boycott of her store after they saw that misleading video of her and Twist? Many of them were far-flung around the world, as is the way with cyber-bullies, but surely some of those haters were local. After all, someone was standing smack-dab in the middle of the Marketplace to film it, right? Maybe Charlee's boyfriend Ozzi could help her figure out who originated the video or if anyone local had been one of the commenters. Dena didn't know exactly what Ozzi did for a living, just that he worked with computers, something to do with software. Charlee always joked about him being a hacker. He always denied it, but never very strongly.

Dena checked the time. It was early, but this was an emergency. She called him.

"Dena, what's wrong?" His voice sounded panicky.

"I hope I didn't wake you, but I need your expertise."

"My expertise? What's going on? Are you okay?"

"I'm fine, but my dog has been stolen. I don't know how much Charlee has told you…" Dena filled in all the blanks for Ozzi. "So, I'm hoping you can help me figure out who took that video."

"Dena, I know we always joke about me being a hacker, but I'm not. I'm really not."

"So you can't help?"

Ozzi was quiet for a minute. "Let me check a couple of things and call you back."

It didn't take long before Dena's phone rang. "Did you find it?" she asked excitedly.

"No, I'm sorry. I checked the metadata, but it's been wiped. There's no way for me to tell who uploaded it."

"What about your hacker friends? Can anyone do it?"

Ozzi chuckled. "Again, we're not hackers."

"But Charlee says—"

"I know." He paused. "Tell you what. I'll ask around and maybe one of my *software engineer* friends can help. Don't get your hopes up, but I'll let you know if I get any information for you."

"Thanks, Ozzi. Whatever you can do. I appreciate it."

Dena didn't expect to hear anything more from him. Even she knew that if the metadata had been wiped there'd be no way to trace anything. He was just being nice to the mother of his girlfriend.

Dena went back to her empanada, her coffee, and her list.

What if the person who took Twist was simply some rando who wanted a beautiful and unusual white German shepherd? How in the world would she be able to track them down? Dena began to deflate. No, she couldn't think that way. It had to be someone she could track down, otherwise finding Twist might be a wild goose chase. And that was unacceptable.

Dena sipped her coffee, thinking, hoping the jolt of yet more caffeine would jog loose a good idea.

What if the sheriff was wrong and Duke Bughata did have a wife, maybe a daughter, who wanted Twist back? If there was some estrangement, perhaps they would sneak in here to lure Twist back. And it might explain why Twist willingly went with them without a bark or any kind of alarm.

But how could the sheriff's department be wrong about that? They had all those databases and resources at their disposal.

Maybe the explanation was much simpler than Dena was allowing.

Could it have been Jain? She adored Twist. Perhaps she had poor impulse control and wanted her for her very own.

Dena polished off the empanada without really tasting it, trying to think of one example of poor impulse control from Jain. None sprung to mind. That girl was the grown-up over at Kober's house, based on everything Dena had heard over the last couple of months.

Kober, on the other hand ….

Dena ran a finger around the rim of her cup, lost in thought, trying to picture Kober committing this transgression. She imagined Kober through every step of the dognapping, beginning with telling Dena the kids were miffed at her because she reneged on her promise to get them a dog of their own when they moved to Sugar Springs and ending with an image of her opening her car door and Twist jumping in. But Kober was so loud. Surely she couldn't have managed any kind of covert operation without waking the entire neighborhood.

The high heels were problematic, too. Dena had never seen Kober wear anything but boots or sneakers. But that didn't mean much. Kober could have donned stilettos to throw her off the track. That's what Dena would have done.

Kober's kids could have thought of that too. They were smart. And hadn't the twins kidnapped a cat once and said it followed them home?

Dena drained her cup. "That would be so stupid, though. I'd find out easily enough." But Dena knew kids didn't always think through events to their logical conclusion. Especially ten-year-old boys.

The twins luring Twist away, perhaps with the help of

older siblings, became Dena's working theory, mainly because it was the simplest to prove, but also because deep down she didn't want to believe there was a dognapper on the loose in Sugar Springs who might mistreat Twist. Finding Twist at Kober's house was the least terrifying option, and the one easiest to determine.

Dena hadn't been inside Kober's McMansion before but had driven by it several times. It was a beautiful property, perfectly landscaped with a four-season garden, and handsome brick and stonework soaring three stories high. Graceful and elegant, Dena thought.

The February sun rose late and cast weak shadows across the neighborhood.

Dena sat in her car at the curb, trying to decide if she really wanted to do this or not. Her theory started out simplistic, but now it seemed positively moronic. She didn't want to accuse Kober's kids of anything. The last thing she wanted was to make anything worse for Kober, piling on to her problems and stress.

All she wanted was Twist. It would be easy enough to see whether or not Twist was at Kober's house. It would take two minutes. Twist was too big to hide under a bed and would come running at the sound of her voice or her knock at the door. Dena wouldn't have to accuse anyone of anything.

Lights were on all over the house, so Dena knocked. She had an excuse ready. If a kid answered and asked why she was there she'd say, *I want to talk to your mom about something.* Not a lie. Although if they asked why it couldn't wait until later at the Marketplace, Dena had no answer. If Kober herself answered, she'd ask to see the humidifier

Kober had told her about. Also not a lie. Dena was in the market for one. Her caffeine seemed to kick in and Dena also realized she could use the same answer if the kids questioned her more rigorously, as clever kids the world over had been known to do.

Pajama-clad Wyatt opened the door, nonplussed to see her standing on their front porch, like she did it every morning. "Hi," he said, then immediately retreated to plop down in front of the television.

Dena stepped inside and closed the door behind her. She heard the twins tearing around the house and when they ran past, she saw they were sword-fighting with toast. Dena pressed herself against the wall to keep from being jousted upon.

After they thumped up the stairs, Dena found herself tiptoeing toward the kitchen and forced herself to stop. Surely it made her look quite suspicious. Just walk like a normal person, she commanded her feet.

Jain sat at the breakfast nook, dressed and ready for school, reading a book.

Dena retreated before Jain saw her. If anyone would ask intelligent unanswerable questions right now it would be Jain.

She glanced around, looking for any signs of Twist— piles of socks, a fine patina of dog hair covering every surface, bags of kibble on the countertop. Dena noticed Wyatt watching her so she smiled at him and quickly left the living room, suddenly feeling ridiculous.

If Twist was here, she'd be running around with the twins, or cuddled next to Wyatt on the floor, or patiently waiting for a tidbit of Jain's breakfast.

Unless she was outside. Or in the basement. Or the garage.

Dena walked down a hallway the opposite direction from Jain in the kitchen. She'd just take a peek.

She spied a door that, based on the footprint of the house, seemed to Dena like it should lead to the garage. She pulled it open.

Steam engulfed her. She heard the shower running.

Before she could slam the door shut again, Kober's head poked out from behind the shower curtain. Her eyes were closed, shampoo running down her face. "Son of a pink pizza! I TOLD you kids this lock was BROKEN and to KNOCK! Can't I get a minute to my—" Kober swiped at her face, shrieking when she saw Dena. Her grip on the shower curtain loosened and it swung open, completely exposing Kober.

Dena shrieked in response.

"What are you doing here?" Kober bellowed, scrabbling for the curtain.

"I … I …" Dena's excuse flew out of her brain. "I … wanted to know if you had any cinnamon rolls."

"In my shower?"

Dena slammed the bathroom door shut, leaning against the wall to catch her breath.

Jain and the boys stood in the hallway, gaping at her, not looking the least bit nervous or ashamed.

Unlike Dena. "Oops," was the only thing she could think to say.

The kids seemed to think that made perfect sense under the circumstances and returned to their various activities.

Surely if Twist was in this house somewhere she'd have come at a gallop when she heard their shrieks. And if any of those kids had anything to do with her disappearance, it would register on their faces. They weren't psychopaths, after all.

Dena wanted to flee, but knew she'd have to explain her presence to Kober eventually. Better sooner than later. She made her way to the kitchen where Jain was filling the sink with soapy water.

"Is your dad here?" Dena asked. It would be unbearably humiliating to meet him for the first time under these circumstances.

"Left yesterday for Denver." Jain scrubbed at a skillet.

After an uncomfortable silence Dena said, "I should probably make your mom some coffee."

"Probably." Jain pointed out the coffeemaker and opened the cupboard, showing a canister of ground coffee. She looked at Dena as if she wanted to ask something, then thought better of it. She pulled the plug in the sink and left the kitchen, calling to her brothers. "Time to get ready for school. Hurry up!"

Dena measured out the coffee and water and pushed the button to start the machine brewing.

She thought about leaving a note for Kober. She thought about leaving town. She thought about leaving the planet. She thought about crawling into a hole to die. Here lies Dena Russo, her tombstone would read. Succumbed to a sudden and fatal attack of mortification.

Finally, Kober walked into the kitchen. She saw Dena sitting there at the breakfast nook. Kober opened her mouth to say something then closed it. She grabbed a cup then turned toward Dena, opening her mouth to say something. She closed it again. Kober poured coffee, then opened her mouth to say something. Closed it again.

"Kober, I'm really—"

Kober held up one finger. "You guys ready for school yet?" she called, leaving the kitchen.

The four children clomped down the stairs, coats and

backpacks swinging. After loud goodbyes, Dena heard the front door slam.

Kober loomed at the kitchen threshold.

"Listen, I can explain—" Dena began.

"Doubt it." Kober topped off her cup and sat across from Dena. "I'm waiting. I'm quite curious as to why you're in my house at this ungodly hour, watching me bathe."

"I wasn't watching you bathe! I thought that was the garage door."

"Alright, then. I'm quite curious as to why you're in my house at this ungodly hour, looking for my garage." Kober sipped her coffee, glaring at Dena over the rim.

Dena took a deep breath. No humidifier story would do at this moment. "I'm looking for Twist."

"And you thought she was here?"

"Not really. But I hoped." Dena told Kober the whole story about Twist's disappearance.

At the conclusion, Kober jumped up. "Son of a flaming red excuse! I can't believe you thought my kids stole your dog!"

"I know, I know. It's ridiculous. I just thought this would be the least terrible option." Dena let out a whoosh of air. "I wish now it *had* been one of them."

Kober stared at her for a long time before sitting down again. "So, if it wasn't one of my precious little hellions, who was it?"

Dena and Kober discussed the pros and cons of the list Dena brainstormed earlier.

"It had to be whoever made that video and plastered it all over the internet," Kober said. "Someone who was at the Marketplace and saw your confrontation with Duke— or at least heard about it—and wanted to punish you for stealing the dog. Or more altruistically, wanted to return Twist to Duke."

"I guess. Maybe." Dena pushed her chair away from the table and stood, rubbing her temples. "I better get ready for work."

"Does that include stopping at everyone's house to watch them shower? If so, I'll go ahead and give Max a call so he can be prepared. Wouldn't want him to have a heart attack."

"I guess I deserve that," Dena said glumly. "Please don't tell anyone about this."

"No promises." Kober stood too, a grin curling the sides of her mouth. "Please don't sneak up on me in the shower again."

"No promises."

———

It was nine o'clock by the time Dena left Kober's house. She parked in her own driveway, but instead of going in the house, walked along the sidewalk toward the gate.

Still being careful not to ruin any of the paw or footprints, Dena checked the yard for more clues, now that the sun was completely up. She picked her way across the yard, through the snow toward the shed on the opposite side.

Her hand flew to her mouth, muting her scream.

Dena

HAND CLAMPED TIGHTLY over her mouth, Dena lost her balance and staggered backward, away from Duke Bughata's body crumpled in the snow.

Dena hadn't seen very many dead bodies, only those at funerals and, of course, Norbert Wallace's last month. But she could tell, even several feet away, that Duke was dead. His skin was ashen and even though she'd only seen him that one time, his face looked bloated.

She backtracked through her steps in the snow, retreating as far from Duke's body as possible while still being able to see it. She pulled her phone from her purse and called the sheriff's office from the sidewalk.

While she waited for the authorities, her mind raced. How long had Duke's body been out here? Was it here when she spoke to Sheriff Johnson earlier? Had she shined her flashlight but just missed it? Until Twist came, she couldn't remember the last time she'd been back here. Her patio furniture hadn't even been unpacked yet, forming a base in the shed under a dozen moving boxes filled with gardening items and tools she wouldn't need until well into spring. Her trash bins were in the garage. She'd had no reason to walk into her back yard, much less all the way around the shed, since move-in day just after Christmas.

She shook her head to clear it. Duke's dead body hadn't been in her yard that long. She saw him ten days ago. She shuddered. Had he been there this entire time?

Maybe Duke had come to get Twist last night, had a heart attack, and Twist ran away through the gate he'd left open. Dena strained to see more footprints in the snow, but only saw her own from earlier, and Twist's pawprints, and those high heels.

Where were Duke's footprints?

———

When Sheriff Johnson arrived with Deputy Chavez and an EMT crew, she pointed at the front door and told Dena to go in the house. Dena did as she was told, but immediately exited from the back door, taking care not to step in any of the high heel footprints, and leaned against the house opposite the shed. She positioned herself so she could see Sheriff Johnson and Deputy Chavez milling around with the EMTs, but Duke's body was hidden from view.

Dena watched them secure the scene, making phone calls and poking around while the EMTs worked on Duke. They didn't work for long, and they weren't in hurry-up mode, confirming Dena's assessment that Duke was already dead. They were still packing up their gear when the coroner showed up. Dena recognized him from when he came to attend to Norbert Wallace's body.

She shuddered, but not from the cold.

Dena saw one of her neighbors talking to the EMT crew out on the sidewalk. She hoped they were vague in the information they relayed about the scene and circumstance. Thankfully, the angle and a slight hill didn't allow anyone to see the specifics of what was really going on. She didn't need the whole town knowing that Duke Bughata's body was found next to the shed in her back yard.

The coroner motioned to the ambulance crew, who returned to the yard with a stretcher. The EMTs, the coroner, Sheriff Johnson, and Deputy Chavez huddled together, heads bent in conversation.

After the coroner took measurements and a series of photographs, the EMT crew picked up Duke's body and placed it into the back of the coroner's covered pickup truck. Dena wondered what her neighbor thought when the ambulance drove away without lights flashing and siren blaring.

Chavez handed something to the coroner while speaking to him. He studied it carefully before handing it back and replying. Chavez and Johnson both nodded. The coroner made his way back to his truck.

The sheriff and the deputy had a short conversation before walking over to Dena. Chavez carried a small box in an evidence bag.

"Do you have a rat problem, Dena?" he asked, speaking so fast it came out as one word.

Dena peered into the clear bag he held. She couldn't read the name of the product on the box, but she saw it had a skull-and-crossbones and said in big read letters, *Kills vermin dead*. She looked up at the deputy with big eyes. "Do you really think I poisoned Duke in my backyard and left the evidence in plain sight?"

Deputy Chavez gave a small shrug.

Dena lowered her voice, even though the gawking neighbors milling about in the street were too far away to hear anything. "Isn't it more probable that someone lured

Twist out the doggy door then stole her, knowing I'd leave to go look for her so they could dump Duke's body here while I was gone?" Dena felt pleased with herself for coming up with that theory on the fly, discounting the fact a killer would be stupid to dump Duke's body here after the sun was already up and the neighborhood stirring to activity. That was neither here nor there, as this was the sheriff's department crime to solve, not Dena's.

"Dena," the sheriff spoke slowly and calmly, "you know we must poke and prod into all corners, even if they don't seem perfectly logical. A dead body was found in your yard with rat poison nearby." Sheriff Johnson held up her hand to quiet Dena before she could squeak out another denial. "We don't even know if Mr Bughata was poisoned yet, but you want us to figure this out, right?"

"Of course I do."

"Then let us do our job. And in the meantime, why don't you go ahead and keep this quiet for now."

Dena tipped her head at her neighbor. "It won't be quiet for long."

"We'll have a word before we go. But I don't see any reason for you to tell anyone at the Marketplace, for example, do you?"

"That's fine with me. But they're going to ask about Twist when I don't bring her into work with me and the discussion might accidentally turn to Duke." Dena glanced sadly toward the shed. Was there anyone who found more dead bodies than she did? If so, Dena felt as sorry for them as she did for herself.

"You'll figure something out." Sheriff Johnson motioned for Chavez to go chat with the neighbor, leaving her and Dena alone. When he stepped away, she said, "Dena, you know I wouldn't be doing my job if I didn't ask, but did you have anything to do with Duke Bughata turning up dead in your backyard?"

"If I say no, will you believe me?" Dena asked her.

"If I say yes, will you believe *me*?" Sheriff Johnson asked in return.

Kober

KOBER NOTICED that Dena had opened her bookstore late—by almost two hours—even though it was Dena herself who wrote in the Marketplace Handbook for Tenants that under no circumstances will anyone fail to open their business during the hours when the Marketplace was open.

Did seeing me naked cause temporary blindness and cause her to seek emergency treatment? Or was she just out searching for Twist?

All the tenants had to agree to each one of the terms in the handbook and initial all of them. After Norbert's ex-wife and executor sold them the Marketplace for a song, they'd had meeting after meeting to hammer out the terms of their agreement with one another in order to keep the Marketplace humming along with as little stress as possible. They negotiated and argued about each clause until everyone was happy with how it read and what it might mean for their particular business.

Temporary blindness was not listed as one of the terms they'd discussed. Nor was a missing dog.

Today Kober listened to Dena apologize to the other tenants in the vendor room for her tardiness without giving any kind of explanation for it. Instead, she dove into a lengthy explanation about leaving Twist at home to get her more comfortable staying there and also because she thought that maybe Twist was potentially scaring away her customers. Kober had to literally bite her tongue to keep from talking. She noticed Dena actively avoided making eye contact with her.

None of the other tenants seemed the least bit troubled by what Kober knew to be an outrageous lie.

Skyler, in fact, recounted the story of the 4H calf she raised as a preteen that followed her around constantly. "It got to be kind of a pain, to tell the truth, so I don't blame you for leaving Twist at home."

Evelyn said, "Personally, I'll miss her, but Balaam will certainly be happy not to have Twist here. I don't think he ever quite figured her out."

Hugo mumbled something about Health Department rules.

Kober knew Dena was lying about Twist, but didn't understand why. What was the big deal to say that a dog that didn't even belong to you had run away and/or potentially been dognapped? She hadn't even had the dog for two weeks, yet seemed awfully distraught about it.

Unless she was just freaked out about seeing me naked. I seem to have that effect on people.

Evelyn

EVELYN'S EYES drooped while Dena was telling them why Twist wasn't with her this morning. She didn't mention why she opened the bookstore so late today, which is what Evelyn was more interested in. But she was too tired to get into it and she was sure Dena had a good reason.

Evelyn hadn't had a proper night's sleep. She woke up in the middle of the night to pee and found Max was gone. Again. Not just gone from his side of the bed, but gone from the house.

Evelyn searched the entire house and even went to the garage to see if the car was still there. It was, but Max wasn't.

She dialed his phone, ready to give him a piece of her mind. But when she heard his muffled ringtone coming from the pocket of his cardigan hanging in the closet, she hung up.

She and Kober had a conversation a while back about Max disappearing. Kober had hinted that maybe Max was having a torrid affair. She had giggled about it at the time.

Seriously … c'mon … Max? Having an affair? That was a younger man's game, wasn't it?

But things looked very different in the middle of a dark, starless February night and Evelyn began searching the house for clues.

She pawed through every drawer in his dresser, every nook and cranny in every closet, the bookshelves downstairs, even the garage shelves.

Nothing.

She went back upstairs, becoming angrier with every location she searched.

Balaam had woken up and followed her around the house, angry now too. He jumped up on Max's pillow, knowing full well he wasn't supposed to be there.

Evelyn shooed him off the bed.

Balaam pointed his tail in the air while he walked over to her. He put a paw on Evelyn's slipper.

"I'm fine. Go back to bed."

Balaam dug his claws into the top of her slipper. "No, no treats." She pried his claws off her foot. "Back to bed with you, sir."

Balaam slunk off to bed.

Evelyn thought she'd do the same. She'd go back to sleep and show Max she didn't even care. But who was she kidding? She was too hyped up to sleep. She stood in the center of their bedroom, trying to think of someplace Max could hide something.

Problem was, she didn't even know what she was looking for. What could that old coot be hiding? Where in the world *was* he? And who was he with?

Evelyn considered taking one of the sleeping pills she knew was in her nightstand. She assumed it was expired, since she got it after her gallbladder surgery three years ago —or was it four? Maybe it would still knock her out for a while. As she reached for the knob to pull it open, she stopped, mid-reach, and hurried to Max's side of the bed.

She stared at his nightstand, the only drawer in the house she hadn't opened. She grimaced at the knob, suddenly afraid of what she might find. "Don't be a loon, Ev," she murmured. "Just look, then go back to bed."

Evelyn took a deep breath then yanked open the drawer. The nightstand wasn't big, but the drawer was deep. She began to rummage around. Loose photographs, receipts, the instruction booklet for the exercise tracker he never wore, an eye mask he got on an overseas flight more than ten years ago, a scattering of coins he probably thought might be worth something someday, and a paperback he'd been looking for last week.

At the very bottom of the drawer her fingers wrapped around a soft plastic rectangle. She pulled it out. A checkbook. Must be the one he got for the photo studio. She almost dropped it back in the drawer. But why would it be buried under all this stuff? She opened it up and didn't see their business name. She didn't even see her own name.

The only name on the checks was Max's.

She flipped through the register, but only saw withdrawals, no deposits. And no annotation as to the recipients of the checks. Just dates, amounts, and some weird doodles. Evelyn peered at the register, trying to decipher Max's writing. The dates were random. A couple checks for various amounts one month, then no checks for several months, then another. She couldn't discern a pattern to it.

Evelyn buried it back in the bottom of the drawer.

Did floozies take checks? Evelyn would have sworn that would be a cash only business, but what did she know?

She briefly considered calling the sheriff's office, but when Max showed up again, she'd have to explain why she wasted their time. She wasn't sure if that would embarrass her or Max more.

Evelyn decided against the sleeping pill, but turned off the lights and snugged up the covers on her side of the bed. She leaned against the headboard and began ticking off a mental list of all the eligible ladies she and Max knew.

If she fell asleep, so be it.

If she scared the bejeebers out of Max when he got home, so be it.

She was still awake at four when Max tiptoed in and crawled into bed.

"And just where have you been?" Evelyn said.

Max jumped. "Good grief, woman! What are you doing sitting in the dark like that?"

"Really? We're going to play that game?"

"What game?" Max switched on the lamp on his nightstand.

"The one where you pretend I'm the crazy one and we avoid talking about the affair—or plural, affairzzzz—you're having. I just want to know who it is. Millie with her pot roast you always rave about? Esther with those double Ds? Bernice with that cute little apartment where nobody tells you what to do and you can be the boss again?"

"Wow, Ev. Just … wow." Max reached for her hand. "How long have you been thinking about this?"

She snatched her hand away. "Long enough. So which one is it? Or is it someone I don't even know?"

"It's nobody, Ev."

"Then where were you in the middle of the night?"

Max looked directly at her. "I've been having some bouts of insomnia so I go out walking until I get tired."

"You expect me to believe that?"

"Well … yes."

"Most people read or watch TV or make chamomile tea when they can't sleep."

"I'm not most people." Max grinned at her.

"Don't I know it." Evelyn narrowed her eyes at him, trying to decide if she believed him. He didn't make a habit of lying to her, in fact, she couldn't remember when —or even if—she'd ever caught him in a lie. "Okay, you old coot. Let me get this straight. You've been having trouble sleeping and instead of doing what normal people do, you go out in the middle of the night, in the middle of February, and walk around these unlit, dangerous, rutted country roads."

"I'm not an idiot. I wear my coat."

"It's still too cold for this nonsense, Maxwell Zachary Milligan."

"Nah, it's bracing. Puts hair on your chest."

Evelyn reached over and pulled open his pajama top. "Liar."

He laughed. "I said *your* chest." Max reached over for Evelyn's pajama top, but she swatted his hand away.

"Max," she said softly. "It's not safe for you to walk out on those dark roads in the middle of the winter. Promise me you won't do it anymore."

"It's perfectly safe, Ev. I like it out there. Besides, I've never even seen a car out there. If anyone was driving on those roads, I'd see their headlights from miles away." He pulled her close and she let him. "It's perfectly safe, trust me."

"You know what happens when that bar out by the highway closes. All the drunks drive home. It's those drivers I don't trust."

Max snuggled up close to her and they were quiet for a few moments. Then Max murmured, "I'm kinda hungry. Maybe I'll go see if Millie has any pot roast."

Evelyn yanked the pillow out from behind him and smacked him with it. He laughed and rolled over to turn off the lamp. When he turned back to his wife, offering his arm, she snuggled into his shoulder. He fell asleep immediately and began to snore.

Walking the dirt roads of the greater Sugar Springs metropolitan area. The old coot. She decided not to ask him about the checkbook. She didn't really want to know. If it was what she suspected, she'd rather he was eating midnight pot roast with Millie.

Dena

DENA FELT uncomfortable about lying to everyone except Kober about Twist. If Sheriff Johnson hadn't asked her to keep quiet about Duke, she would have gathered up all the tenants and told them everything about everything. If there was anything she learned from Norbert Wallace's murder, it was that amateur sleuthing should be a team sport.

Regardless, it was a burden keeping both secrets and it made her sick to her stomach. She knew, however, that if she said one word about Twist disappearing, it wouldn't be long before they were talking about Duke's body in her back yard. How could it not be related?

Evelyn had been yawning all day and dragging around the Marketplace, but when she had asked Dena if *she* was feeling okay, Dena turned the question back on Evelyn to dodge answering. But also because she was worried about her.

Evelyn told her that she was exhausted because she'd been up all night, waiting for Max. "Get this. The old coot wanders around Sugar Springs in the middle of the night when he can't sleep. In February."

Dena was now worried about Max as well. "That doesn't seem safe."

"Try telling him that."

"I wouldn't dare."

"Smart girl." Evelyn poured another cup of coffee. "I just don't know what I'm going to do with him."

Dena thought about Twist disappearing in the middle of the night too. She wanted to race to Max and ask if he saw anything unusual while out wandering. Maybe he saw who took Twist, or who dumped Duke's body. She knew she couldn't, though. Besides, Max was no dummy. If he saw someone luring Twist into a car in the dead of night, he would have said something, maybe even stopped it from happening in the first place.

And there was absolutely nobody in Sugar Springs who wouldn't report seeing a body being dumped in someone's back yard.

Dena couldn't even talk to Charlee or Lance about any of this. They'd ask too many perfect questions and she'd blurt out things she shouldn't. They were always good for solace and/or shelter, and Dena was millimeters away from running away to Denver to hide. She knew she couldn't. Better that she not risk picking up the phone and hearing their voices.

She groaned. Even if this investigation allowed her to run away to Denver, she couldn't anyway. Despite all the drama, today was the day Boyd Drummond, the ice cream guy, was supposed to show up to start setting up his shop. She had to be here to facilitate. Or whatever the Marketplace manager was called upon to do. Dena hoped she would figure it out eventually.

She was glad for small miracles, though, and Boyd

hadn't made his appearance before she got to the Market-place for the day.

She vowed to keep busy, locking herself in her book-store if need be so she wouldn't be tempted to blurt out anything that might ruin the investigation into Duke's death. She couldn't risk doing something the sheriff specifi-cally told her not to do. A little white lie about Twist's disappearance and keeping her mouth shut about Duke wouldn't kill her. Besides, Duke's death, while unfortunate, had nothing to do with her and she felt confident that the sheriff's investigation would reveal the same. Okay, she pretended to feel confident, even though everything seemed a bit like a precarious house of cards at the moment.

With the sheriff's department up to their neck investi-gating Duke's death, she knew there would be no inquiry into Twist's disappearance. Even though Dena had forced Sheriff Johnson and Deputy Chavez to look at the high heeled prints in the yard, and take photos of them before they left, neither was interested in talking about it. Twist was important to Dena, but her disappearance didn't trump Duke's death.

It didn't lessen the knot in the pit of her stomach, though. Where was Twist? Was she being treated properly? Was she inside someplace warm with food and water?

She offered up a prayer, hoping it was sufficient.

Dena tried to put the morning's unfortunate events out of her mind. Instead, she busied herself searching for Boyd's file with all his paperwork and documentation for the opening of his ice cream shop at the Marketplace. It wasn't with the other tenants' files in the file cabinet. She searched her front counter, including the shelves under her front counter.

She went into the vendor room to see if she'd left it in

there. She didn't see Boyd's file, but she did see a new haiku on the white board.

> Opening late is
> Supposed to be a no-no
> Who needs rules, right?

Touché. She deserved that, but decided not to mention it, instead, asking the other tenants if they'd seen Boyd's paperwork around. Nobody had.

Her shoulders slumped when she realized she must have completely dropped the ball and hadn't generated any of the documents yet. Boyd Drummond and the Scoops Ice Creamery didn't even have a file yet.

Dena scrambled to make a folder and begin printing out documents. Had he emailed any of the signed documents she'd asked him for? Increasingly frantic, she searched her email for any attachments he had sent her.

While in the middle of this chaos, her phone chimed with a video call. Assuming it was one of her kids, Dena punched at it saying, "Whatever it is, I can't right now. I'm—"

"Dena?"

She almost dropped the phone when she heard the faint voice of her friend Georgia from Santa Fe. Dena had left so many unanswered texts and ignored voice mails that she almost gave up on the fact she'd ever hear from Georgia again.

Dena stopped dealing with Boyd's paperwork and plopped herself on the stool at her front counter. "Georgia! Oh my gosh ... it's so good to hear from you! How are you?"

"I'm okay."

Georgia's voice sounded flat and monotone. Dena

looked closer at her face and hair. No make-up, no jewelry. Her curls were flattened, like she'd slept on them for three days straight. She didn't look or sound like herself. Granted, she'd been in a coma and was now recuperating at home, but still. Was this the new normal for Georgia?

"How long have you been home from the hospital?"

Georgia looked past the camera, as if she stared at a big calendar in the sky. After a pause she said, "Not sure."

"Couple weeks? Couple days?"

Georgia again looked past the camera and nodded.

"How are you feeling?"

"Fine."

Dena felt her queasiness bubble up again. Georgia did not seem fine. "Georgia, what medications are you on? Can you go get the prescription bottles and show me the labels?" Dena hoped that by doing that she could also see who or what Georgia kept looking at just out of range of the camera. But Georgia didn't move.

"My pills are brought to me."

"Georgia, is there somebody there with you? Can I talk to them?"

Again, Georgia looked just past her camera, then shook her head. She was just about to say something when the lid of her laptop slammed shut.

Dena immediately dialed her back, but her call went unanswered.

Since Georgia hadn't moved, who disconnected the call? And why?

Dena tried calling some of their mutual friends in Santa Fe, but got through to exactly none of them. When Dena left town, it had been under a bit of a cloud. One could even say she had been chased away by these so-called mutual friends. When Georgia had her hiking accident and ended up in her coma, Dena became persona non grata with their group of friends. They wiped Dena away as if she never existed. In all probability, they had blocked Dena's number en masse and her increasingly frantic calls never even went through.

Dena considered calling Sheriff Johnson for advice, but she knew her time and attention was being taken up with Duke's murder.

Instead, Dena went next door to the bakery.

"Kober, can I borrow your phone?"

Kober had her hands full meticulously frosting a twelve-layer red-and-white torte. Without taking her eyes off her work, she gestured with her butt. "It's over there."

"I'll bring it back in a minute."

"No prank calls!" Kober bellowed after her.

Back at the bookstore, Dena used her own phone to look up the number for Beige Ann, then dialed it on Kober's phone. Beige Ann might be the best chance Dena had. Perhaps only chance.

"Ann?"

"Who's this?"

"Don't hang up ... it's Dena. I just got a weird video call from Georgia. Have you seen her recently?"

There was a long pause and Dena wasn't sure Ann hadn't hung up. Finally, she said, "The other day."

"You saw Georgia the other day? How did she seem to you?"

"Perfectly fine. No thanks to you."

Dena didn't want to rehash for the millionth time that she hadn't pushed Georgia off that hiking trail, no matter how many times they accused her of doing so.

"Can you go over to her house and just check on her? I'm a little worried. Somebody might be over there already, but—"

"Then why would I barge in?"

"Because … like I said … she didn't seem right and I'm worried about her."

"So *now* you're worried about her." Ann didn't sound beige right then. She sounded a bit red and huffy.

"Listen, Ann, I know I'm not your favorite person in the world, but please, just go over and check on Georgia to see if she's okay. Then just text me back on this number. All I need is a little thumbs-up emoji and I can quit worrying. Please?"

"I don't really care if you worry or not." Ann disconnected.

Dena wanted to throw the phone. Instead, she hammered her fist on the counter. She jabbed at the keypad on Kober's phone, pounding out a text message to Ann. "You're not doing it for me! You're doing it for Georgia!" Dena added emojis as punctuation—angry face, head exploding face, crying face, expletive shouting face, shocked face. She reconsidered and erased them all then added three praying hands emojis and hit send.

Kober

KOBER GLANCED up when Dena came in to return her phone. She'd finished the torte and was carefully boxing it up. Before she closed the lid, she showed it to Dena. "Would you pay forty dollars for this?"

"No."

Kober recoiled, wincing, and Dena hastily added, "Not because it isn't gorgeous and most likely delicious, but because it's just me so I'd have to eat the entire thing. Which I would. Probably in one sitting. So no, I wouldn't even pay five bucks for it." She had a twinge of guilt thinking about that empanada. Which she paid for. And ate in one sitting.

"Would you pay five bucks for a cupcake?"

Dena hemmed and hawed.

"I guess that's my answer."

"Again, nothing against your cupcakes. But I really should be watching my pennies as well as my waistline." Dena pointed to Kober's chalkboard price list. "I thought you had your pricing all figured out."

"This isn't a used bookstore," Kober snapped. "I can't

just charge half off the cover price." Kober erased a series of prices from her board. "Sorry. That didn't even make sense."

"I took it in the spirit it was intended. Are you worried about money again?"

Skyler joined them with a laugh. "Is there someone who's not worried around here? I thought that was part of owning a business, to worry about money."

"Seems to be for me," Kober said.

"Me too," Dena said, silently noting her additional worry about Twist.

"Oh, good. Glad I'm not alone," Skyler said.

Kober used a pair of tongs and lifted one of her gigantic peanut butter cookies in the air and waved it enticingly in front of Dena and Skyler. "Think I can get five bucks for one of these beauties?"

Neither woman piped up quickly enough to suit Kober so she groaned and returned the cookie to the tray.

"What's going on, Kober?" Dena asked.

"Nothing. I'm just worried about this place."

"That doesn't sound like nothing," Dena said. "You don't have to minimize your feelings. Not with us anyway."

Skyler nodded. "But why are you worried? You've got good traffic, happy customers, lots of referrals."

"And even if I don't buy a torte, I know everything that comes out of that oven is beyond delicious." Dena waved her arm toward the display shelves.

"Thank you. Both of you. I'm just … I don't know … worried about the future. Like, what if I can't sustain this place? I know I have momentum right now, but everyone is going to get tired of me eventually."

Skyler laughed. "They might get tired of you, but they'll never get tired of your goodies."

"Very funny."

Skyler had been reading Kober's chalkboard menu. "You know what you don't have on here? Wedding cakes. People always need wedding cakes."

"Always?" Kober asked sarcastically.

"You know what I mean. You wouldn't believe how many of my girlfriends are planning weddings right now. And they're spending a fortune—an absolute fortune—on their cakes. You need to get in on that action. You need to offer fancy wedding cakes." Skyler tapped her temple. "You're lucky you know a genius."

"I *refuse* to make wedding cakes." Kober knew the vehemence of her statement shocked Dena and Skyler, but she didn't feel like explaining.

Skyler shook her head. "You don't know what you're missing. One enormous fancy cake every month would probably pay for your lease here."

"Bakeries do tend to make wedding cakes, you know," Dena said softly.

Kober changed her demeanor completely, smiling at them. "I just don't want to be greedy, preying on women at their most vulnerable." She went back to her chalkboard and started writing in prices. Maybe four-ninety-nine for the cookies, if five seemed like too much, she thought. She tried to make it artistic so maybe people wouldn't realize she was trying to scam them over a penny.

Skyler took the chalk from her. "May I?"

"Be my guest."

Skyler was naturally artistic and had lovely handwriting. Kober knew these were both traits she did not possess. Her writing looked more like it came from a hoof than a hand.

While Kober and Dena watched Skyler transform a boring old chalkboard menu into a thing of beauty, Kober's phone chirped.

"I think this might be for you." Kober pointed her phone screen toward Dena. "Making friends wherever you go." The entirety of the text message was an upraised middle finger.

Dena grabbed the phone. In all caps she wrote, IS GEORGIA OK???

Ten seconds later there was a thumbs-up. And immediately afterward another upraised middle finger.

Dena returned the gesture to Kober's phone and stalked from the bakery.

Kober called after her in an over-the-top New Jersey tough guy accent. "Yo! It's a good thing you've got classy friends like me and Skyler now!" She pretended to pick her nose and Skyler stuck a hand down the back of her pants and scratched her butt. Then they laughed like maniacs.

She was loathe to say it out loud, lest they use this weakness against her and learn she was all soft and squishy under her highly cultivated crustiness, but Kober was glad she had a couple of classy friends too.

<h1 style="text-align:center">Skyler</h1>

AFTER SKYLER FINISHED MAKING Kober's menu board beautiful, she showed her an easy way to change the prices if she wanted. All she had to do was wet one finger and erase the first number. Of course, that meant she had to increase or decrease items by full dollars, but that seemed to be what Kober wanted to do. Skyler assured Kober she'd come fix it, though, if anything got messed up.

Back in the cheese shop Skyler puzzled over why Kober was so deadset against making wedding cakes. Kober may not be able to make her menu pretty, but it was obvious she could work miracles when she decorated cakes.

It seemed to Skyler that wedding cakes would be a natural fit for the bakery. But what did she know? Kober could do what she wanted; she knew what was best for her own business.

Just like she could with her cheese shop. She'd stopped into the bakery between customers because she'd wanted to ask Kober yet again what she thought about her charcuterie classes. It was silly to keep asking everyone, especially since she'd already advertised and even had some folks sign up, which was a definite plus, since the class was tonight.

She knew she was being ridiculous, but she still wasn't sure about what she was doing. Honestly, how much validation did she need? She felt so needy.

Skyler didn't know whose opinion she could trust anymore.

Evelyn loved everything—except that stupid feta cheese.

Max told her he was one thousand percent behind everything she did, which she knew meant he was just sick of hearing about her worries. Totally valid, of course. So was she.

Hugo agreed with everything she said.

Jake. Well, she didn't know Jake well enough to trust his opinion, did she? But he had agreed that the class sounded like a good idea. She blushed, remembering how she thought he was swooping in for a kiss when he wasn't. Obviously he wasn't blowing smoke in an attempt to get in her pants or anything. Skyler rubbed both hands over her face, wondering if she was destined to turn scarlet, henceforth and forever, every time he delivered her cheese.

Dena, on the other hand, wouldn't give her an outright opinion most of the time, simply asked thought-provoking questions so Skyler could do some soul-searching for the answers only she could realize. Skyler loved Dena, but man, she could be exhausting. She wondered if she did the same thing to her kids.

But Kober. Kober she could trust to tell her the truth, no matter how painful or distasteful. Unfortunately, Skyler had asked Kober about the charcuterie classes so often that now, whenever Skyler brought it up, Kober honked loud, like a goose.

It only took three or four times before Skyler got the message that Kober was sick of the topic.

She was glad now that Kober had been distracted by her own problems when she popped into the bakery to ask about those darn classes again, saving her from another round of shrill honking. It was a shame, though, that Kober didn't see the brilliance of her wedding cake idea.

Skyler brightened. She'd keep telling Kober to sell wedding cakes until she started honking about that.

Perhaps Kober would see the brilliance of Skyler's ideas if she was successful with the charcuterie classes. Ooh! Maybe Kober could start doing baking classes! She'd have to mention it to her.

But for now, Skyler had to suck it up and get organized for tonight.

She stacked up the cheese boards her students paid for as part of their tuition. Skyler ran a finger over the subtle logo she'd had carved into the round wooden trays when she ordered them. They were plain, but classy. She'd already decided if these classes took off, she'd invest in some more intricate boards. Maybe commission some with little drawers to hold a set of cheese knives and tiny forks.

In between customers, she made a list of all the cheeses, crackers, and other filler she'd make available for her students to use in the creation of their own works of art. She could use it as a supply template for future classes, assuming this one went well.

She began to gather everything off to the side so she wouldn't accidentally use something for tonight if a customer came in and wanted her to do up a cheese board.

Skyler knew she had enough varieties of cheese, thanks to the hunky Jake, along with his vote of confidence, but she worried about olives. She added extra figs, dates, cashews, almonds, and golden raisins to her supply, just in case her Kalamata, Castelvetrano, and Manzanilla olives weren't enough.

Skyler hoped the charcuterie gods were accepting supplications. *Please let this work out.*

Hugo

HUGO WAS STILL BEATING himself up over his interaction with Skyler and Jake earlier. It irked him no end that seeing Jake flirting with Skyler could make him feel so insignificant.

He had as many good qualities as Jake did, didn't he? Sure, he didn't raise exotic animals on a ranch and walk around with llama poop on his boots, but wasn't that something for the positive column?

Hugo flexed his arm and stared at it. His forearms were as sinewy and muscled as Jake's were. At least one was, anyway. He held both arms in front of himself and compared them. The fact one was three-quarters-of-an-inch bulkier had to be erotic, right? Just because his muscles came from mixing and piping chocolate and not the great outdoors didn't make him any less ... sexy.

Aw, who was he kidding? Only himself. Skyler didn't see him as sexy, no matter how hard he tried or how big his arms were. He knew Skyler only saw him as friendship material. Maybe she even thought of him like she would a younger brother, although he knew for a fact that he was ten months and six days older than she was.

He wished he could reset the clock to the very first minute they met here at the Marketplace. Then he'd be able to feign surprise at seeing her again, and not going along with it when she thought they were meeting for the first time. He was so shocked when she hadn't remembered him that he couldn't even mumble anything about meeting at the FrouFrouFood trade show all those years ago.

Skyler was the reason he left his high-end hotel job in New Orleans to come to this podunk town. Sugar Springs had grown on him these last few months, but he wouldn't be here if he hadn't known this was where Skyler was opening her cheese shop.

He'd been following her blog since they met, long before she was able to open her place, and long before the chocolate shop was even a twinkle in Hugo's eye.

When they happened to sit next to each other in the crowded "So You Think You Can Restaurant" seminar, they made small talk while waiting for it to begin. Skyler confessed to him she was trying to learn how to run a cheese shop, but feared she'd never be able to get it all together. She had to cobble together the funding and learn everything about running a business. Her degree in art and her upbringing on a dairy farm only trained her to love cheese and to be poor, she'd told him.

Hugo had been smitten with her from that very moment. He didn't want to come on too strong and scare her away, though, so he didn't ask her to join him for a drink at the bar or share a meal or anything. All he did was make sure he just happened to be where she was during the long weekend of the conference. And subscribe anonymously to her blog, of course.

Why was he such a putz? Why didn't he ask her to

dinner right there during that seminar? Why didn't he use his real name when he subscribed to her blog? Why didn't he email her after the trade show? She gave him her business card, after all.

Such a putz.

Instead, he followed her budding career silently, like a creeper and a stalker, from afar.

And now it was too late. She was under the spell of Jake, the intrepid llama rancher.

Jake probably emailed her all the time.

Dena

"THE FUN STARTS NOW!" a man's voice boomed.

Dena jolted her attention from her computer toward the promenade where the voice came from. She hurried through the bookstore and saw the most enormous man she'd ever seen dressed in a bright Hawaiian shirt, cargo shorts, and flip flops. He was built like a refrigerator. Not just a regular one, but a commercial side-by-side.

He stood in the center of the promenade holding a large cooler by both handles. It had no lid and Dena could see it was filled with small paper cups with wooden spoons sticking out of them. He greeted everyone in his Boston accent, "Hahwahya? Good to see ya!"

This had to be Boyd Drummond, ice cream showman.

He jabbed the cooler toward everyone within ten feet of him. "Free samples! Taste the world's best ice cream this side of Fenway Pawk! Made by yours truly!" Boyd bent low to offer cups to children, then swept and danced around, offering samples to taller people. "Whatever flavah you want, I can make!" For being so huge, he was surprisingly nimble. He included a loud guffaw with every cup given away.

Dena shouldn't have been surprised that Boyd was potentially more exhausting in real life than he was over the phone.

"Hey! Turn that frown upside down!" Boyd pirouetted over to a man sitting in one of the overstuffed chairs scowling at a receipt a teenager held out to him. "You can't be sad when you eat ice cream!" The teen grinned and took a sample cup, then took another when Boyd elbowed him hard enough to lose his balance. Boyd held out the cooler to the man in the chair who stared at it for a moment, then beamed.

"I love ice cream."

"Everybody does!" Boyd boomed.

The man grabbed a cup and immediately spooned a bite. He closed his eyes in ecstasy. "Mmm."

"Have another!" Boyd shoved the cooler in front of his face and the man took another cup.

He and his son toasted each other with all four of their cups of ice cream. The boy said, "Cheers!" while his dad said, "Here's Mudslide in yer eye!" to which Boyd howled with glee.

By now all the other tenants had congregated in front of the bookstore, watching Boyd holler at people, cajoling them with good-natured teasing to pronounce his ice cream the best they ever tasted.

From anyone else, the constant barrage of blaring demands would seem like bullying, but the crowd ate up Boyd as happily as they ate up his ice cream samples. When his cooler was empty, he shouted, "Bring all your friends to my grand opening tomorrow! Scoops Ice Creamery! Somewhere in this building! Not sure where ... just follow your nose! It'll be the most delectable aroma in the place!"

Dena felt Hugo stiffen beside her, clearly miffed at the idea that Boyd's ice cream could possibly smell better than his chocolate shop.

"You must not have made the acquaintance of the Sugar Springs Bakery!" Kober bellowed, walking toward Boyd.

"I have not!" he bellowed right back at her. The only difference between them was that Kober had a scowl on her face, while Boyd's grin threatened to split his face. "Glad to meet you, bakery lady!"

Boyd handed Hugo the empty cooler then wrapped Kober in a bear hug, causing her eyes to practically pop out of their sockets. Whether that was from surprise or physical force, though, Dena couldn't tell.

Dena took one step forward and planted her feet before speaking quietly. It was a trick she used on her children when they were young to encourage them to modulate their voices. "I'm Dena Russo. I own this bookstore." She waved behind her. "We've spoken on the phone."

Again, Boyd's agility startled Dena and she found herself wrapped in a bear hug of her own.

"Dena Russo! I am delighted to meet you!"

Dena's first instinct was to push away, but the longer the hug lasted, the more she enjoyed it. Boyd's embrace reminded her of her beloved Uncle Doc, whom she hadn't thought of in years. She hoped Boyd wasn't going to fling her up in the air, though.

When he finally released her, Boyd spoke to the group of tenants, voice not modulated in the least. "Come out to my cah and give me a hand!"

Everyone was so surprised by literally everything about Boyd Drummond that they all shuffled off toward the door to the parking lot. Boyd reached into the back of a van and handed Hugo two boxes to carry, then gave Kober, Evelyn (after bestowing a kiss upon her hand), Max, Skyler, and Dena each two four-foot-long plush ice cream cones, all different colors. Dena carried a chocolate scoop in a waffle cone under her left arm, and a vanilla soft serve with wavy fabric peaks and a cherry on top under her right arm.

She led the way through her bookstore into the vendor room and through the back door of Scoops Ice Cream, directly behind the bakery and at the other end of the Marketplace from Hugo's chocolate shop. Everyone piled their stuffed ice cream cones on the floor in the center of the ice cream parlor. Hugo dropped the boxes next to the pile.

"Thanks, you guys!"

"Can you tone it down, bud? We're standing right here." Kober stuck her index fingers in her ears.

If Kober thought he was loud, he must be louder than Dena thought.

Instead of being offended, Boyd let out another belly-laugh. "I thought I *was* toning it down!" He dropped his voice to a stage whisper. "Here I was trying to be on my best behavior."

"Everyone, I'd like to officially welcome Boyd Drummond to the Marketplace family." Dena pointed at the other tenants as she introduced them. "Max and Evelyn Milligan own Step Into History, the photo studio—"

"Bet you don't have an outfit in my size!"

"Skyler Olsen owns Really Grate Cheese—"

"My dairy sistah!"

"Hugo Dekker owns Zoet Chocolates—"

"You should wear a zoot suit instead of an apron!"

"And Kober owns the bakery."

Kober pushed her hair back into place.

"You look feisty. Are you feisty?"

"Try me."

Boyd put up his dukes and danced around like a prize-fighter then laughed. "Glad to meet all of you." Boyd swept everyone into handshakes or hugs, sometimes both.

"Excuse me!" A woman's voice called. "Can I get some of these cupcakes?"

Kober hurried back to the bakery calling, "I'm coming!" On the way out, she shot Boyd a dirty look for distracting her from her business, as if he was the only one capable of that.

"What kind of accent is that?" Max asked.

"Boston, born and raised," Boyd said proudly.

"What brings you to Colorado then?" Evelyn asked.

Boyd took a deep breath, expanding his chest so much it threatened the buttons on his shirt. "Followed Joey Baggadonuts—"

"That's somebody's name?" Skyler's eyes widened.

Boyd guffawed. "That's everybody's name in Boston." He shrugged. "I followed him out here, but it turned out I loved Colorado more than I loved him." Skyler began to say something, but he spoke over her. "I didn't want to be greedy and have the perfect state and the perfect man, so I sent him on his way and found myself in Sugar Springs. Bought a little house right downtown—"

"Oh!" Evelyn nodded. "You're the one who popped the top of the old Barker place."

Boyd nodded, leaning in toward her. "I'll let you in on a little secret. I'm a big guy. Needed a big house. Got a houseful of big stuff. Six burly guys are almost done moving it all in as we speak. Then they'll be over here with the rest of the stuff I need for Scoops."

"Well, we'll let you get settled in," Dena said. "We all have stores to run, but if you need anything, just let us know. Kober's just opposite you, Hugo's at the other end from you, Skyler is next to Kober, then me, then Evelyn and Max. We usually keep our back doors unlocked."

Balaam sauntered by and before he knew what had happened, Boyd had scooped the startled cat up into his arms. "And who is this pretty kitty?" Boyd had his face right in Balaam's. "We're going to get along famously!"

Balaam screeched and struggled, finally hissing a warning and slashing a paw at Boyd before vaulting to the floor and fleeing the ice cream shop.

Boyd yelled after him, laughing. "You just wait until I get the ice cream going! You'll change your tune!"

"No, he won't," Max rasped.

"That's Balaam," Evelyn explained. "Not much of a people person."

"We'll see," Boyd said.

The other tenants left, leaving Dena and Evelyn to bring up the rear. They watched as Boyd tore open the strapping tape on one of the boxes and pulled out a ball of twine.

Evelyn pointed at it. "If that's for Balaam, don't bother. He'd only strangle someone with it."

Boyd guffawed. "It's to hang my ice cream cones."

"If you need scissors, I have a pair," Dena said.

Boyd rummaged in the box a bit more. "Nope. Found 'em." He waved a pair of scissors in the air.

"I'll leave you to it, then."

———

After an hour or two, all the other tenants had stopped into the bookstore separately to complain about Boyd hanging his ice cream cones from the ceiling all around the promenade. He must have had another full load in his van because plush cones in every flavor with every topping seemed to hang everywhere.

"Those huge ice cream cones?" Skyler had whispered. "He hung one in front of my shop!"

"He's taking up more than his share of space, Dena," Evelyn had told her.

"Should I go put chocolate samples in his store?" Hugo had fumed.

"Son of a soft serve!" Kober pointed out into the promenade. "Are you seeing this? Who does he think he is? I have half a mind—"

"You should," Dena said. "Go tell him to keep the ice cream confined to the ice cream shop."

Kober looked at Dena like she was nuts. "You're the Marketplace manager, not me!"

Dena sighed. "But you seem to be the angriest about this."

"I'm the angriest about everything. Doesn't mean I want to confront him about it."

"Well, I don't want to confront him! He's only been here two hours."

Kober stared at her. "And for that entire time, you've been the Marketplace manager. Weird."

Dena stared back, trying to look indignant but couldn't maintain it. "Fine. I'll talk to him. But you owe me a brownie."

"Ha! For what? Doing your job? Fat chance." Kober sashayed back to the bakery, leaving Dena to ponder what to say to Boyd.

She considered pulling down the wayward plush cones. She considered asking everyone else to pull them down. She considered pretending they fell.

Ultimately, she simply walked into the ice cream parlor and said, "Hey Boyd, you can't hang all those stuffed cones everywhere. Gotta keep them within the confines of your shop."

"Ah, I'm a chowdahead. I didn't even think! So sorry. I'll get them down right away. I just ran out of room for them in here." He waved an arm around and Dena nodded. "They didn't look this big in the catalog."

"Maybe if you raise them up? Or group them in the corners? Or maybe hang them on a slant?"

Boyd contemplated Dena's ideas. "Yeah, that might work. Like over there?"

"And maybe there."

"Or I can give some of them away."

"That's a good idea, maybe as part of your grand opening tomorrow." Dena glanced around. "Speaking of which, are you seriously thinking you'll be ready tomorrow? There's no rush, you know. You can take the week if you like. It is February in Colorado, after all. Not really peak ice cream time."

"No reason to delay. My guys will be here any minute with the freezers and the cases. Then making the ice cream doesn't take long at all. I'll have at least six flavahs ready before you even leave tonight."

Dena raised her hands in surrender. "Whatever you say. I know as much about the ice cream biz as I do being an astronaut. Just enough to wind up in a black hole."

Boyd guffawed.

As she left the ice cream parlor, she called over her shoulder, "Don't forget to take down those cones in the promenade."

"Doing it right now!"

Dena returned to the bookstore, almost tripping over Balaam, wondering if she made a terrible mistake in leasing space to Boyd, despite his excellent bear hugs.

She wasn't sure the Sugar Mill Marketplace was big

enough for him and his supersized personality. Unfortunately, she hadn't found anyone better. That is, with a heartbeat and disposable income. She went over the numbers again in her head. They all needed Boyd's money coming in to share the costs of running the Marketplace. They'd just have to live with his overwhelming exuberance.

"Maybe now they'll find somebody else to be Marketplace manager," she mumbled to Balaam.

He narrowed his copper-colored eyes, but didn't look at her. Probably still trying to make sense of the fact Boyd picked him up like he was a cat or something.

———

A couple of hours later, Kober's kids burst into the bookstore looking for Twist.

Dena held her finger to her lips and pretended to be on the phone while she hurried over to the bakery.

"You didn't tell them about Twist?" Dena spoke through clenched teeth, her face pinched with anger. "You're their mother!"

"Please, please, please can you tell them? I can't. They'll look at me with their big brown eyes and … I just can't. You do it." Kober looked at Dena with *her* big brown eyes. "I'll give you some of those cinnamon rolls you were after this morning and I won't even make you look at me naked." Kober narrowed her eyes. "You owe me."

Dena knew Kober had a point and relented, blowing out a breath. "Fine."

"You're the best."

"You're the worst."

Kober smiled and tiptoed behind Dena back to the bookstore. She stayed out of sight, listening from the doorway.

Dena made a show of saying goodbye to the nonexistent person on her phone. "Hey!" she said to the kids. "Did you guys hear we're getting an ice cream shop? Behind your mom's bakery on the backside of the Marketplace. The owner's name is Boyd and he was giving out free samples a while ago." She smiled wide, hoping to entice the kids to forget about Twist.

"Where's Twist?" Jain asked.

Dena made a sad face, but tried to temper it so they didn't know just how heartsick she really was. "She got out of the fence and ran away."

"No, she didn't," Wyatt said with a frown. "That doesn't sound like her at all."

"Yeah, she's way smarter than that," the twins said in unison.

"You're right." Dena didn't want to lie to them. "All I know is the gate was open and she wasn't in the yard."

"Have you looked for her?" Jain eyed Dena suspiciously.

"Sheriff Johnson and Deputy Chavez are keeping an eye out for her." Dena knew that truly was a lie. But it didn't matter because it was clear the kids didn't believe her about any of it. She shot a look at Kober cowering out of sight at the back door of the bookstore, listening in.

"We'll go look for her," Jain said. "C'mon."

Dena saw Kober duck out of the doorway.

The boys trooped behind Jain to get permission from their mother. Even though they moved with purpose to find their four-legged friend, the spring was out of their step.

Dena's heart clutched.

Kober

"YES, of course, go look for Twist," Kober told her children. "If you find her, take her wherever is closest, our house, Mrs Russo's, or back here. Only until it gets dark, though, then I want you home. And zip up those coats ... it's colder than a snowman's tush out there!"

The kids dutifully zipped their coats and pulled on hats and gloves before racing out of the Marketplace.

Kober walked across the promenade and watched out the window while the kids hurried through the parking lot and disappeared from view.

She knew Dena was right. She should have been the one to tell them Twist was missing, but she also knew those kids would soon have more than their share of loss and she didn't want it to begin with her. She was a big, fat chicken. Selfish, she knew. Completely, utterly, fantastically selfish.

But what else could she do?

Dena would get over it, and she did owe some kind of penance for that shower fiasco this morning.

Kober wondered how much longer she could hold that over Dena's head.

Maybe forever, if she played her cards right.

Balaam

BALAAM SAT IN THE BOOKSTORE, knowing but not caring that he was in Dena's way.

He had slowly and meticulously wandered every corner of the Marketplace and now this bookstore—twice —but had seen no sign of that … that Twist creature.

She was here, then she was not. Had he simply imagined her? Was she only a wretched nightmare?

Balaam sniffed around and finally found the exact location where that thing had done the unmentionable to him —booped his nose. More than once, too.

He tiptoed toward a plush bed pushed against the wall. Balaam glanced over at Dena, sizing her up. Too tall.

There was only one answer.

It wasn't my imagination.

That creature, that Twist, had indeed been here.

But where was she now?

Not that he cared, of course. He was simply curious, despite knowing how that never ended well for his species.

It didn't make sense. How dare she boop his nose and then just disappear like that? How could he be expected to exact revenge? Where would he achieve satisfaction if he couldn't put her in her place, like he'd done to every other creature in this building?

Balaam worried he was being made a laughingstock. First, the nose booping, then that man picking him right up off the floor. The gall.

What was this world coming to if cats weren't in charge? Up was down, black was white. Nothing was making sense all of a sudden.

Next they'd tell him mice were to be his friends, rather than lifeless trophies to drop at the feet of his adoring, grateful people.

Skyler

FRIDAY NIGHT after the Marketplace closed, Skyler greeted and held open the outside door to the ten students who had signed up for her after-hours charcuterie class, locking it behind her. She led them toward the front of her cheese shop where she'd set up some long tables with stylish drapes in the middle of the promenade. The tables weren't decorated with flowers or place settings, but rather, were covered with an enormous variety of cheese, crackers, olives, nuts, dried fruit, fig jam and other spreads.

On the table in front of each chair was one of the branded wooden cheese boards each student received as part of their fee. They would assemble their board, following the few instructions Skyler had planned to give them. Then she'd encourage them to take photos before helping them wrap it tightly to transport home.

"I want to officially welcome all of you to the very first charcuterie class sponsored by Really Grate Cheese." Skyler pointed at the sign in front of her shop. "That's me, I'm Really Grate—I'm Skyler. Sit wherever you want, everyone gets a cheese tray to take home."

When everyone had shed their coats and sat in front of a tray, one woman said, "I'm nervous. I've never done this before."

Skyler smiled in a way she hoped was calming, because she felt like a set of fully exposed nerves herself. "Charcuterie design isn't anything to be nervous about. There's no right or wrong way to design a cheese board. The perfect cheese board is *your* cheese board. Consider me your cheese admiral, helping you navigate the charcuterie seas."

Everyone laughed and Skyler felt the tension immediately dissipate.

Skyler pointed out and described all the goodies spread before them on the tables. She was thrilled when everyone began taking photos. Hopefully, the shop would get some tags on social media. "In a traditional platter, people would arrange a blue cheese, a soft cheese like Brie, and a hard cheese like cheddar. But if you want to use all cheddars or all Bries, then go for it. It's dealer's choice around here. There are a few design ideas I'd like to offer you, so you have the theory to fall back on. But again, it's just design theory. It's like building a house. There's the foundational aspect, that's your tray. Then the items you'll choose, which I guess would be like the rooms in your house and then the flourishes—the way you decorate—that make your cheese board yours and yours alone."

Skyler passed along her three unbreakable rules of charcuterie design. "One, make sure everything can be easily reached, so nobody has to reach over the board to get to some hard to slice cheese in the middle of the tray. Two, along with your cheeses, provide items that are sweet like jams or honeys, spicy like seasoned nuts or peppers, and briny like olives or pickles. And three, garnish, garnish, garnish. Use herbs, fruit slices, lettuce blankets, even edible flowers tucked in around your boards."

After Skyler finished with her instructions, she told them to go ahead and get started, then went into the shop to open the wine. She poured a glass of merlot for each of her students, placing them on a tray, then stepped into the vendor room and quickly downed one for herself.

"I saw that." Max wagged a finger at her. He and Dena leaned against the doorjamb at Dena's back door.

"You startled me! I thought everyone had gone already."

"Trying to get everything done," Dena said. "An impossibility, but a girl can dream, right?"

"Just straightening up." Max tipped his head, indicating the promenade. "How's it going out there?"

"I don't want to jinx anything, but I think it's going really well."

Dena indicated the glass of wine she just tossed back. "Cause or effect?"

Skyler laughed. "Just a pre-celebration drink. Want one?"

"Better not. Evelyn's waiting for me." Max glanced through Skyler's shop to her students. "On the other hand, maybe I should stay and take some notes from you, maybe a bit of your mojo will rub off on me."

"I'd love a glass," Dena said.

They followed Skyler into the cheese shop and she poured the three of them each a half glass of wine and they clinked glasses. When Max raised an eyebrow at the small amount, she shrugged. "Sorry. Don't want to run out."

Max raised his glass. "Here's to your huge influx of cash and that it doesn't trigger an FBI warning or anything."

"I'll drink to that!" Skyler sipped her wine this time.

"Cheers." Dena raised her glass too.

"Seriously, though, I hope you have a good CPA," Max said. "They won't steer you wrong." Dena nodded, while Max added, "They're worth more than a two-headed calf!" He tipped his glass back and finished the remaining wine before heading back to the studio.

Dena polished off her wine too. "I'm glad it's going so well tonight. You were worried about nothing."

"That's kind of my modus operandi." Skyler giggled.

"I guess it's working for you, then," Dena said with a smile as she returned to the bookstore.

Skyler took their glasses and set them in the sink, then picked up the tray with the wine glasses for her students. Their eyes lit up when she went around the table with the stemware.

"This is such a fun class!" one woman gushed.

A young couple clinked their glasses together. "Happy anniversary," they murmured to each other.

"I'm telling all my friends they should sign up," one man whispered to Skyler as he took a glass. "This is a great thing to do on a first date." He tilted his head to the woman sitting beside him, engrossed in placing olives meticulously on her cheese board.

After Skyler delivered the wine, she walked around again, this time studying their cheese boards. "All of these are shaping up to be so gorgeous! But remember, a little goes a long way. Don't be greedy with one ingredient over another. We call it a cheese board, but remember about all the other stuff!"

Skyler complimented two women on how they both placed their items in a curving manner across their boards. "We didn't really talk about specific designs, but I personally like these curving shapes." She pointed to a man's board. "But look how he's doing his in a squared off pattern like that. It's really attractive! And again, you can do any shapes or designs you like, different for every event. I saw one once for a Super Bowl party where the cheese formed the shape of a goalpost."

A man raised his hand. "What should I do about that fig jam? I want to put it on my tray, but I don't have a container for it."

Skyler bustled over and showed him how he could scoop some on to one of the bigger crackers or make a little boat from the smaller crackers. She even showed him how to use the jam underneath so it acted as a bit of natural glue. "Of course, when you do this at your house, you can find all kinds of little jars or bowls or even small leaves of lettuce to use."

The students were all laughing and helping one another with ideas for their cheese boards and Skyler was as relaxed as she'd been all week. She was making the rounds with another bottle of merlot when she saw Boyd Drummond tromping through her cheese shop toward the promenade.

She felt her serenity begin to crumble.

"What's going on heah? I thought the Marketplace closed at seven." He nodded at everyone, saying, "Hah-wahya, hahwahya?"

His voice boomed and he startled one woman so much that she accidentally mixed her carefully placed smoked almonds with her carefully placed Manzanilla olives. "Oh my!"

Skyler hurried toward Boyd, intending to pull him from the promenade into her cheese shop to explain this was a closed class, but she zigged while he zagged and circled the other side of the table, inspecting and commenting on everyone's work.

Skyler breathed a sigh of relief, however, when everything he said was complimentary and encouraging to her students. Loudly complimentary and encouraging, of course. When she finally caught up to him, she gently gripped his elbow and steered him away from the class and back into her shop.

"Is there something I can help you with, Boyd? I thought you'd be long gone by now."

"Just stretching my legs. Seems everyone is still here, except Max and Evelyn. Is this how it always is on a Friday night here? If so, maybe we should stay open longer!" Boyd's chuckle turned into a guffaw, but Skyler didn't get what was so darn funny.

"Before the Marketplace opens and after it closes is often the only time we have to get paperwork and our orders done. You'll find out soon enough, though." Skyler smiled, to show him she wasn't trying to be smug or anything. She always hated it when people older or further down whatever path she was on said stuff like that. Her older cousins were the worst. No matter how old Skyler got nor how many things she accomplished, she was never as old as they were and couldn't possibly know more than they did. It infuriated her and she'd vowed long ago that she'd never do that to anyone else. "I'm here late tonight, though, because of this class. It's my very first one and so far it's going better than I expected." She couldn't stifle her enthusiastic pride and gave an excited little face scrunch.

Boyd swept her up in a bear hug. "That's wicked awesome! I'll get out of your hair and let you get back to it now."

"Are you really going to open your ice cream parlor tomorrow?"

Boyd nodded. "I'll be in early to mix up some more flavors and then I should be all ready to go." He turned to leave then immediately turned back to her. "Hey, listen,

Skyler, I'm sorry about putting those ice cream things all over the place. I just wasn't thinking."

Skyler touched his forearm. "Absolutely no problem."

Boyd gasped loudly, making Skyler jump. "I have an idea!" He hurried away and Skyler returned to her class.

In a couple of minutes everyone heard Boyd bellow before they saw his bulky form. "In honor of Skyler's inaugural cheese class, anyone want a stuffed ice cream cone?" Boyd hugged a plush waffle cone with a scoop of Neapolitan topped with rainbow sprinkles tight to his torso.

Every hand but one shot in the air.

"Hmm … who has a birthday this month?" Boyd asked.

"Mine's February third!" the anniversary man said.

"Mine's the seventeenth!" the woman on the first date said.

Boyd handed her the plush cone. "Today's the thirteenth, so yours is the closest. Enjoy!"

The woman beamed first at Boyd, then at her date. "Thank you!"

Skyler smiled. That guy was getting so many First Date points.

Dena

NORMALLY WHEN DENA worked late at the Marketplace it was as silent as a kindergarten on Sunday. Tonight, though, the hum of Skyler's charcuterie class students was welcome background noise while she worked. She felt like the laughter and pleasant voices kept her blood pressure from spiking as she completed and corrected Boyd's paperwork. He'd told her he'd done it, but he hadn't. Or at least he hadn't completed it correctly. In what world was it acceptable to simply sign your name to documents without filling in the required information?

All afternoon she tried to pin him down to finish it up, but whenever she came near him, he shoved a new ice cream sample in her mouth and then began glad-handing anyone in the vicinity. Then, before she could corral him, he was off to the grocery store or to deal with his movers or something and she couldn't find him for hours.

He'd make an excellent politician, Dena thought. All style, no substance.

But now, on top of dealing with Boyd's documents,

Dena had to watch Hugo staring forlornly at Skyler, while she attended to her class.

She shoved away from her front counter and marched into the vendor room where Hugo sat, strategically perched where he had a clear view through Skyler's cheese shop.

Dena stood in front of him, hands on hips, blocking his view. "We've talked about this Hugo. You must stop stalking that girl!"

Hugo tried to peek around Dena, but she sidestepped back into blocking his view every time. She could be an NFL linebacker if she kept this up.

Finally, he sighed. "Maybe I am a bit … stalkery … but it's not what you think!"

"What is it I think, exactly?" Dena didn't move from her linebacker stance.

"Skyler and I knew each other from before."

Dena dropped her arms in surprise. "Before when?"

"Before we came to Sugar Springs. She just doesn't remember."

At this, Dena dropped into the chair opposite him. "What?"

He nodded. "We met several years ago at a trade show. We hung out that whole weekend—" At Dena's questioning look, he quickly added, "No, not like that. We went to the same seminars and compared notes afterward, got the occasional cup of coffee, stuff like that. But then when we met up here, she didn't even remember me."

"How did you both just happen to end up here?" Dena asked suspiciously.

Hugo looked at the floor. "I guess that's the stalkery part. The minute I found out she was moving here to open a cheese shop in the Marketplace, I erased myself from the New Orleans food scene and arranged for a new life in

Sugar Springs. I was just so disappointed and embarrassed that she didn't even remember me. And now too much time has passed and it's ridiculous and awkward." He looked up into Dena's eyes, perhaps searching for sympathy, she thought.

Boyd blustered into the vendor room with three huge cups of ice cream. He plopped himself down with a loud OOF and pushed ice cream in front of them, keeping one for himself.

Hugo and Dena stare up at him, perplexed.

"What?" He pointed a plastic spoon at Hugo. "I've been watching you all day. You seem sad. You can't be sad when you eat ice cream." Boyd pointed the spoon at Dena. "And this is an apology scoop. I know I bagged on all that paperwork. It's just no fun!" He pointed at Hugo's ice cream. "Chocolate fudge swirl. Thought I'd go straight to the chocolate horse's mouth for a taste test."

Hugo took a bite and proclaimed it delicious.

Boyd pointed at Dena's ice cream. "Huckleberry pie."

Dena took a bite. "Is that real pie crust?"

"You know it."

"It's fantastic." Dena and Hugo dug a spoon into the other's cup. Both made yummy noises.

"What flavor do you have?" Hugo asked Boyd.

"Key lime." He pushed it toward them and they each took a spoonful.

They savored a few bites in silence then Boyd said in a relatively tempered voice, like perhaps he was trying to whisper, "I couldn't help but overhear, Hugo. You're not alone in the lovelorn club." He took a big bite. "Wanna hear my sad story?"

Hugo nodded.

"I packed up my life and followed my guy like a devoted puppy to Colorado—"

"I thought you said you liked Colorado better than you liked him?"

"I decided I didn't like him about eight seconds after he said he didn't like me which was about eight seconds after we got to Colorado."

"I don't think you need to try so hard to get people to like you," Hugo said quietly. "He just wasn't the one for you."

"And maybe Skyler isn't the one for you," Dena said.

Hugo didn't look up from his ice cream, simply gave a noncommittal shrug.

They all took bites of their ice cream.

"I bounced around all the big cities along the front range trying to figure out what I wanted to do. Denver, Fort Collins, Boulder, Colorado Springs," Boyd said. "I finally decided I wanted the slower pace of a small town. I drove through Sugar Springs last year and just loved it. But then I had to decide how I could support myself here. I'd invested in a friend's ice cream parlor way back when and when he ran it into the ground, I lost my investment, but got all the equipment and recipes. It sat in storage until I stumbled on the info about leasing space here. I always loved ice cream," Boyd patted his ample belly, "as you might have noticed, so the rest is history. If a fat guy who loves ice cream can't make a go of an ice cream parlor, then I don't know who can!" He guffawed.

"Maybe someone who completes paperwork?" Dena said with a wry smile.

"I said I was sorry!" Boyd started to get up. "Do you want more ice cream?"

Dena waved him back down. "Hugo's right. You don't need to try so hard to get us to like you. You'll find we're an easy-going bunch here."

"If you don't count getting accused of murder all the time." Hugo quirked an eyebrow at Dena.

"What's that now?" Boyd asked.

"Long story," Dena said. "But seriously, take it down a notch. Or ten."

"I'm just nervous meeting new people." Boyd scraped the last bit of his ice cream from the bottom of his paper cup.

"You don't seem nervous. You seem gregarious and extroverted," Hugo said.

Dena collected their empties and dropped them into the trash. "Yes, exactly. Like a gregarious and extroverted stick of dynamite."

Boyd returned to the ice cream shop, but before Dena left the vendor room, Hugo said, "I wanted to tell you … I went out last weekend."

"A date? Really?"

"Well, no. Not really."

"Thanks for bringing that up, then." Dena groaned theatrically and threw her hands in the air.

"I just meant that I went into the Springs to a club, keeping an open mind about meeting someone."

"And did you? Meet someone?"

Hugo laughed. "I guess you could say that. She was a mess, though, and I found out later that she was a barfly who's always on the make to find a sugar daddy."

"You do own a chocolate shop," Dena said with a smile.

"The irony was not lost on us."

"Us who?"

"The bartender and this other guy at the bar. She tried to get her hooks in him too, so we bonded over that."

"Another sugar daddy?"

"He was an interesting guy. Has a shoe design business."

Dena perked up. Maybe he could tell her something about the high heel shoe prints in her yard. She couldn't explain anything to Hugo, but said, "That does sound interesting. Women's shoes?"

"Yeah. Are you in the market?" Hugo pulled out his wallet. "He gave me his business card." Hugo handed her the card.

"Maybe. Thanks."

Dena returned to the bookstore and opened her laptop. She typed in the website address on the business card. It took a minute to load, but when it did, Dena saw an impressive online catalog of the most exquisite and unique women's shoes and boots, vastly out of her price range.

She scrolled and scrolled, drooling at the gorgeous hand-painted footwear collections, each one different, but showing the same artistic flair.

None looked like the high heels worn by Joanne Dunning the book buyer, and none resembled those red and black Oxford pumps or the cobalt blue Victorian-looking boots from those two customers who were so enamored by Twist.

Dena sighed, but kept scrolling through the pages and pages of eye candy, fostering quite a case of unrestrained shoe envy. Her eyes began crossing and she knew she should stop torturing herself with things she didn't need and couldn't afford, completely losing sight of what she'd been looking for in the first place.

But then, out of the blue, a photo filled the screen with a style that looked very familiar. She stared at it until she felt dizzy from concentration before she remembered. Like a photo in a child's View Master machine, it was as if she clicked the lever and saw the boots in the promenade of the Marketplace. It was the day Duke Bughata came in ranting at her and hammed it up by falling to the floor so melodramatically outside her bookstore. "You are all my witnesses," he'd told the crowd.

And in that crowd, Dena pictured the woman wearing those boots.

Kober

EVEN THOUGH KOBER'S kids were still moping around about the missing Twist, they all agreed to pitch in at the bakery. With Valentine's Day landing on a Saturday, it was all hands on deck that morning.

All hands except for Nic's, that is. He called to say he was stuck in Denver. A client meeting went too long, some contract had to be rewritten, or the corporate giraffe escaped, or something. Kober had quit listening. She knew when Nic called late in the afternoon from Denver, they probably wouldn't see him for three more days. She'd given up getting mad about it, telling herself at least they wouldn't have to argue over the remote, and she wouldn't hear him snore all night.

But seriously? This particular weekend? That hurt.

Even though Kober tried to keep it from them, Jain figured it out and gathered the boys to present their home-made Valentines to her. After Kober gushed over their artwork, Jain whispered in her ear, "Everything will be okay, Mom."

Kober whispered back, "I'm supposed to be the one who tells you that."

"But I already know."

Kober presented them with enormous heart-shaped brownies and a box of fancy truffles she bought from Hugo. He even decorated it with a glittery gold bow which Jain immediately tied in Kober's hair.

Then they had all cuddled together on the couch, gorging themselves on sugar while they watched Star Wars movies.

Who needed romance when you had cuddly kids, chocolate, and a George Lucas franchise?

This morning, however, Kober fought a sugar hang-over and wondered why her kids did not. They remained sad about Twist, but jumped into the car without whining or dragging their feet on the bakery's first Valentine's Day. She wondered how she got so lucky with the four of them.

Kober sent the twins out to do parkour—because that was much more helpful to her than their "help" in the bakery—while Jain manned the cash register and Wyatt bagged and boxed the items chosen by the customers. Kober busied herself at the oven and mixing bowls, keeping a close eye on what was running low.

"Hey, Mom!" Jain called. "There's a customer who has a question for you."

Uh oh, Kober thought. She racked her brain to remember which items had nuts and which did not. That seemed to be the most common question she got. Jain had pointed out that she should have a Nut-Free Shelf, but Kober hadn't quite gotten around to it yet. Maybe if it slowed down today, she could get Jain to organize that.

Kober stepped toward the young woman Jain indicated. "What can I help you with?"

"I was here last night taking that cheese class—"

"Oh, how'd that go?"

"It was fantastic!" the woman gushed. "And I was sitting right outside your bakery and everyone was telling me how good everything was that you make—"

"How nice of them!" Kober placed a hand on her heart.

"So I wanted you to make my wedding cake!" The woman ended on a note of triumph, delighted with her idea.

The smile slid off Kober's face. "Nope. I don't make wedding cakes."

"But you have to! Everyone says your cakes are the best!"

"That's nice of them, but—"

"And I have a huge budget."

Kober cocked her head. "How huge?"

"Sooo huge."

Kober stared at her for a long time. The woman seemed to understand deep in her bones that if she spoke or moved in the slightest, Kober might get spooked. They both stood very, very still.

Finally, Kober went to get her order pad. "Okay, but I have some questions you have to answer first. What flavor are you thinking?"

"Can you do vanilla with raspberry filling?"

"I can."

"Then that's what I'm thinking."

"Next question. How long have you known your fiancé?"

"Three years."

Kober closed up her order pad. "Not long enough."

"Wait! We've been dating for three years, but we've known each other since middle school."

Kober slowly opened her order pad again.

"How many people?"

"Have I dated? Gosh, I'm not—"

"How many people for the cake?"

"Oh. Maybe fifty? We're not completely sure yet."

"Does this guy live and work in the same town as you do?"

"Not always. He's a corporate trainer and travels around a lot."

Kober gripped her pencil tighter.

"Am I to deliver the cake or will you pick it up?"

"I think we'll pick it up."

"What about kids?"

The woman frowned. "To pick up the cake?"

"Have you discussed having kids yet?"

"Oh. Yes, but I'm sure he'll come around after the wedding. He's just scared."

Kober made a guttural noise and shoved her order pad and pencil in the pocket of her apron. "Tell you what. I'll give you anything you want in this store for free if you don't get married."

The woman laughed but Kober didn't. She watched while the woman wandered to the display case and studied the cakes in there. "I love how you did the swirls on this one. I'd like you to do that on mine."

The woman kept yammering about cakes and weddings and décor and bridesmaids and happily ever after, but Kober only listened with half an ear. She thought about her own wedding, and subsequent years of marriage. Their wedding had been magical, and most of their marriage had been too. Something had changed, but Kober couldn't pinpoint exactly what it was.

But she was absolutely certain this poor woman in her bakery was delusional if she thought she'd have a happy marriage to some clod who was never home and had to be talked into having kids.

But who was she to protect this delusional woman who obviously didn't want her protection? Kober pulled out her order pad and began doing the math, reaching a price for this delusional wedding cake. Then she doubled it, added a fifty-dollar tip, and announced the price to the woman, assuming the exorbitant price would get her out of any involvement in this wedding.

The bride-to-be didn't bat an eye.

They finalized the rest of the details and the woman paid a deposit of fifty percent of the outlandish price.

With enormous eyes and dropped jaw, Jain watched Kober ring it up at the register. Kober elbowed her daughter and whispered, "Close your mouth. You'll swallow a fly."

Kober walked the woman to the promenade. As she watched her leave the Marketplace, Kober wondered if it was more important to make enough money to take care of her children or to stick to her principles.

After much thought, Kober decided if she had more money she could better stick to her principles.

Dena

FRIDAY NIGHT, Dena had clicked the photo of the boot on the website and enlarged it, filling her screen with the detailed image. As she had studied the sharp-heeled knee-high boot design, she became more and more convinced it was the one she saw worn by the woman in the grungy hoodie. In the enlargement, she could see the boots were hand-painted. Red, gray, black, gold, and white swirls large and small made up the major motifs of the design. Peeking out from the larger areas were smaller designs: tiny flowers, dots, swoops, and swooshes, and even some miniature skull-and-crossbones with happy little smiles.

After she saw the prices on Gunther's designer shoes, though, the grungy hoodie the woman wore with them made no sense. Perhaps it was an affectation, like Silicon Valley tech entrepreneurs who dressed like they were still in college. But a Silicon Valley tech entrepreneur at the Sugar Mill Marketplace? It didn't make sense, but it would sure explain the viral video.

Convinced that what she was seeing was significant, Dena had located the "contact me" page on the website and within three minutes had emailed Gunther, Hugo's new friend.

She drummed her fingers with anticipation, waiting for Gunther's reply. But when a response didn't appear in her inbox after ten minutes, she had to assume Gunther hadn't been sitting at his computer twiddling his thumbs, waiting for someone to message him through his website.

She continued to obsessively refresh her email all Friday night until she went to bed, remaining hopeful that Gunther was the key to tracking down the woman who wore those boots. He surely kept records of who bought and wore his outrageously expensive bespoke boots.

Immediately upon waking Saturday morning, she checked her email for any word from Gunther.

Nothing.

Her stomach had been churning all night with anxiety that Gunther held the clue she needed to find Twist and perhaps help solve Duke's murder. The only thing keeping her from retching while she tossed and turned, was the absolute certainty that when she woke, she'd finally have some definitive answers she could take to Sheriff Johnson.

She toggled between the website and her email, willing it to light up with a message.

Making coffee, she told herself, "It'll be there after the pot brews."

Popping a slice of bread in the toaster, "It'll be there after this bread browns."

Turning on the water in the shower, "It'll be there after I get ready for work."

She sat forlornly in front of her computer screen, but then brightened and dialed the phone number for Gunther's studio. It rang three times and her optimism faded. But on the fourth ring a man's voice said, "Gunther's Designs."

Dena was shocked into silence.

"Hello?"

"I'm here. I emailed you last night but thought I'd try calling."

"I just got in. Haven't had a chance to check my email. What can I do for you?"

"I'm interested in a pair of boots I saw on your website."

"Which ones?" he asked.

"They're tall, with a swirly pattern on them."

"The dark ones or the rainbow ones?"

"Dark."

"Ah yes. Let me just make sure they're still available. Then we can—"

"I can't afford them, but I wanted to ask you about the other ones you've sold," Dena said.

"There are no other ones," Gunther said. "Each of my designs is completely unique."

Disappointment crashed over Dena. "Oh. But I was sure I saw a woman wearing that same boot just last week."

"Hang on a sec." When he came back on the phone he said, "I just read your email and I see the confusion now. The boots you saw *are* one-of-a-kind, but I did donate a similar pair for an auction last year. I don't usually do that, but I made an exception that time."

"Who won them?" Dena asked breathlessly.

"No idea. I gave them to the Neighborhood Business Alliance. They ran the auction."

"You don't keep any records of who buys your boots and shoes?"

"I keep meticulous records of who buys my boots and shoes. But nobody bought these. I donated them."

"So ... no records at all."

"Nope. You might try the NBA, though."

Dena was momentarily confused as to why the National Basketball Association would be a resource, until she realized he was speaking of the Neighborhood Business Alliance.

"Okay, thank you for your help."

He laughed. "What exactly was I helping with? If you saw these boots that you liked, you can buy them online. Just click the button."

"Your boots are exquisite, but so is the price. If I could, believe me, I'd click the heck out of that button. But I wasn't actually looking for the boots. I was looking for the woman who wore them."

"I wish I could help." Gunther paused. "Unless you plan on conking her over the head and stealing them."

"No, nothing like that. I'll call the NBA and see if they can help." Dena disconnected, despairing that they'd have some raffle-winner's information. But even if they did, why would they share it with her?

Regardless, it was her only real clue so far. Maybe her one chance to solve this mystery. She looked up the number for the NBA and dialed. But the recorded message said they were closed over the weekend and would be back in on Monday morning.

It was a chance, of course, but Dena felt it slipping further and further away.

Dena

THE ONLINE PETITION calling for the boycott of her bookstore was in full swing, it seemed, because business was painfully slow, especially for a Saturday. Those customers who did come in seemed miffed she wasn't offering gift wrapping. When had Gift Wrap Saturday become a thing? Maybe around Christmas or Hannukah, but just on random Saturdays? Online shopping sure had screwed everything up. Dena worried she'd never understand the retail business world.

She watched Boyd bustle around the promenade with more free samples. This time they covered an attractive tray instead of a huge cooler. She had peeked into his ice cream parlor a couple of times during the day and was surprised to see long lines waiting to buy his sweet treats. Impressed, Dena let out a long whistle. If this was the business he did in February with no advertising, imagine the crowds he'll be bringing in by the time July rolls around.

She hoped she'd still be around to see it.

Around two o'clock Dena went into the vendor room

to heat up some soup in the microwave. The new haiku made her smile.

> Ice cream is a treat
> To indulge your tastebuds in
> All the livelong day.

But Jain was sniffling in the corner, obviously crying, with Evelyn hovering over her. Dena wondered if she and Kober had gotten into it, mother and daughter style. She was sure it must be difficult for Jain and Kober to work together all day, as different as they were.

She had decided to stay out of it and simply heat up her soup and skedaddle back to the bookstore. Before the microwave beeped, though, Evelyn said to her, "Jain is upset about Twist."

Dena put a comforting hand on Jain's shoulder. "I'm sorry. It's hard, I know. You'd grown so close to her."

"But you have to remember," Evelyn said to Jain. "Twist wasn't Dena's dog to begin with. Duke was always bound to come back for such a lovely animal. He shouldn't have done it so dramatically, of course, getting her in the middle of the night like that."

Dena's head snapped toward Evelyn. "What are you talking about? Duke is—" She stopped herself from blurting out the news about Duke.

"It's just good that nothing violent happened." Evelyn seemed not to have heard Dena. "People can be so weird about their pets. And Twist must have been happy to go with him, since Dena would have heard barking and such otherwise."

"Jain?" Kober yelled from the bakery. "I need you! The cash drawer is stuck again. How'd you get it open before?"

Jain trudged into the bakery, snagging an ice cream sample from Boyd as he entered the vendor room.

He offered a cup to Dena, but she shook her head.

Once again Dena's thoughts tangled up with questions about Twist's disappearance and Duke's murder. She knew the two incidents weren't coincidental, but what was the connection? Where was the proof? Would she be able to find it in time to call off the internet trolls intent on destroying her business? Would the sheriff? Would she ever see Twist again?

Hugo hurried into the vendor room with a Tupperware of his own, and Skyler walked over to pick up something from the printer tray.

"Are you okay, Dena? You don't look so good," Skyler said. She led Dena to a chair and pushed her down into it. "Do you need some protein?"

Hugo removed Dena's soup from the microwave then placed his own food inside and punched the numbers to get it busy zapping. He glanced over at her while he tapped his foot impatiently for his food to heat. "You've seen better days."

Evelyn elbowed away Boyd and the ice cream he was pushing in Dena's face. She placed Dena's soup on the table and handed her a spoon. "Here. Your blood sugar is probably low." She raised her voice. "Max? Can you bring in one of those old lady drinks of mine? The chocolate, though. The vanilla ones taste like armpit." To Dena she said, "My doctor insists. Something about electrolytes, I think. They're always harping about some darn thing anyway, to make sure I get enough calories. Do I look like I don't get enough calories?" Evelyn laughed and placed both hands across her belly. "Don't you worry, dear. We'll get you fixed up in a jiffy."

Dena gazed at the spoon Evelyn held out to her. "Soup

won't be fixing this, I'm afraid." Dena knew her stomach churned because of worry about Twist's disappearance and Duke Bughata being murdered in her own literal back yard. She expected the small-town gossip balloon to have inflated to gigantic proportions and exploded all over Sugar Springs by now, but it seems nobody had heard about Duke's murder. She had been biding her time until someone else brought it up so she could honor Sheriff Johnson's admonition to keep it quiet.

"Well, then," Evelyn said, "maybe it's the potassium. Max? Did you hear me?"

Max hurried in with a can of ready-to-drink chocolate nutrition shake.

Dena accepted it from him but set it down on the table without opening it. Instead, she blurted out, "Duke is dead! I found him in my backyard."

Nobody said anything. Then everyone began talking at once, declaring outrage, expressing shock, offering compassion and concern.

Kober careened into the vendor room. "What in blue blazes is everyone yelling about?"

Evelyn whispered to her, then quieted everyone down. "Dena, are you okay? You've been bottling this up inside? No wonder you're feeling poorly!" She popped the top of the protein shake and held it in front of her until she took a sip.

"Why wasn't there an article in the paper about it?" Hugo asked, pulling out his phone. "Remember how Aja and Cap published all that nonsense when Norbert died?" He began scrolling.

"I found him on Wednesday morning. It's only been three days," Dena said.

Evelyn gasped. "Three days! You poor dear."

"When has that stopped them?" Max rasped.

A customer poked her head in from the back door of the chocolate shop. "Um … is there anyone working in here? I was hoping to buy some truffles. Today is—"

"I know what day it is," Hugo snapped. "But this is more important than truffles."

"Honestly!" the woman huffed. "I've never—"

Boyd walked over and smiled at her, placing one arm around her shoulder. "Let me help you. Hugo is … dealing with something here." Boyd steered her back into the chocolate shop.

"Thank you," Hugo called. "And I'm sorry!" He didn't move, however, simply continued to scroll on his phone. "There's nothing online, either," he finally said.

"Maybe Aja and Cap learned a lesson about jumping the gun and gathering the facts *before* they post articles," Skyler said.

"But it will get out, and it'll be another black mark for the Marketplace," Hugo said morosely.

Evelyn held out the protein shake again, but Dena shook her head.

Jain and Wyatt appeared at Kober's side and began whispering to her.

"She said what?" Kober asked them.

Jain remained close to her mother, but announced in a sturdy voice, "Wyatt and I heard Ms Russo say, *Don't worry. Duke Bughata will get what's coming to him.*"

"Not again!" Dena buried her face in her hands and her words came out muffled. "I didn't have anything to do with this." Why had she ever moved to Sugar Springs, Colorado? "Nothing bad could ever happen here, my eye!"

Dena

LATER THAT AFTERNOON, Sheriff Johnson and Deputy Chavez stopped into the bookstore. The sheriff waited until the lone shopper left, scurrying out without buying anything as soon as they made eye contact.

"Seems a police presence isn't conducive to selling books," Dena said pointedly.

"I'm sorry." Sheriff Johnson spoke slowly and quietly, stepping closer to Dena. "I understand three people heard you threaten Duke Bughata's life."

"Who else told you that besides Jain and Wyatt?"

"You know I'm not going to tell you that."

"I didn't kill Duke."

Deputy Chavez spoke faster and louder. "But you don't deny you threatened his life?"

"I didn't technically threaten his life. I was talking on the phone to my accountant and I was … frustrated, so yes, I did say Duke would get what was coming to him. I had in mind an IRS audit, though, instead of a murder. And really? I thought we already discussed this. Why would I kill him in my own backyard?"

"Why indeed." Deputy Chavez gave a knowing look and flipped open his notepad.

"Dena, you know how this works. We're investigating a murder. We find out you had angry words with, and about, Duke. You stole his dog—"

"He *abandoned* his dog." Dena felt her fingernails digging into her palms.

"You found Duke's body." Sheriff Johnson held up her hand before Dena could speak. "Yes, in your own back yard. But that doesn't change the facts."

Boyd tromped noisily into the bookstore carrying three cups of ice cream.

Sheriff Johnson gave him a startled look, but Deputy Chavez grinned, grabbed a cup, and dug into his orange sherbet.

Sheriff Johnson murmured, "That looks delicious, thank you" before giving her swirl of vanilla soft serve a judicious lick.

Boyd whispered in Dena's ear while he handed her a cup of caramel swirl, "You can't be sad when you eat ice cream," then retreated from the bookstore.

She stared at it queasily.

———

Neither Sheriff Johnson nor Deputy Chavez had much more to say to her and Dena had even less to say to them, other than reiterating she had nothing to do with Duke's murder and to please let her know if they heard anything about Twist or the identity of the real killer.

Fat chance, she'd thought, glumly aware that there was a time when questions such as these wouldn't even be on her radar.

They left the bookstore soon after they finished their ice cream. Deputy Chavez finished Dena's too.

Dena kept her distance from the other tenants the rest of the day, and they kept their distance from her. She knew they probably just didn't know what to say to her, but she was glad nevertheless. She didn't know what to say to them either.

She felt terrible that the Marketplace was going through turmoil again, but surely they had to know she had nothing to do with it. *She* hadn't summoned Duke to the bookstore to start yelling at her. *She* hadn't uploaded a viral video. *She* hadn't killed him.

Unfortunately, she hadn't solved any of the mysteries swirling around her, either.

Just as she was gathering her things to go home to a long-anticipated glass of wine, Jain slowly approached her. She couldn't look Dena in the face.

"I don't think you killed anyone." Her voice was scarcely more than a breath.

"Thank you." Dena embraced the teenager.

After a bit, Jain pulled back and spoke in a much harsher tone, much closer to how she sounded earlier. "I think whoever killed that man also stole Twist and I hate them!"

"I do too!" They embraced again and both began crying.

"I thought I heard more sadness around here!" Boyd pressed two chocolate soft serve waffle cones in their hands.

"I'm going to be as big as a house if you keep this up, Boyd," Dena said, licking a drip traveling leisurely down the cone.

"Then you need to turn your frown upside down!"

"I wish it were that easy."

"You'd be surprised as to what ice cream can accomplish," Boyd said determinedly.

Dena wondered if that was his mantra because it was true or because he wished it was true. Regardless, it hadn't accomplished much so far, unless her upset stomach counted.

Kober and the boys came looking for Jain. "There you are!" she said.

"No fair!" the twins hollered in unison. "Why does she get ice cream and we don't?"

Kober looked at the red-rimmed eyes of Dena and Jain and began to reprimand the boys.

Boyd spoke over her. "I was just coming to see what flavah you boys wanted. Come with me and we'll load you up."

"Can we get sprinkles?" Wyatt asked, hurrying after them.

"Darn tootin'! As many as will fit."

Kober remained with Jain and Dena in the bookstore. Jain offered her a bite of her ice cream, which Kober accepted.

"That man sure knows his ice cream," Kober said, licking her lips.

Jain smiled. "He told me ice cream is better than medicine."

Kober studied their faces while they enjoyed the ice cream. "He may be right. You both look better than when I walked in."

"Sugar high," Dena said. "Too bad it doesn't last."

Dena

AT HOME that evening Dena couldn't focus. She'd never admit it, but she could sure use some more ice cream. It wouldn't help her focus or figure anything out, but it would help her not care about it all for a while. Was a sugar high the accomplishment Boyd meant?

Her thoughts kept circling around Twist and Duke Bughata. Jain was right. Somebody like Duke—or whoever might have been in those high heels—didn't deserve Twist, but Duke didn't deserve to die … or did he?

Dena hadn't found out anything substantial about him, and now she was a suspect in his murder.

What did Duke's death have to do with Twist disappearing, anyway? Was her first thought correct, that the dognapping was simply a distraction so someone could dump his body there, knowing she'd go search for Twist?

That seemed so far-fetched, and maybe she couldn't think of another scenario because of the deep and abiding sugar withdrawal she was suffering, but what else could it be?

She felt like she was back at square one, though. She hadn't been able to find out anything about Duke before and had done everything she could think of to find him. And now, she'd lost Twist, probably her bookstore, and perhaps even her freedom if the sheriff decided to arrest her for Duke's murder. She didn't have an alibi, and there were credible witnesses who'd testify she threatened Duke's life.

Dena knew she needed to talk to both Charlee and Lance about this and reached for her phone. Before she could dial, however, the screen lit up with a video call.

Georgia.

"Hi! How are things in Santa Fe?" Dena forced her voice to be chipper. She didn't want to get into all this with Georgia while she was still recuperating.

Georgia squinted and moved her face up close to her computer screen. Instinctively, and ineffectively, Dena moved her own phone further from her face.

"Why'd you push me off that trail, Dena? Tell me the truth right this minute."

"Georgia," Dena said patiently. "I told you before, I did no such thing. Let's not rehash this."

"You lured me out there and left me to die."

Okay, rehashing it was. "I left you because there was no cell service and I had to get a ranger."

"But did you? Did you really? Those other hikers had no problem getting me down the trail."

"Yes, hikers, plural. I couldn't do it myself."

"You didn't even try."

"How in the world would you know? You were completely out of it. When I saw where you landed, I knew I needed help."

"You pushed me and left me to die."

Dena listened incredulously to this surreal conversation. Georgia spoke so matter-of-factly. She wasn't hysterical. She wasn't rambling or glassy-eyed like the last time they spoke. Her voice wasn't as animated as usual, but Dena didn't quite know how one should sound when one was accusing a friend of a shove off a mountain trail.

"You left me to die," Georgia repeated before disconnecting.

Dena stared at the dark screen. "This is just great. Exactly what I need right now, on top of everything else." She jolted with a sad, sickening thought. Had something permanent happened to Georgia during her recovery, or during the fall? Traumatic brain injury? Stroke? Was that why she hadn't remembered they already discussed this?

She panicked, scrolling for Helen's number in Santa Fe. She could check on her in person like Beige Ann did. Dena had a troubling thought. Maybe Ann hadn't checked on Georgia at all the other day.

Would Helen take Dena's call, though? Helen used to be her friend too, until Thanksgiving weekend, that is. Dena thought about those practical jokes Helen had pulled at Thanksgiving, pranking everyone in attendance. She'd poured that huge glass of vodka and drank it down. They found out later she'd replaced the vodka with water. And freezing that spoon in the mashed potatoes so you'd pull out the entire thing. It was funny at the time, and Dena found out later that Georgia had been in on it.

Was this another of their pranks?

Dena stopped scrolling.

Georgia must be trying to get back at her for that rat. Dena thought she'd gotten over it, but she and Helen must be cackling about it in Georgia's fancy living room right now. Helen was probably the person off screen who slammed the laptop shut that last time. Probably because she couldn't control her laughter and didn't want Dena to hear.

Dena spoke to the dark screen of her phone, as if Georgia's face was still there. "Well, it's not funny, but I hope you finally got it out of your system. I've got real problems to concentrate on."

Dena

EARLY SUNDAY MORNING, Dena heard knocking on her front door. Bleary-eyed, she pulled her chenille robe tight around her and cinched the belt. She opened the door, expecting to see Sheriff Johnson and/or Deputy Chavez.

"Oh, it's you."

Aja and Cap Capitano from the *Sugar Springs Courier* stood on her front porch. Aja had her reporter's notebook open. "Can we talk to you?"

"About what?" Dena asked innocently. She knew full well they wanted to talk about Duke's murder but she wanted them to say it.

Aja narrowed her eyes and jotted something in her notebook.

Cap said softly, "He was found in your yard, Miz Russo."

Dena sighed and stepped aside. "Might as well come in. I need coffee. You want some? It's not free-range or anything." She knew they were hipsters, but wasn't sure what level they'd achieved.

She brewed a pot, biding her time in the kitchen while

she gathered her thoughts. She joined them in the living room with steaming mugs placed in front of them. She'd been trying to figure out a way not to talk to them at all, but knew, if history was any indication, they'd print a story regardless. At least maybe she could give them some real facts, and perhaps spin it in such a way so as not to blow back on the Marketplace in any way. A tall order, she knew.

"Do you have any hemp milk?" Aja asked.

"I do not. But I do have some yarn in the other room."

Aja frowned. "Why would I want yarn in my coffee?"

"Exactly."

The corners of Cap's mouth twisted up and Aja shot him a look.

"Dena—can I call you Dena?" Cap asked. After she nodded, he continued. "Can you tell us about finding Duke Bughata's body?"

"I had been out looking for my dog, Twist—"

"You mean Duke's dog," Aja clarified.

"And when I got home, I went in the back yard to see if I could figure out anything else about her ... disappearance. That's when I saw him."

"Can you describe him?" Aja looked up expectantly.

"I'd rather not."

"Understandable," Cap said.

"At least tell me how he died," Aja said.

"You should talk to the coroner for that." Dena sipped her coffee and wished she had some more ice cream. Where was Boyd when she needed him?

"What do you think happened?" Cap asked.

Dena slowly ran her index finger around the rim of her mug. "I wish I knew."

They asked a few more valid, sensible questions, as if

they were actual journalists. Dena answered truthfully, but didn't offer many facts, since she didn't have many.

She couldn't help herself and finally said, "Did you guys get visited by three ghosts or something? You're acting very differently than you did when Norbert died."

Aja and Cap exchanged sheepish glances with each other.

Cap said, "We may have been a bit, let's say, overzealous. We jumped to too many conclusions and could have been more … discerning in our decisions."

"I've got to say, that's refreshing to hear," Dena said. "I was surprised you weren't banging down my door the minute you heard about Duke."

"Um … we are," Aja said with a blank face.

"But his body was found Wednesday," Dena said.

"We took a little Valentine's Day getaway." Cap looked at Aja with puppy eyes.

Gross.

"We just got back and came right over here, as soon as Cap's granddad called. Haven't even unpacked."

Valentine's Day! Dena laughed, startling Cap and Aja. So that's why Kober and Hugo were all worried about having enough fresh strawberries, cherries, and red food coloring. No wonder the bakery and chocolate shops both had lines out the door for the last couple of days.

"I really need to check the calendar more often," she said to the perplexed journalists.

Dena

MONDAY MORNING DENA repeatedly called the Neighborhood Business Alliance until someone answered the phone. She told them she was looking for the woman who won the boots that had been donated by Gunther's Designs for a raffle or auction some time last year.

The woman on the phone listened politely then said, "Even if I had that information, what kind of dummy would I be to pass it along to you? It would violate about a thousand privacy laws. And what would happen to me when you confronted that poor woman in a dark alley and stabbed her for her boots?"

Dena wondered if there was something in her voice that made both this woman and Gunther assume she would murder someone over a pair of expensive boots. She was just about to ask for more information about the Neighborhood Business Alliance, when she realized the woman had hung up on her.

Despair settled upon her while she perused the NBA website once again, hoping this time something would jump out at her that might help her locate the woman wearing Gunther's boots. She scrolled and clicked, seeing only what she'd seen before. Vague but lofty mission statement. A carousel of highlighted businesses which slid past one after another. A section of a Colorado Springs map outlining the territory of the NBA. Dena had never been in that part of town, but she assumed it was a funky collection of upscale and boho businesses, if Gunther's Designs was any indication.

One thing she still didn't see, however, was a list of all the businesses in the Alliance.

Dena called back without identifying herself. "Is there a list of all the businesses in the Neighborhood Business Alliance?"

"Not as such. If you're inside the boundaries of the NBA, you belong. It's simply a consortium of business owners who join forces to create awareness of the eclectic shopping, dining, and services in the area. We band together to organize events and experiences for the consumer."

"I see. Thanks."

Dena enlarged the map and tried to see all the businesses that way, but it was not optimal. When she enlarged it, the type got fuzzy, but when it was smaller, the business names stacked up on top of each other rendering them impossible to read. It didn't matter anyway. Dena didn't even know who she might be looking for. There was absolutely no reason for her to think that one of the businesspeople in the area won those boots. If the events were put on for the community at large, like the woman had told her, then absolutely anyone could have won them.

———

Dena walked into the vendor room with heavy limbs later that morning. Her eye was immediately drawn to the white board.

Four days without a murder!

Underneath was a new haiku.

> We thought the murders
> Were a story for last month.
> Surprise! We were wrong.

None of the other tenants were in yet, but it would be useless to ask who wrote this one anyway. By now, everyone had certainly written at least one, Dena included. The authorship didn't matter anyway. The haikus always seemed universal, the sentiment shared by every tenant at the Marketplace.

She got a pot of coffee going then poured a cup to sip sitting on the stool at her front counter.

Since her obsessive quest to find the woman in the boots went bust, Cap and Aja's visit yesterday was able to find a bit of room to worm its way into her brain. She began turning everything over in her mind, with just the teensiest bit of worry that the *Courier* would flat-out accuse her of murdering Duke in cold blood. It could still happen, of course, but she seemed to see a shift in their journalistic integrity. Or maybe their maturity. Perhaps both. But their business model depended upon eyeballs. And what attracted more eyeballs than a murder with a local slant, involving a current resident who had been in the news much too often lately?

Nothing, that's what.

She thought about all the conversations and newsy tidbits she'd heard recently. Hugo "erasing" himself from New Orleans. Max extolling Skyler about employing a good CPA since her business seemed to be taking off. And what Evelyn had said about Duke being greedy and wanting the bookstore back now that she had improved it. She glanced around and gave a rueful laugh, wondering if that could possibly still be true. There had been very few customers since that video went viral.

Was that the cause or were people more focused on their Valentine's Day shopping than on used books? Dena imagined there was only a small subset of people who luxuriated in unwrapping the gift of used books on the most romantic day of the year.

Dena loved those people, however, and wondered how she could market directly to them. She'd never been a chocolate-and-flowers kind of gal, even when her husband had been alive. She was more of a book-and-a-snuggly-place-to-read type.

She thought of the few times she'd read with Twist curled next to her on the couch, or at her feet so she could slip her cold toes under Twist's warm fur.

Her heart clutched at the thought of Twist. "How could he just leave her behind?" she murmured for the zillionth time. Did he leave Twist with her on purpose because he knew he was in danger? What in the world had Duke gotten himself into so deeply that it got him killed and Twist dognapped?

She thought about the bookstore financials being in disarray. Dena finished her coffee and set her cup aside before firing up the ancient computer. She must have missed something.

If Duke's murder had something to do with his original visit to the bookstore, there had to be something else on there like those anagrams of Duke Bughata's name.

Sheriff Johnson only wanted facts and evidence, which Dena didn't have. The IRS only wanted their back taxes paid. The angry internet trolls only wanted—well, Dena didn't know what they wanted and perhaps neither did they. But they wanted something. And she probably didn't have it either.

Dena knew it was up to her to figure out what kind of monkey business Duke was up to. She thought briefly about calling Ginger again for help, but she couldn't bear to drag her CPA into this quagmire. The fewer people she implicated, the better. Besides, she and Ginger already talked about it and Ginger said she didn't have Duke's business records any longer. Ginger had no more help to give.

But Dena had the ancient computer so she scrolled backwards—slowly and thoroughly—through every payment recorded. She vowed to go back and forth until she found something to help Sheriff Johnson figure out who killed Duke, and perhaps exonerate her with the IRS.

She soon came across an automatic payment to a Susan Rode. The name wasn't familiar to Dena and she didn't remember it being there before. Hunched over the computer, she stared at it for a long time. She gasped, straightening on the stool and almost losing her balance.

Susan Rode was an anagram for Dena Russo.

The more she thought about it, the more she was certain that payment had not been there the last time she went through these accounts. And if Duke was dead, only Ginger could have altered the records. She had remote access to Dena's financials via this same computer program.

Dena didn't know what was going on, but it was crystal clear to her that Ginger was involved.

She picked up her phone to call Sheriff Johnson but didn't dial because she heard the sheriff's voice in her head softly and slowly demanding evidence, something she seemed to be a stickler about. Dena still had none. Just more questions.

She poured herself another cup of coffee, returning to the bookstore and closing the back door behind her. She didn't want the other tenants to overhear anything they shouldn't.

Dena jotted some notes to herself about the points she wanted to make, hoping she might trip up Ginger and she'd say something to incriminate herself.

After she'd rehearsed a bit in her mind, and sipped some coffee to calm her nerves, she stared at the cup shaking a bit in her jittery hand. Maybe coffee was the wrong way to go. Too late now.

Dena dialed Ginger's number.

Before Dena even said hello, Ginger said, breathless and fast, "Ohmygod, I was just going to call you! I have proof that Duke—maybe with someone else—was trying to scam you!"

"What? Tell me everything."

"It's too much over the phone. Plus, I have documents to show you."

"I can't leave the bookstore. Can't you bring them over here?"

"I have client meetings I can't reschedule today. When can you get over here?"

Dena thought for a moment. Jain could watch the store after school, maybe with Wyatt's help on the off chance that business picked up today and it got busy. "I can be there around four o'clock."

"Okay. I'll show you everything and then we'll call the police from my office. I think it would be Colorado Springs' jurisdiction anyway."

"Sounds good." Dena thought about the payment to

Susan Rode. "I'll bring you the documents I have too. That's why I was calling. See you later."

Dena printed everything off the ancient computer that she found suspicious, feeling ashamed and remorseful for jumping to the conclusion that Ginger was not on her side. Luckily, she had most of the day to gather her documents. Sheesh, that ancient computer was clunky. Dena envisioned tiny elves scurrying around inside the computer, placing each letter individually before allowing a page to print.

The elves cooperated, albeit sluggishly, and she was ready to go by the time Jain and Wyatt enthusiastically agreed to babysit the store.

"We're each gonna get twenty bucks?" Wyatt asked.

Jain elbowed him in the ribs. "Don't be rude," she said through gritted teeth.

"That's not rude at all. Just good negotiation tactics." Dena smiled.

"Sweet! We're negotiating? Then I want fifty bucks." Wyatt had the confident look of a Wall Street CEO.

Dena turned her back on him, stepping in front of Jain and addressing only her. "Happy to have you on board, Jain."

"Hey! Not fair." Wyatt wiggled back in front of Dena. "I'll take twenty."

"Way to negotiate, nimrod," Jain said.

Dena

DENA SET up her GPS with Ginger's business address in Colorado Springs. While she drove, Dena wondered if the image she had of Ginger in her mind matched the reality. She really hoped she'd have curly red hair. Would she be tall and willowy? Dena was almost always wrong about the voices she heard when she listened to NPR. She tried to avoid seeing photos of the journalists who lived inside her radio, preferring the portrait conjured by her imagination.

It was the same when she read Charlee's mysteries. Charlee used very sparse description of her characters, allowing her readers to create each character for themselves. But whenever Dena mentioned something about one of the characters, Charlee almost always laughed and told her that was not at all how she pictured them.

In the end, it didn't much matter what people—fictional or real—looked like, only what they did and said.

And Ginger hadn't done or said anything particularly curly or red-headed.

But she *had* found some more dirt on Duke, perhaps

even something that could explain his murder and get Dena off the hook.

Anxious to hear what it might be, she stepped on the gas.

The GPS told her to exit the major street she was on. As she meandered her way through a commercial district, she saw a sign in front of a refurbished bungalow with several businesses listed. One was Gunther's Designs. She thought about stopping in if she finished early enough, but then laughed when she remembered the prices she saw on his website.

She glanced at her GPS and saw she was only eight minutes from Ginger. Perhaps she was in the Neighborhood Business Alliance district and could shed some light on the auction event. Maybe Ginger even knew who won the boots and Dena could get another step closer to finding Twist.

Ginger's office was in the center of an outdated tired-looking strip mall with a parking lot full of potholes. Her neighbors included a nail salon, a Chinese carryout, a laundromat, a print shop, an eye doctor, and a martial arts studio. The location might have seen better days, but the crumbling parking lot was busy, attesting to a thriving scene. So thriving, in fact, she had trouble finding an empty spot. It certainly didn't match the upscale area where Gunther's Designs was housed. Maybe Ginger wasn't in the NBA district after all.

Dena pulled open the door under the simple "CPA" sign to find a plump brunette sitting at a desk talking loudly on the phone. Her face was partially hidden by a large computer monitor and a lush houseplant with trailing leaves covering a tall plant stand. Dena knew this was Ginger because she recognized her voice. She pulled off her coat and gloves and smiled to herself while walking across the room to the chair Ginger had indicated with a pointed finger above her head. Again, she completely mismatched Ginger's voice to her image. It made her wonder how people pictured her when they heard only her voice on the phone. She thought of both Gunther and the woman at the NBA who accused her of plotting the murder of the woman in the boots. They probably pictured her differently than a tall middle-aged woman with nary a prison tattoo.

Dena looked around the office while she waited. A credenza lined the wall near the front door. Ginger's desk was next to it. Two armchairs with upholstered seats sagged in front of Ginger's desk at either corner. None of the furniture matched. It was a bit more ramshackle than Dena preferred for her CPA, but outdated furniture and worn carpet weren't deal-breakers for her. There wasn't much of a personal nature on Ginger's desk. No framed photos or weird tchotchkes like a collection of Hot Wheels cars or plastic dinosaurs or erasers in silly shapes.

But one thing caught Dena's eye.

An Increase Your Vocabulary Word-A-Day calendar, showing a date exactly two weeks earlier.

Dena couldn't take her eyes off the calendar. The word was "impeccable." She heard Duke's voice when he was yelling at her in the bookstore ... exactly two weeks ago ... when he'd used the wrong word and she had to translate in her head. *I curated an impressive selection of used books. I bought shelves, I even built some. I trained my employees to an implacable degree...*

He must have read that page on this calendar without actually learning it, then came directly to Thrice Sold Tales to confront her about that bogus clause in her contract. Had he been sitting in this very chair earlier that morning? It didn't make sense. Why was the calendar facing the guest chairs and not Ginger sitting at her desk?

Ginger finished her phone call and stood, coming around the corner of her desk next to the credenza.

Dena watched, mouth agape. It was the woman in the photo with Duke and Twist as a puppy. She closed her mouth and tried to maintain a nonchalant air even though every nerve was sending fireworks through her body and every muscle tensed hard as steel.

"You must be Dena Russo. I'm so happy to finally officially meet you." She held out her hand to Dena who shook it numbly. Ginger then sat in the guest chair between Dena and the front door.

As she crossed her legs, Dena saw she wore hand-painted knee-high sharp-heeled boots with red, gray, black, gold, and white swirls. As her vision narrowed to a pinprick, Dena gaped at the miniature skull-and-crossbones with happy little smiles.

Gunther's design. The boots worn by the woman videotaping the confrontation with Duke in the Marketplace. The prints in the snow.

Ginger had stolen Twist. Did she also kill Duke like both she and Jain had theorized?

Dena faked a coughing fit to try and buy some time to think. She steadied her breathing. She needed to keep her cool. Maintain her composure. Not let on what she was thinking. Ginger didn't know she knew about the boots or about Twist. Something was terribly wrong here, but Dena didn't know exactly what.

"Can I get you some water?" Ginger asked with concern.

"No, please don't bother." In one quick motion, Dena arranged the strap of her crossbody bag on her chest then stood to collect her coat and gloves. "I must be catching something. I don't want to make you sick. I'll get out of here. You can show me the documents another time." Dena would drive straight to the Colorado Springs Police Department and call Sheriff Johnson for advice.

"Don't be silly. You're already here. And I come from hardy stock. It takes more than a little cough to lay me low."

Dena returned to her seat and choked out, "Okay," covering it with another fake cough. Way to keep your cool, she thought. She needed an alternative plan to get out of there.

"How was traffic?"

"Getting heavy. Probably should think about getting back on the road pretty quick. Maybe I should have a look at that documentation you talked about? Better yet, maybe just make me a copy and I'll take a look at it when I get home." Dena stood again, glad she was already wearing her bag.

Ginger waved her back toward the chair. "No need. I already forwarded it to the police. You and I can get to know each other better now. Let them deal with all the ugliness."

Dena relaxed a bit, knowing the police were already involved. Maybe she completely misunderstood the boots and the calendar page. She couldn't imagine how, but she was willing to consider it.

Ginger seemed weirdly calm, not at all what she was like when Dena spoke with her on the phone. "What … ugliness exactly? When will the police be here? You never said—" Dena heard a noise and glanced toward the hallway behind her. "What was that?" The noise seemed familiar.

"I didn't hear anything."

Dena was quiet for a moment, listening. "Is she stealing your socks too?"

"Ugh. Constantly! That dog is a menace." Ginger clamped a hand over her mouth. "You got me."

Dena was so surprised that her ploy worked she couldn't move. Barely breathed. Until Ginger stood. Then Dena flinched.

Ginger walked across to the hallway and opened a door.

Out bounded Twist, tail wagging full speed, and rushed at Dena in the chair.

Dena bent to hug her, eyes filling with tears, crossbody bag crushed into her stomach. Twist's tail thumped against the leg of the chair while Dena murmured and cooed to her. She kept her face buried in Twist's neck while she tried to figure out what to do. She couldn't very well just spring from the office and run away with the dog. Who knew what Ginger would do?

She decided to bluff, pretend that Ginger wasn't involved at all in anything. And maybe she wasn't, despite so much evidence to the contrary. Dena would pretend Duke was the one and only bad guy. After all, that's what Ginger had told her on the phone. She'd play along until she could get herself and Twist out of there and she could tell Sheriff Johnson all the half-formed clues and evidence and let her figure it out. Perhaps Ginger had somehow been hoodwinked by Duke and was perfectly innocent.

"You've taken good care of her." Dena straightened up, but Twist didn't leave her side. Dena kept her hand on Twist's back. "That Duke Bughata." Dena tried to make her voice sound disgusted and angry. Which she was, of course, but needed to keep a tight lid on her fear and hysteria to sound convincing. Plus, she wasn't entirely sure who she was disgusted and angry with. "He shouldn't be allowed to have a dog. Why didn't he come back for her?"

"What?" Ginger frowned. "Why would he?"

"Because she's his dog?" Now it was Dena's turn to look confused.

"I thought she was your dog."

"I never saw Twist—or Duke, for that matter—before the day he came in the bookstore yelling at me."

"Wait. You're not his girlfriend?"

"His what?"

Ginger stared at Dena then shook her head and smiled. "Go figure. He was actually telling me the truth for once. I thought he gave you the bookstore because you two were romantically involved."

"The only thing Duke Bughata has given me is a pain in my—" When Dena saw Ginger's smile morph into a sneer, she suddenly felt certain in every atom of her body that not only did Ginger steal Twist, she also killed Duke. But why? Out of jealousy? She couldn't let Ginger know her suspicions. "Men, amirite? He must have wanted the bookstore back to … I don't know …" Dena scrambled for some plausible reason, "cover some gambling debts or something. I bet that's the angle the cops are working to solve his murder. We can tell them that when they … get … here." Dena's skin prickled and every one of her muscles twitched. How could she have been so dumb? Ginger never called the police. She never intended to. Dena didn't have the bandwidth or the time to feel sorry for herself right then. She needed to make sure Ginger didn't have an inkling that Dena suspected her in any of this. Dena consciously worked at relaxing her face and making her voice light. "Duke was a shady character and he—"

"I should have believed him. He said he just wanted his cash cow back."

Dena took offense. "You thought I was the cow? Not the bookstore?"

"No offense." Ginger shrugged. "I just knew he'd screw something up so I told him I'd handle it. But then the idiot got it in his head to use my name to report himself missing."

"Why report himself missing?"

"If I had to guess, I'd say so it would cast suspicion on you and you'd get scared and give him back the bookstore." She peered at Dena. "Or go to jail."

Recognizing the look of hostility on Ginger's face, Dena realized that Ginger had been biding her time, waiting to see if Dena was going to figure anything out and if she did, Ginger would lure Dena to her office and kill her like she'd killed Duke. Dena didn't know why and she didn't much care. She just wanted to get herself and Twist out of there.

The obvious way for Dena to get out of this mess was to make a break for it, but that seemed impossible at the moment. Ginger was smack-dab between her and the door. Grabbing her coat and gloves, getting Twist to follow her, and running out to her car parked clear across the lot while presumably getting chased by this madwoman didn't seem realistic. Of course, she could take off without her coat and gloves, but it was her favorite coat, and Lance had given her those gloves.

Dena shook her head. Did she have a Plan B?

Maybe she could catch the attention of someone walking past. There seemed to be lots of foot traffic in this strip mall. Dena glanced out the window. Unfortunately, many of them were kids and teenagers wearing martial arts uniforms, going to their classes.

Maybe Twist could help somehow. Dena remembered the "go next door" trick that Jain and Wyatt had been teaching her. She wondered if Twist had retained anything about the lesson or if it was simply a fun game she played with the kids. She'd only seen her do it once, and barely that. Dena had been preoccupied and distracted when Jain and Wyatt had demonstrated it for her. She wished now that she'd paid more attention.

Despite the hostility Dena had seen on Ginger's face, Ginger didn't seem too concerned by Dena's presence, even getting up to take another phone call from a client. She leaned casually against the front of her desk. Ginger snapped her fingers at Twist while she explained something about taxes to her client on the phone. Twist walked over and sat at her feet. Maybe Dena had misinterpreted the entire situation. She reached for her coat, preparing to walk right out the door. She could snap her fingers for Twist too.

Without missing a beat of her phone conversation, at Dena's movement, Ginger reached through the trailing leaves of the plant on the corner of her desk. She slid out a handgun which she aimed directly at Twist.

Dena dropped her coat and settled back into her chair. She hugged her purse.

Ginger nodded at her the way a teacher might nod at a clever student. She continued her conversation, pointing the gun at Twist the entire time.

Furtively, Dena snuck one of Ginger's business cards from the holder on her desk. Dena slowly dug out a pen from her purse. Sliding the card to her knee, she wrote HELP in big bold letters across both the front and back of the card.

Dena palmed it, wondering how she was going to get

Twist out the door with it in her mouth and without Ginger taking a potshot at her.

Maybe she could hold up the card to the passersby. Would they be able to see that it said HELP? Was there a glare from the setting sun on the glass? Could anyone see inside the CPA office at all? Was she too far from the window?

Even though Dena tried to be sly about it, Ginger apparently saw her glancing repeatedly to her right out the front window. Ginger finished her phone call then nonchalantly dangled the gun by one finger and walked toward the door.

Twist stayed where she was.

Dena expected Ginger to lock the door. Instead, she opened it and peered out in both directions.

This was Dena's chance.

Dena sprang from her chair and held out the business card to Twist, saying urgently, "Go next door!"

Twist grabbed the card between her tiny front teeth and pushed past Ginger to the sidewalk out front.

Dena grabbed her coat and followed, presuming that Ginger would chase after the dog. Instead, Ginger blew a loud, wet raspberry and said, "Good riddance. That dog made an unholy alliance with all my socks. Let her go steal someone else's footwear."

There was a scuffle while Dena tried to push past Ginger and follow Twist.

Ginger blocked her escape and locked the door.

Dena lunged for the gun. She snatched it from Ginger with shaky hands and pointed it at her. "Stop right there."

Unconcerned, Ginger continued walking toward her.

"I said stop!"

"You dope. It's not loaded."

Dena knew nothing about guns, but she looked at it to

see if she could tell whether or not Ginger was telling the truth. She couldn't. She shook it like a Christmas present, thinking bullets might rattle. They didn't. She aimed it at the floor and pulled the trigger. It clicked.

By then, Ginger was back at her desk. She held out her hand for the gun.

"I think I'll just hold on to it, if you don't mind," Dena said.

"Suit yourself." Ginger stared across at Dena. "Now your fingerprints are all over it."

Gah. Dena used the sleeve of her coat to rub the gun. When she looked up, Ginger was still staring at her. What was she planning? The fact the gun wasn't loaded gave Dena hope that maybe this situation wasn't as bad as it felt at the moment. Because it felt dire.

Nobody knew where she was, the police hadn't been called, and she was sitting here with a killer behind a locked door.

When had her life turned into this?

Dena

DID Twist even go next door with Dena's SOS in her mouth, or was she long gone, loping down the street, tasting her freedom, sniffing fences and lightpoles?

Dena tried to recall the businesses along the strip mall. What was to the right of Ginger's office, if Twist even decided to go next door? She groaned inwardly. Next door was the martial arts studio. What were the odds anyone over there would even notice the business card, read it, and take *any* kind of action? Slim, at best. They'd probably just chase the dog away and get on with their class.

Dena knew she had to stall as long as possible, for two reasons. One, to give anyone a chance to take action on her HELP plea. And two, because she had absolutely no other ideas. She continued with her earlier ploy to make sure Ginger thought only that Dena suspected a bit of financial shenanigans, and not anything about Duke's murder. Realistically, Dena knew that was a longshot. Ginger had to think Dena was a tad bit suspicious of her, what with finding Twist locked up here, their earlier conversation about Duke, and pulling out a gun. But

Ginger remained an enigma. Dena had no inkling what she might be thinking or planning.

But maybe it was time to find out. "I can't believe Duke didn't pay his taxes."

"Who told you that?"

"The IRS lady downtown."

Ginger's eyes bugged out. "You went to the IRS? What kind of goody-two-shoes are you?"

"It's okay, you couldn't have known what he was doing."

Ginger stared at Dena for an uncomfortably long time.

Dena groaned as the realization hit. "You totally knew what he was doing, didn't you?" Her plan was backfiring spectacularly.

Ginger stared for another beat. "I had to kill him, you know. He threatened to turn me in to the IRS. If they started an audit, they'd find all sorts of things I'd rather have kept secret." She sighed deeply. "And now you're telling me *you* went to the IRS? That's deeply troubling and very unfortunate."

Dena waved her hand, slicing the air nonchalantly. "Oh, you know how the IRS is. I'm sure they've already forgotten about it."

"Did you fill out any forms?"

Dena pictured IRS Form 3949-A she'd been so adamant about filling out. "Just the one."

"Very unfortunate."

"There hasn't been any follow-up or anything, I'm sure it's fine."

Ginger stared at Dena. "You don't know how anything works, do you?" Dena kept her mouth shut, hoping this was a rhetorical question. "Duke found out I was taking a little frosting off the top. He thought he was the only one doing that. I learned my lesson, though. No clients get to skim from their books. They get too greedy and then there's not enough for me. He took too much so the bookstore wasn't turning a profit anymore. That's why he had to close it. Then he sold it to you. I made the mistake of telling him it was doing great—"

"Great? Hardly."

Ginger laughed. "You business types, think it's all about you. He completely misunderstood too. What I meant was that now that he wasn't skimming, I could skim more so the bookstore *was* doing great ... for me, anyway."

"So that's why he came into the store yelling at me." Dena shook her head. "He thought it was profitable and wanted it back, just like Evelyn said." Another truth dawned on Dena. "Oh! And that's why attorney Finster was nervous when he saw the contract. He was telling the truth when he said that Duke must have gone in and doctored it to show I was supposed to pay him five hundred dollars a month. If he couldn't skim it from his profits, I guess he decided he could extort it from me." Dena puckered her lips in disgust.

"That evil little genius." Ginger leaned back in her chair with an appreciative smile on her lips.

"I don't think Finster was in on it," Dena said.

"No, not Finster ... Duke. He told me to call Finster at a precise time one day, but told me it was about something completely different. It must have been so he could buy time to change the contract."

"Finster told me he stepped out to take a call and figured that was when Duke altered the contract. But it doesn't do any good to just change one copy of a contract," Dena pointed out.

"That's a 'he said, she said' situation. Who is a jury going to believe ... two fine, upstanding citizens with a long history of doing business in Sugar Springs, or some interloper who's obviously in over her head running a business and thought erasing an important clause of her contract could save her money?"

Dena had to concur, Duke and Finster would come off looking much better than she herself would. She slumped in her chair, more and more deflated. "So, my gas bill. Is that fake?"

"Of course! Your payment to the gas company," Ginger used air quotes, "goes straight to my bank account."

"You'd ruin your life over fifty-nine dollars a month?"

"Dena, Dena, Dena. You think you're my only unobservant client? You'd be surprised how many people just hand over their financial lives to their CPA. In fact—"

Ginger was startled by an entire class of green belts and their sensei banging on the front door of the CPA office. Dena saw Twist's nose poking and booping at the door.

The sensei held up the business card and yelled, "Everything okay? We got this note from a dog!"

Ginger waved and smiled through gritted teeth. She stood up and came around her desk, calling loudly, "Everything's fine." She didn't go near the door, however. Instead, her back to the door, she got directly in Dena's face and hissed, "No monkey business." She gripped Dena's arm and walked her through the office, continuing to wave and smile at the martial arts class while moving away from the windows and door.

Dena began yelling and wrenched her arm away. She lunged for the door, but Ginger hustled her through the office, out of sight. Dena felt herself being manhandled down the hall.

Off balance with every step and rough push, she fought against Ginger's tight grip on her, kicking and flailing wildly with all her strength. Dena had an image of being pushed out a door into the alley and thrown into the trunk of Ginger's car, never to be heard from again.

The thought that there might be a back door gave Dena a burst of energy. She fought harder but still managed to find herself in a hallway, out of view of any potential rescuers.

She wedged herself beside a file cabinet.

Ginger yanked her out.

Dena wrapped her hand around the handle of the file cabinet. Her other hand grappled for purchase on a water cooler. Her right foot hooked around the corner of the filing cabinet. Her left foot kicked at Ginger's ankles.

Ginger was dancing around so only about every third kick of Dena's landed.

Dena lost her balance and the file cabinet drawer flew open.

Both Dena and Ginger spun in a crazy dance.

Dena heaved on the bottle of water, tipping the entire five-gallon bottle to the hallway floor.

They slipped and slid. Dena continued to kick and flail like a squirmy kid avoiding a bath.

Ginger lost her grip on Dena.

Dena waterskied down the wet hall toward the back door. She twisted the dead bolt, but before she could fling open the door, Ginger grabbed a handful of her hair.

Dena's head jerked backward. She lost her balance. "Ow ow ow!"

The two women fell into the pool of water on the floor, splashing and squirming, two angry wolverines.

Dena pulled herself to her hands and knees and slid away from Ginger's grip.

She made her way to the back door. Reached for the

knob. Turned it. Came face-to-knee with a sea of white-clad legs.

The adult Tae Kwan Do class stood before her in the alley.

Unseen arms lifted her up and out of the way while everyone else thundered into Ginger's office.

Twist began licking Dena's face.

When her vision cleared, she used Twist to struggle to her feet.

Ginger was prone, on her back, in the puddle of water.

The class stood over her.

Police sirens and flashing lights filled the darkness.

Dena

THE NEXT MORNING Dena and Twist walked into the vendor room. The whiteboard was full of haikus.

> Why didn't Sherlock
> Holmes pay taxes? Because of
> His smart deductions.

> Tax cheats annoy me.
> They make my twenty-three kids
> Irritated too.

> The definition
> Of a corrupt CPA?
> Loophole named for her.

> What is the difference
> Between tax evasion and
> Avoidance? Prison.

She smiled at all of them, but the final one made her laugh out loud.

> Dena Russo is
> Brave, foolhardy, and a
> Fine amateur sleuth.

The other tenants began trickling into the vendor room when they heard her reading the poetry to Twist.

Dena filled in the blanks about Ginger for them, having only given them the highlights via a group text the night before, since she was exhausted by the time she got home.

They asked two million questions, but Dena only had one hundred answers. "I don't know how Ginger was able to fly under the radar with the IRS for so long, except for the fact that most of her clients ceded too much control to her, and some of them, like Duke, were in on her scams."

"How did she get Duke into your back yard?" Kober asked.

"I'm not entirely sure, and we may never know, but I'm pretty sure she used that broken branch I found on the sidewalk to brush away their footprints walking into the yard. That's why there were only her footprints from my back porch leaving the yard, making it look like I was the only one walking out there."

"But why not brush away her footprints too and just leave Twist's?" Evelyn asked.

"She was trying to frame me, I guess. Plotted against me from the very beginning. Although it would only take someone two seconds to know I don't wear heels like that." Dena shrugged.

"I'm sure it was more of an elaborate plot than that," Hugo said. "You're probably not giving her enough credit."

"And you're probably giving her too much," Kober said. "Most crooks are idiots."

"Duke must have still been able to walk," Skyler mused. "There's no way she could have carried his body all the way across your yard."

Dena nodded. "I think she poisoned him somewhere else, maybe just in her car parked at my curb. When he was getting woozy, she walked him into the yard where I found him. Then she dropped the rat poison nearby where Vince found it."

"Maybe they were doing some weird stake-out thing in her car parked at the curb and she had a thermos of poisoned coffee." Hugo nodded at his brilliance.

Dena and Evelyn both shuddered.

"Poor Duke," Dena said. At the surprised looks on everyone's faces she clarified. "I mean, what he did was despicable, but he didn't need to be murdered for it. Especially because Ginger got it so wrong. She thought he and I were romantically involved, for heaven's sake."

"Jealousy makes people do weird things," Kober murmured.

"Like buy an ice cream parlor," Boyd said.

"And keep odd hours." Evelyn cut her eyes at Max as he walked into the vendor room. "Where have you been, anyway?" she asked him.

"I have news," he announced. "Not as interesting as Dena's here, but still. I got us a new tenant! Well, almost."

"Who?" Evelyn asked. "Millie's Sexy Pot Roast Rendezvous?"

"No." Max rolled his eyes. "Pham's House of Noodles. I've been raising money all over town."

"Pham?" Evelyn wrinkled her brow.

Max nodded then explained to the others. "Pham is Vietnamese, in a wheelchair. You might not have seen him around town, since it's hard for him to get around. He has that big place out by the highway."

"With all the toys in the yard?" Kober asked.

Max nodded. "He has adopted and fostered a thousand kids over the years. But I got to talking to him a while back and he told me his parents owned a noodle shop before the war and it was always his dream to have one again. Never enough money, though."

"Probably because of all those kids," Hugo said.

Evelyn turned to Max. "Is that why you've been sneaking all over town in the middle of the night?"

"I told you, that's just insomnia." He cocked his head at her. "What do you think I could do in the middle of the night, anyway? Help Pham plant secret noodle trees?"

"Why didn't I see fundraising flyers around town or anything?" Evelyn asked suspiciously.

"I wasn't asking for nickels and dimes. I've been getting corporate grants and micro-loans for him."

"Why keep it from us?" Dena asked.

"More importantly, why keep it a secret from me?" Evelyn said.

"Sheesh," Max rasped. "I wasn't keeping it a secret. You told me I'm in charge of money stuff and I knew you liked Pham and would approve. I also knew that if it didn't work out, you'd cry and you know how I hate to see you cry."

Evelyn nodded. "That's fair."

"Besides, you had your hands full with the studio." Max glanced around at the other tenants. "You all had your hands full. I didn't want to get anyone's hopes up."

"That explains the checkbook I found," Evelyn said.

"What checkbook?" Dena asked.

"Oh, nothing. I just found a checkbook at the house. That must have been how Max was keeping track of the donations. Isn't that right, Max?"

Max didn't say anything for a moment, but then quickly agreed, saying, "Sure. That's right."

Dena was surprised Evelyn let his comment pass because Max was clearly hiding something. Skyler must have thought so too because she shot a questioning glance in Dena's direction. Dena didn't think Max would need a simple checkbook register to track corporate grants for Pham, and apparently neither did Skyler. But maybe they didn't have all the facts.

Dena made a mental note to ask Max about it later. If there was something weird about the fundraising Max was doing for Pham, as Marketplace manager, Dena needed to know. She wasn't even sure how that would work. Were they giving gifts to Pham, or was it some sort of investment on their part?

Max and the others wanted to hear more about Dena's adventure with Ginger until she told them everything she could remember. After a while, they began drifting into their own spaces to begin their workdays.

Dena had just begun to fire up her ancient computer. Today was the day she had to stand on her own two financial feet. She planned to scrutinize every transaction and verify its appropriateness before adding it into a new dedicated point-of-sale program on her laptop. It had integrated inventory tracking, robust customer management, and a simple interface that she already felt comfortable with. Nobody else would have their fingers in her financial pie.

She envisioned how happy she'd be the minute everything was transferred satisfactorily. She was already planning a *Destroy the Ancient Computer* party.

Her phone pinged and she saw there was a new online edition to the *Sugar Springs Courier*. Dena groaned, pushing the button with trepidation.

"Thrice Sold Tales and Dena Russo Completely Exonerated," the headline read.

Dena's knees weakened and she dropped on to the stool to finish reading the article. It was too good to be true. Aja reported the actually true, factual facts of everything that had happened without innuendo or titillation, even ending the article with a cheery, "Be sure to visit the bookstore and the Marketplace to offer your congratulations for Russo's stellar sleuthing and bravery."

That article in addition to Sheriff Johnson's assurances that the IRS wouldn't come after her based on Duke and Ginger's criminal wrongdoing made her almost as happy as having Twist with her again.

Dena read the article twice more and was beginning a third pass when she heard voices in the store.

"Are you open yet?"

Dena looked up to see three separate groups of shoppers. Two older women. A woman with two toddlers and a baby in a stroller. A middle-aged couple holding hands.

Twist greeted all of them with a happy wag of her tail.

"Yes, yes, I am!"

Dena directed the woman with the kids to her children's section. Twist followed them. "Look, Mommy! A doggy!"

"I see. She must be the store assistant," the woman said.

The older women were looking for mysteries, so Dena pointed out the table with Charlee's books.

"Something ... cozier?" one asked while the other began thumbing through one of Charlee's more suspenseful and ripped-from-the-headlines titles.

"I have a huge selection of cozy mysteries. I've shelved them into subgenres." Dena led her to the stacks.

"Ooh, crossword mysteries!" She pulled a book off the shelf. "That looks fun!"

"That's a Colorado author. My daughter knows her," Dena said. "Let me know if you need any more help."

Twist wandered toward the mystery section, tail wagging.

When Dena returned to the couple, they were on opposite sides of the store. The woman said, "We're on our way back home and thought we'd stop in. He's looking for books about Colorado, and I'm just browsing."

Twist appeared at the woman's side and she bent to rub her ear and pat her on her side. "Beautiful dog."

Dena didn't quite know how to respond to this compliment, even though she received it regularly about Twist. After all, Dena had absolutely nothing to do with how Twist looked. Sometimes she'd say, "She's smart, too," or "I bet her parents were gorgeous," but now she simply said "Thank you" on Twist's behalf.

Dena pointed out the Colorado history first editions that Quint O'Dell curated, then turned back to the woman. "Where did you hear about the Marketplace?"

"We read about it in your local paper. Seems you've had an interesting couple of weeks."

Dena laughed. "I guess you could say that."

"Is your assistant here the one from the article?" The woman took a knee next to Twist and Dena's muscles tightened. But the woman began cooing to Twist and didn't seem to care about the viral video or anything else she'd read about Dena and Twist. After a bit, the woman wandered off to browse, Twist padding along behind.

Dena returned to her stool, relieved that perhaps shoppers would be returning to the store. She never liked to hover, preferring to give customers their freedom to browse. She kept an ear tuned toward them, though, in case she could offer help.

Another woman marched up to the front counter. Dena looked up to see an angular, severe-looking woman, around forty, Dena guessed, with a right front tooth that overlapped her left front tooth. She seemed dangerously thin and wrapped in the drabbest clothing Dena had ever seen.

Before Dena could ask what she could help her with, the woman said, "I'm here about the job."

"Who told you there was a job here?"

"Isn't there?"

"Yes, not for the bookstore, though. For the Marketplace. But I haven't even advertised for it yet."

"Evelyn told me to come in and talk to you."

Now it made sense. "Of course." Dena didn't have any kind of employee application or form prepared yet, so she pulled out a yellow legal pad and clicked her pen. "What's your name?"

"Kateri Warcloud."

"Do you live in Sugar Springs?"

"I live across the river in a house with my grandmother."

"In the forest?"

Kateri nodded.

Twist wandered out from the children's section and watched their job interview as if she were watching a ping pong match. It was very similar. Fewer dropped balls, though. And no trash-talking.

"Computer experience?"

"Lots."

"Spreadsheets?"

"Of course."

"Design work?"

"Some."

"Are you looking for full-time work?"

Kateri paused and Dena's stomach dropped. She really needed someone full-time.

Kateri chose her words carefully. "I can work full-time, as many hours as you need, but I also take care of my grandmother, so I will need some flexibility."

Dena breathed a sigh of relief. "I am nothing if not flexible." They talked more about Kateri's skillset and the needs of the Marketplace manager position. It was a gratifyingly overlapping Venn diagram.

The only slight misgiving for Dena was Kateri's clipped, short sentences and *just the facts* manner of speaking. Dena wrote that off as nerves, simply a by-product of a stressful job interview. Perhaps Kateri was actually a blabbermouth and was really trying to reign that in. At any rate, it wasn't a deal-breaker for Dena.

She briefly wondered if she should discuss Kateri's potential employment with the other tenants, but instead, thrust out her hand. "When can you start?"

After Kateri left, Dena glanced down at Twist sitting at her side. "Looks like I have two assistants now."

Balaam strutted into the bookstore. When he came around the corner, he saw Twist who immediately jumped up to greet him with a nose boop. Balaam arched his back and hissed, scrambling backward.

Twist hurried toward him and booped him again.

Dena watched with delight as Balaam backed up after each of Twist's boops, looking more and more astonished and resigned about the boopery. She considered whether she should rescue Balaam, but before she could make any decision, her phone rang.

She saw a video call from Georgia in Santa Fe. Hm. Calling to apologize for her wild accusations? Calling with more wild accusations? There was only one way to find out.

"Hi, Georgia. How are you doing?"

Afterword

Thank you so much for reading my books! If it wasn't for readers, I'd look too much like a toddler banging away on a keyboard for no reason.

I hope you were delighted with your visit to the Sugar Mill Marketplace. If so, check out the rest of the series!

Your reviews help authors drive book sales *and* help readers find new books and authors. Please consider popping over to the **PLOTTED** review page and dropping a few words. I'd really appreciate it!

Subscribe at BeckyClarkBooks.com to Becky Clark's *So Seldom It's Shameful* News for free series starters for both the Mystery Writer's mysteries and the Sugar Mill Marketplace mysteries. You'll also find fun short stories, a Christmas play, up-to-the-minute info about releases and sales, and the scoop about becoming a member of my Review Crew.

Acknowledgments

The theme of PLOTTED is "greed." Of course, the opposite of greed is generosity, and it's because of generous people that my books get written and read at all.

Many of these generous people hang out with me in my private Facebook group, Becky's Book Buddies. They're also part of my Review Crew, making sure they shout about my books from their rooftops and otherwise offer some noisy buzz for me. They interact with me in the Cozy Mystery Crew group on Facebook, and they visit our group blog over at Chicks on the Case.

I heart all of them and enjoy our interactions so much!

Huge thanks to **Tammy Barker** for letting me pick her brain about accounting and business practices. Any inaccuracies are all mine, because she's a grown-up and lives in the real world and I am an author.

If you looked up the word "generous" in the dictionary, you'd see a pencil sketch of **Jessica Cornwell**, editor extraordinaire. She is generous with her corrections, advice, *and* her praise. It makes my cold little heart thaw a bit whenever I see her comments telling me not that I shifted tense again, but that a passage made her laugh or cry. And again, any mistakes that seep through are because

I got my grubby fingers all over the manuscript after she signed off on it.

Also by Becky Clark

If you enjoyed this little taste of the Sugar Mill Marketplace series, check out the rest of the series today. And while you're at it, get up to speed with Charlee Russo in the Mystery Writer's mysteries.

Sugar Mill Marketplace mysteries

Booked #1

Plotted #2

Bound #3

Mystery Writer's Mysteries

Fiction Can Be Murder #1

Foul Play on Words #2

Metaphor for Murder #3

Police Navidad #4

Crossword Puzzle Mysteries

Puzzling Ink #1

Punning with Scissors #2

Fatal Solutions #3

The Dunne Diehl Mysteries

Banana Bamboozle #1

Marshmallow Mayhem #2

Nonfiction

Eight Weeks to a Complete Novel—Write Faster, Write Better,
Be More Organized

About the Author

Award-winning author **Becky Clark** is the seventh of eight kids, which explains both her insatiable need for attention and her atrocious table manners. She likes to read funny books so it felt natural to write them too. She surrounds herself with quirky people and pets who end up as characters in her novels. Readers say her books are "fast and thoroughly entertaining" with "witty humor and tight writing" and "humor laced with engaging characters" so you should "grab a cocktail and enjoy the ride."

For entirely too much information about her, visit BeckyClarkBooks.com. While you're there, subscribe to her mailing list for **oodles of fun and free stuff**.

Follow her on Amazon and BookBub to get up-to-the-date info on new releases and sales. Join her private group "Becky's Book Buddies" on Facebook for shenanigans and fun. Put her books on your GoodReads shelf to make all your friends jealous.